EARTH AS IT IS IN HEAVEN

AN AURAL NOVEL

BY KARL ELDER

Pebblebrook Press

Sheboygan, Wisconsin 2016

EARTH AS IT IS IN HEAVEN

Published by Pebblebrook Press,
an imprint of *Stoneboat*
PO Box 1254
Sheboygan, WI 53082-1254
Editors: Rob Pockat, Signe Jorgenson, Jim Giese, Lisa Vihos
www.stoneboatwi.com

Earth as It Is in Heaven: An Aural Novel ©2016 Karl Elder
Library of Congress Control Number: 2015956196
ISBN: 978-0692567999

Cover illustration by Charles Dana Gibson
In days to come the churches may be fuller (circa 1894-1908)

Printed in the US

In memory of
Lucile Fessler
Marion K. Stocking
Mark Strand
and
Lucien Stryk

A warm thank-you is due to Robert Schuricht, whose endowment in the support of my work has contributed to the publication of this novel.

My appreciation extends to Signe Jorgenson, Katherine Amundsen, Amanda Smith, and Rob Pockat for their diligence at copy-editing and proofreading what I imagine to have been among the most challenging of manuscripts and galleys.

Be it known also that the characters of *Earth as It Is in Heaven* are of my making and are in no manner consciously emblematic of persons living nor deceased.

—K.E.

After ecstasy, the laundry.
—Zen saying

EARTH AS IT IS IN HEAVEN

It were the Schoolteacher come to call it such as Anarchto-pia what with all the goings-on. Next to Termite-Town-Constable and Pyro, she were the nearest our kind ever knowed to a mayor, beings there weren't no man nor gink about to run for office or nothing. Not with her around. On account of that lady put a hold on your heart just like she done all the other ginks. It weren't so much what she said in school. It was having to stay after, her eyes burning holes clear through you to make you believe she'd be your one true love for the rest of your born days. "Knowledge is power," she'd say, the two of you just sitting there, one of you squirming.

I got me a library card after about the third spell. I knowed Nooner Johnson would be headed up to the county seat that Saturday, since I heared him talking in the barber shop, so I just flat-out asked him ifing I could hitch a ride in the beat-up pickup of his with the floorboards like swiss cheese. He weren't surprised none when I tell him what I wanted it for—the ride, I mean. He had the Schoolteacher always in the back of his head too, he said, just like all the other ginks, even with him being married and with a pack of kids of his own.

We pull up to one of them parking meters, and Nooner,

he asks me to stay in the truck because he don't have change. I spose he wants me to pull away or something in case a policeman come along, but I weren't about to what with no license. Heck, I weren't old enough for a permint, let alone the real thing. It's while I sat there I begun to think on how peculiar-like our town was. A man could drive to the post office without worry whether he had pennies in his pocket.

I don't know why I remember that one ride back to the barber shop so well, cepting to say you know how there are some things that sticks out and for what is no reason. Take the ball diamond, for a fact. Lord knows why a picture of home plate, a piece of metal that it was, would shine in your mind till you were umpteen years old and probable-like for all your days thereafter, beings it made it that far. But that morning was bright, and it was clear. There's a trace of snow on the ground. You could turn your head full circle and there would be nothing in the way for miles but the road, the railroad tracks, telephone poles, and a few barns so distant as to start you thinking on the hotels on the Monopoly board.

I heared Wally Phillips on WGN, though not in Nooner's truck beings there was a hole in the dash where oughta be the radio. I caught sight of Old Floyd the Hydralectric's head through the barber shop winda, and Nooner and me, we went in just sos we can razz the old Devil a bit, because he likes it, but it was me what got poked fun at.

"What—no great American novel?" says Bob the Barber, seated in his chair like a fool on a throne, what he used to say hisself.

I shrugged.

"Jesus H. Christ, Nooner, you drive the gink all the way up to Lawless, and you don't give the boy time to browse?"

Nooner din't say nothing, just sips on his Royal Crown.

This goes on and on. Quiet–like. About halfway through his pop, final–like Nooner burps. He turns his head to Floyd, says, "Getting any nookie, Floyd?"

Floyd grins some more.

Though it were of a Saturday morning, we all just sit there—Floyd, Nooner, and Bob the Barber. All cepting Wally Phillips and me. We lean on the machine.

"Where's the customers, Bob?" I says.

"Don't know," the Barber says with a grin what is the mirror to Floyd's. "Maybe the size of Floyd's head scared them off."

Nooner got soda in his nose on that one.

Maybe that's all why I remember the ride back from Lawless so good. That and because, now when I think on it, it's maybe the only time I saw one of the critters—me there with my library card in my pocket and Nooner's silence echoing in my ears. What's he always staring off about, I wonder, on account of he were a gink of hers too, when all of the sudden I seen this shadow about the size of a coon's out of the corner of my eye on the snowbank before we cross the bridge.

"What the heck's that?"

"What?" Nooner says.

"Back there," I says, all akimbo in my seat.

"I din't see nothing."

I dropped the subject and thought on the Schoolteacher, what weren't nothing new but sort of a hobby–like.

She had her hooks in me, all right. Part of it was how she

dressed, no makeup or nothing. I swear she had only one pair of shoes, chunky heels, black and masculine-like with about a dozen pair of eyelets and these skinny black shoelaces. I saw them a lot. In the lower grades you din't get to look up much. You spent most your time reading or figuring or pretending, one or another, but you don't look up. I spose she wanted to save her ultimate weapon, the eyes, for later.

For now you was ascared of her and you loved her. Though it were rare, she could smile. Lord, could she smile big. The tears would well up in your eyes when you seen that. Right there and then you knowed you'd been pardoned all your sins.

She might touch you, too. It'd be so brief as not to be felt none, but later you'd feel it and you wouldn't want to scrub that place but wash around it like it was the kiss of Marilyn *Man*roe. Oh, how you loved her. You were seven. She was forty-seven maybe, and you wanted to marry her. Not that you wanted to make out with her none. I mean who would want to kiss a woman who you hardly never seen nowhere but that country schoolhouse and in church until you was thirteen? You couldn't picture her nowhere else, especial-like because of the navy blue dress and polka-dot scarf she wore. I'd come to school most days early and there she'd be, dusting the globe or washing the blackboard in a polka-dot scarf around her neck. It would almost make you ascared, a woman like that, so smart and all, cleaning house in a building ever one knowed was doomed because ever kid in the district heared his or her old man talking agin consolidation. But the hardwood floor shined just like the one in church. I guessed it always had and always would, even after the bulldozer bust it to boards. There was good, black dirt underneath and there weren't no way one of them farmer neighbors wasn't going to put it to use. I'd stand outside on a day the clouds would sail by like an armada in the encyclopedia and wonder how in heaven a man could kill this, the chicken-wire backstop, the dust-worn baselines, the storm shelter and the big oak—all that fluffy white, the blue, the sweet black and new green of a April morning after a rain all so exact-like reflected in the big thin windas she kept as clean and clear as spring water in shade.

And her house? Like I says, I never seen the inside till I was thirteen, but it was real plain and tidy everwhere but the bookshelves, on account of, you see, she lived across the road in the parsonage because we had no live-in preacher and she was the caretaker there too. Some said she din't sleep none what with the school and church to upkeep, the schoolyard and graveyard to mow. Still, she were a Lady, and Ladies don't yawn. Not this one no how.

All us ginks yawned, though. She had us reading by October in first grade and writing autobiographies in the second grade. I heared tell diagraming sentences is something you don't do till eighth grade in most districts, but we begun in fifth. Then there was them story problems—ifing a hen laid a dozen eggs ever ten days, how many miles a hour could it take to reach Lawless ifing she traveled by the South Pole and her eggs was the size of the average cucumber in Borneo? I guess she borrowed us facts. And by golly you'd better pay her back. On top of all this she'd sprinkle a few of them Latin and Greek roots. By the time chores and supper and such was over, you'd drop in the sack like a rock to the bottom of the crick.

If you don't learn it here, she'd say, you sure weren't going to learn it in that new high school in town where there was bells, slamming lockers, clocks to watch, thirty pupils per class, and all the makings of a teachers' union, whatever she meant by that. No gink never had the nerve to remind her she was fighting a uphill battle. Our fathers was farmers. The only newspapers we seen was of a Sunday. As long as a man could add and subtract and sign his name for the Banker, there weren't time for no Romeo and Juliet. It was different for the Wilson girls, though. Different for the Olson girls and the Heaths. It was different for Becky and her sisters. Fact is it was different for any girl, even Helen and Peg, beings they was what the Schoolteacher called motivated-like. What girl in her right mind would want to grow up to marry one of us ginks?

I admit I studied on that question as much as any book lesson. I thought on Nooner, Digger, and Bob the Barber. They lived out that way when they was kids. They had her too. It always seemed they made something of theirselfs. They understood stuff like no ordinary man. There was per usual a *Post Dispatch* on the bench in the shop or in the Barber's lap when he weren't cutting hair none, what was considerable-like, and it weren't open to no funny papers neither. She was proud of them, you could tell. She'd say to us sometimes when in the middle of a history lesson the son don't have to do what the father done. I remember the first time I heared that I thought she was talking God and Jesus, it sounded so natural-like, beings she learned some of us Sunday school too.

Maybe *learned* ain't the word. Come to think on it, I don't rightly know how to say it, what went on in that one room schoolhouse, I mean. It was more like a coach, I come to find out, when I met the Bear first practice at the high school. But there was more. She had her talons in you, and as long as she flew in that room, though you was ascared, up so high and ever thing, you knowed you din't want her to let go because you was afraid of falling too. But you din't fly always. She'd sit you down and go preen-like in a corner and expect you to take up with one of the younger ginks.

There's that afternoon Bird Dog Benson whispered something about that lazy old witch off in the corner staring-off, and though he were two years my junior, I begun swinging. She pulled me off and broke yet another ruler on my rear, me yelling at Bird Dog, "You cow-plop, you're just a cow-plop like your old man, and you'll never understand," though at the time it weren't what I understood what had me into my fit. I was nine. She was maybe forty-nine.

Maybe it was inevitable-like I come to understand. Things was sour on the farm. There was the accident. Pop fell from the mow. While he did walk away, the look on his face told me he was walking away from hisself. He'd wanted out, you could tell for a long time. With Mom gone to the care of the School-teacher after trying to birth for him and me a baby sister, a son what can't cook begins to understand when a day after his Pop falls from the mow he sees him stiff and sore and heared him mumble, "To hell with the *family farm*."

Wasn't two months we had our sale. The Banker figured what we still owed, and Pop figured he better find a job and fast. So he took what they had left up the highway at the plant, janitor on second shift, thinking I'm old enough to fend for myself of an evening. I spose that's how the whole town become my second old man—or at least the ginks who hanged around the pool table in the back of the barber shop. That and for a fact we rented the house on the old Corvus farm along the crick halfway between the schoolhouse and town. It was then Pop thought on how I should own a rebuilt Schwinn, and a trip into town suddenly weren't more than five minutes. Wasn't long after I owned my own cue, an old warped one Bob the Barber give me as long as I'd keep it home nights because it was bad luck and on account of it fit me like a new suit, he said, beings I was getting tall and lanky and a little stooped and all. I reckon that's one present that paid for itself. You can bet, before I swore off pool, I paid for the dang table. Finally I got smart and started playing the other ginks for the time on the table. Soon I've equal my money back and Bob has hisself a living income in the back. The old ginks said I was a natural and there was ginks from other towns who bought haircuts and soda pop too, coming to watch. Eight ball mostly. And a little rotation. But when this sharp come down from Lawless and showed me nine ball—fifty cents on the five and a dollar on the nine—sudden-like me and my Pop had us a new source of income. Somehow the Schoolteacher got wind of it, asked me about it. She flat-out tells me hustling pool weren't what she talked when she said the son don't have to follow the father's footsteps. I took one quick glance at that brow of hers and seen it was on the verge of scrunching up and figured I'd best tone it down a bit. So I does. From then on I played mostly fourteen-point one continuous for the time and—Lord forgive me for what Nooner called a waste of a

Godgiven talent—a nickel a point, cepting, when I'd think on those eyes, a penny a point.

That was the year of my first sexy dream. But it weren't that what made me feel so growed up. It weren't even I was paying my own way. It was now I had a name. Most ginks din't get one sprung on them what was to last their whole life until they was in high school or beyond. Oh, there was Bird Dog, all right, but that was really his old man's name and we just called him that on account of he got some name from the Bible even he couldn't say. Anyway, Nooner had his. And then there was Digger. And Cromangon Man. Bob the Barber give me mine. "Stick," is what they says, when they says it.

THE FIRST BOOK I took of the library's was by what I figured was some professor. Who else would be wearing a monkey suit and a pool cue at once? And wouldn't you know, it weren't but a week later, sitting in the shop, flipping the channels on the Motorola, I catch a glimpse of a picture of the same professor, ceptings he din't sound like no professor. That night I was set on opening that book. I read it straight through. I darn near cried when it was over.

It was Digger wanted to know why I been moping around of late, beings Bob the Barber noticed my game was off, that I ain't played nothing but trick shots all week and hardly never for no moolah. I din't say me a word. I din't feel like talking about it to nobody, especial-like no gink, though I din't want to go and hurt his feelings and ever thing.

I'll tell you what, there was only one person in this world I knowed I'd talk to about it, and I weren't half sure I could handle that for fear ifing I told her what was really on this gink's mind, she'd reach across and snatch me bald headed, crew cut or not. I get on my bike and just pedaled, dropped my stick off at the house. I knowed where I was going, sure as shoot, and parked the bike in the stand next to the schoolhouse.

A gink's got to notice things sometimes, he thinks to hisself, so I kind of run the palm of my hand across the top of that stand, feeling the rust-worn pipe under the Rust-Oleum, reminding me of Digger's hearse. I din't look up at the parsonage, but cut across the road anyways, towards the cemetery. The grass, it was cut so nice.

ME, I ALWAYS go to Baby Sis's stone first. It's easier, I guess, when you never knowed them, ceptings I at least felt her kick once when, toward the end before the labor, Mom put my hands on her stomach. But I din't want to think about that none. I just wanted this to be over with, so I just stood there looking on Baby Sis's stone, knowing it'd soon be over with and done. After a time I shift my weight to another foot, trying to think on that. Final-like, I hear her voice from a ways away, beings it could fill a room or the whole outside, coming from ever witch way at once, a slight rasp in it like a crow's caw. "Charles Cousins, is that you?"

I turn around and look right at her. It was a lot easier when you could see her whole self. "Yes Mam."

"I'm just surprised. I don't think I've ever seen you this side of the road but of a Sunday," she says. She was walking towards me.

"No Mam," I says.

"What's the matter, Charles?" she had to go and say. And I'll be darned ifing I din't start bawling right then and there.

She put her hands on my shoulders. Those hands. Right there and then, and I'll be danged ifing I'm not going to need a handkerchief to tell you on this, but she pulled me to her, my spine stiff as my stick, me leaning forward there on her, arms limp, like a scarecrow's, I spose.

She wanted me to come in sos I could compose myself, she says, but I knowed she's being nicer to me than that, that what she really wanted was to worm it out of me what's on my mind. She's got curiosity, the Schoolteacher, and I know she'd never be satisfied till I spilled it all. But I weren't about to, even though I din't know it.

She took me to the parsonage, and the white of that house she painted on herself seemed to vibrate even when I'd my head down and my eyes half closed half the time. There was old books in there all over the walls that sort of slow-like come into view like it was dawn coming on or a TV show about to start, and there was magazines, Lord, were there magazines! She must have subscribed to about a dozen and there weren't any of no *Ladies' Home Journal* sort. I ain't seen nothing like it outside of a library in Lawless, but I din't make a thing of it. I din't want to give her the idea she was weird or nothing.

She offered me tea. Tea. I told her no thanks, but I wouldn't mind a Royal Crown seeing that it was a hot day and all on my bike. She brought ginger ale. Wow. What do you say about a Lady like that? I thanked her, even though it tasted some like Ivory Flakes smells.

"How's your father, Charles?" she just up and asked.

I'd to tell her the truth. You couldn't lie to her none or you'd get the eyes. I looked up and looked at her forehead what was real high. I kept my eyes there. "He's OK, far as I know."

"Does he like his job?" she says.

I said I guess he did but I din't get to talk to him much about it with me being asleep when he got home and him being asleep when I got to school.

"Well, there's Sunday, isn't there?"

"Yes Mam," I says.

"Well, maybe this summer you'll get to see him more."

I told her I sposed so. And then dang it, I started bawling again.

She come over and sits down next to me on her couch, but this time she don't touch me none. She reached in her apron and pulled out these neat-folded tissues, peels one off and hands it to me.

"You miss the farm," she said.

"No," I had to tell her, because I had to tell her the truth. "Pop ain't got nothing, nothing to do with this."

"*Hasn't*, Charles, *hasn't*," she says, I remember.

So I says to her, "Pop hasn't got nothing to do with this," I said. I used to disremember when I was talking to her I ain't talking to no local born.

"Well, Charles, what is it then?"

"It's me," I says and thunk to myself I knowed she'd worm it out of me. "I read this book."

I was sure it was coming.

"What book?" she says.

"A real hard book," I says.

"And?"

"And I got it, I understood ever dog-gone word of it. I could see it all just like it were a movie in my mind."

"*What* book?" she wants to know.

I make her promise she wouldn't get mad.

"*Billards*," I blurt out and kind of cringe, specting the title to maybe rock the book shelf behind us and drop one of them fat ones on my head. But she din't say nothing. The Schoolteacher, she were true to her word. And I figured on account of I'd gone this far, I'd may as well tell the whole story.

It was beautiful, I told her. I told her she's got to realize it ain't pool. That the table ain't got pockets. That there's three balls, a cue ball and two object balls. What you do mostly is shoot the cue ball and hit one of the object balls and then go three cushions and touch the other object ball. Ifing you do that, you get a point and another shot. It's beautiful, I says to her.

She don't say a thing, looking at the floor, those eyes of hers jerking and dancing at the same time.

I tell her what really made me ascared, though. It was while I was studying on those angles it was like the cue ball come alive, that I knowed exact-like how much stroke to use, what the sound of the cushions would be. I knowed it all and I never laid eyes on a billard table in my life.

And there was more I just couldn't see how I knowed because I flunked in the second grade and all. Reading that book, leaning over them pictures, it were like that mirror of the inside of my head turned into a winda and behind it, silent-like, I seen me. And either I'm to be—and that's what made me the most ascared—or *had been* the bestest billiard player who ever lived. But that I have to practice. Now, how can that be, she had to tell me. Ifing I *were* the greatest billiard player ever, how is it that now I should have to practice to make me what I already were?

She looked at me, but not with her eyes. It was a look I'd seen only from Mom. I hated it when her eyes then become her own, when for a second it was like my Mom was going to speak to me from outside, under the lawn.

"You're acting, Charles, like you don't know between fantasy and real," she said.

I couldn't believe it. I knowed she was listening. I'd have bet a year's supply of pop from the Barber's machine she figures on I'm telling her true. Saying what I seen in that book were a fantasy's like saying a wet dream ain't real. I knowed right there I could go home and stare in that book, and I would be like I'd felt a cue in my hand for ever second I would come to hold it, or had held it.

"You've created—"

I jumped up. "I ain't created nothing but what I can create, *has* created, whatever, on that danged felt with my cue!" I spun and I run out.

I pumped the pedals like I'd swallered a steam engine. All I could think on was the eyes. But I weren't mad at her.

They, the eyes, they begun to soften, just a hint, I seen, when I yelled at her.

THE EYES, THEY was green. They was hazel. Blue. It all depended on the light. It depended on what kind of mood you was in and what kind of day the Lord seen fit to make it. Not only did the Lord make the next day sort of sunny-like but he made it a Sunday. Her eyes was blue. Helen and Peg was there, in Sunday school, them with their ugly acne and new breasts. They played a game on me all the time, one I couldn't quit, so I just couldn't keep from church, no matter what. We'd be sitting there in a basement room of the church around that table with the Schoolteacher giving us our lesson and I'd be getting real hot in the face and ears and collar and I'd have to swaller. Then there'd be that hand under the table on my knee, Helen's or Peg's, it din't matter much witch because they'd trade off Sundays. You'd start to squirm a little and pretty soon there'd be no room in your pants to breathe. You felt like you had to excuse yourself to go to the bathroom, but you din't dare. And about the time her palm was pressing down real hard on this tent pole you had in your lap, you'd be wishing the two of them din't have brothers and at the same time thankful they did, specting any second God would split the table with a lightning bolt from the ceiling. And all the time you had to be thinking whether the eyes was on you or not. They, the eyes, wanted to talk to me after, on this very Sunday, I could tell, but I had to fast beat it out of there what with no suit coat on account of because I rode my bike.

I took a spin into town after I goes to the bathroom at home and picked up a Sunday *Post Dispatch* for Pop. Me and him loved them funny papers when they was in color. Pop din't go to church much anymore, and it seemed I couldn't blame him none what with the Lord taking away his only wife that he loved and his baby girl he hardly laid eyes on. We never talked much, but we sure did laugh over them Sunday funnies. That afternoon we got to thinking on how much fun it would be to own a color TV. He said he'd try to work some overtime sos we could go halves or maybe him more than half since my birthday was coming up and he always wanted to buy me a big present from a big store in Lawless, beings I were his only son and all. I says to him I thunk that that would be right nice, now that I'd some income. What I disremembered was I din't feel like shooting nothing but trick shots lately, not with what I knowed now when I looked at that book. Now I'd have to be earning a living instead of just showing off. I could see it in my play, me taking these shots with no anticipation. I mean ifing you're playing 14.1 continuous, you got to know where the cue ball is going to stop after you make a shot. But that's only the problem ifing you're good. When you're the best, then you don't have to know where it's going to land. You land it where you want it. Bob the Barber said it right. He said I was playing belligerent-like. Instead of taking the easy ball, I'd soup the cue ball up with all this juice and all and call balls out of the pack. Oh it's pretty all right. All manner of colors rolling around like an airplane view of your carnival at the Centennial. But it ain't smart pool. Once in a while I'd miss. Then instead of winning a game to fifty by fifty, I'd win by twenty-five. It cut my income in half.

"What the hell's the matter with you, Stick?" Bob the Barber says, perched up on his throne after-hours of a Wednesday. "You're playing with Floyd's head, like you got water in the brain."

"To heck with color TV," I says and rode home and wanted to tell Pop the deal was off, but I falled asleep.

The next day being Thursday, all the stores shut down in the afternoon, all but the post office, on account of some special government rules, the Barber always says. Anyways, I done something I ain't never had the courage for before, I played hooky with my cue and about busted it climbing in the bathroom winda from the alley behind the shop. I thought on that—what would make the barber madder, me breaking in like this or busting my stick? I shot trick shots. A ton of them. I even made a new one up. By the end of the afternoon, I got it pat.

I about croaked when I heared the key in the latch of the front door. Though I were practically shooting in the dark, I just knowed he, the Barber what I'm talking about, knowed I was in there by the sound of that key and the footsteps, quick and smart-like, on their way toward the back room. I bolt for the bathroom but decide I'd never make it out in time with my stick in one piece. I turn to face the music and flip on the bathroom light sos the Barber could see it were me and everthing and not be ascared.

"Charles Cousins," I heared this voice what fills the building, what had stopped short in the doorway, "What-on-

Earth-do-you-think-you're-doing?"

I could have filled my pants. Her feet was spread wide and her knuckles was on her hips, her elbows stuck out as far as they'd go in front.

I hugged my cue. "Nothing," I says. "How did you know I was in here?"

"Your bike," she snapped, and I flinched.

"Yes Mam, but—"

"Never mind," she shouts.

I said to myself it must have been the post office, a package from God, beings he wanted me to pay for my sin. I leaned on my cue in a corner and braced myself on the wall.

"Turn around, Charles!" she yells.

I spun back, you can bet.

"Look at me, now. Does it appear to you I have a paddle in my hand?"

I swallered. "No Mam."

"Then what were you doing in that ridiculous posture?"

I told her I guessed I din't know.

"Charles Cousins," she said, a little of the edge gone from her voice, yet still standing there, mad as a cat, "I haven't spanked you since you were nine years old."

"I spose I'm about due," I says.

First thing next morning I got made the example of. It took her ten licks and two rulers, and you know, I felt more sorry for her than me. I bet to myself she had to pay for them rulers out her own purse. Still, it stung enough that I knowed I weren't about to pull me another stunt like that for a time. But the big change that come over me was swearing off pool, standing there in the shop the night before like a whipped pup, growing on fourteen. Sudden-like she were more older too, maybe fifty-four.

SATURDAY MORNING I waked, I'll not forget, staring at my stick propped up in the corner. I knowed I was going to have to make myself busy, and so after some breakfast, I check on Pop, seeing he were still gone from this world, and I knowed that no cartoons or nothing was going to satisfy me. So I busies myself with something I ain't never done of a Saturday. I was having me a real blast working them Latin and Greek roots. It was then I read something I'll remember even in my grave, it struck my funny bone so hard, and even though I never did get it wrote down. There in that new list she handed me the day before was the Firechief's name. I about split me a gut, wondering on Old Pyro, whether he got hot when he heared the ginks calling him that behind his back. And like I say I was about to write it down, ceptings Pop and me, we was always short on paper, and I was hunting around my bedroom trying to lay my eyes on some when I caught a glimpse of this grocery sack sticking out from under my mattress. I pull it out slow-like, this strange feeling coming on. I know I ain't never seen it before cepting maybe under the kitchen sink where we keep them for garbage and all, and yet here it is in my bedroom, all folded up with some pencil drawed on it. I look down at what is in my hand—little clouds, a whole string of them in the shape of a fishhook, or an almost capital

"C." Now it weren't them doodles that got my heart pounding so. It was two words scribbled, *stoop* and *mailbox*, *stoop* at the top of the C and *mailbox* at the bottom, on account of, you see, ain't nobody in the world makes x's and o's quite like that, the Schoolteacher the other day'd said, standing over my shoulder. And I felt the fret coming on sos I quick shoved that sack back under the mattress, feeling a pencil under there too. I begun pacing around real nervous-like, trying to think on when I done it, knowing full well I'd never have an answer you could right away figure on. We just ain't lived in that house that long.

I right away I went outside in the front yard and near paced me a path out there, stopping ever so often to take a glimpse of the mailbox or the front door, what was nailed shut on account of who needs a front door on a farmhouse where there ain't no women. I went back in and I counted the clouds. Something told me there'd be thirteen. I run to the tool shed, grabbed me an old pair of clippers and a shovel and set to work.

Before long, I'm standing with my back to the mailbox in the middle of counting when Pop showed up in his robe and shoes.

"Morning Charlie," he said.

I don't know that I said it back. I was counting, all right. I'd counted to thirteen about a hundred times, each time coming up with the same figure, thirteen clouds, bleached near white as chalk and about the size of cowplops, in the form of flagstone steps stretching across the front lawn.

"Where'd you get them, Son—the crick?" he says.

I remember looking on his face like it might as well been

on the moon.

He kept at it. "It's a right fine idea. You really done spruced the old place up."

"Ain't no idea of mine!" I yelled at him and run for my bike agin the house. "Can't you see they was already there? I just dug them up!"

I rode out on the driveway, not even thinking about turning left when I got to the mailbox. But I done it, anyways. And kept on pumping.

I'D WORKED UP an awful sweat, standing there over Baby Sis's stone, figuring on I'd be there a while, anyways, since there weren't no sign of the Schoolteacher's car, what was a good thing. What was I going to say to her anyways? She'd just tell me it was all some dream, I says, knowing I'm fooling myself but wishing I weren't so that maybe she could talk me out of believing what I done that morning with my own two hands.

I couldn't take no more, standing there in that spot, so I kind of moseys over toward her front lawn and sits under her big maple, looking away to the schoolhouse sos she wouldn't think I was evading her privacy none, even though it was April and the ground was damp and it were too cool what with my sweat to sit in the shade. I knowed she wouldn't be gone long. I could maybe hear her radio, I thought. I seen a couple cars come by and slow down a bit before they drived on, but I just looked at the ground, thinking they would see it was natural for me to be propped up like that agin the tree trunk.

Finally she pulls in, not even looking at me. She got out, slung a sack of groceries under her arm and begun for the parsonage. Halfway there, she surprised me some when she said, "Come in, Charles, and get up off that damp ground."

I din't want to sit on her sofa, beings my jeans was sort of soggy in the crotch and all, so I follow her into the kitchen.

She begun storing her groceries. I couldn't blame her none for being still mad at me, so I din't say nothing to her till she put it all away, though I was shaking with being ascared when I thought on how I was going to tell her.

She fixes me tea, and I said my piece, told her the whole truth. When I'm done, she come over beside me and she put one hand on the back of my neck and the other she put on my forehead. She holds them there a real long time. Lord Jesus, she held them there. She said she was calling my Pop, and I was to stay there the night. She could crack that whip of hers, all right, but she din't carry it always.

Next afternoon, Pop and me, we had a heart-to-heart, like the Schoolteacher said we oughta. He told me he'd been seeing a lady and her three kids up by work, and I tell him I done swore off pool.

"For your whole life?" he wants to know.

I told him I din't know about that but the Schoolteacher wanted me to get my education, and I reckoned she was right. I mean she din't think it proper for me to be playing for money or nothing, beings I was only growing on fourteen.

"Is that all?" he said. "I mean what did you do over there all day and all morning?"

I din't know how to tell him I swore off Helen and Peg

too. "We went to Sunday school."

"But you din't have no Sunday clothes."

I said the Schoolteacher said that din't matter as long as they was clean, and she made me wash them.

Pop thought that was all right but what'd we do yesterday.

I told him we washed clothes.

"You mean you washed them *with* her...her brazier and ever thing?"

"Yep."

"You weren't embarrassed or nothing?" he says.

"Not when she weren't," I told him, witch was mostly the truth.

"Son, that's a strong woman," he up and tells me. "You'd best listen to what she has to say."

I din't tell him I already had or that part of what she had to say about my heart-to-heart with Pop was not to speak until spoken to about me walking in my sleep. She was afraid Pop wouldn't understand, and I din't doubt her none, beings I sure as sugar din't neither.

She fixed me a big lunch and supper, but she made me earn my keep, cleaning house besides helping her with the wash. All the while she was asking questions-like, cept when she was studying on my answers.

She give me a sketchpad and pencil after supper and told me to draw whatever I want.

"What for?" I had to ask.

"Draw," she said.

I drawed.

I felt kind of dumb—like on account of I knowed she

was real good at it, teaching us ginks on it and all, though we mainly only copied what she done. Now I had to come up with something on my own. I couldn't concentrate there in the kitchen with the radio so soft in the back of my head, and I told her so.

She give me my mother's eyes. Then she just stared at me—not with her eyes but eyes that was hazel and says she was remembering on something. It was a pitiful look, her sitting there, just staring at me and then ever so slightly shaking her head. When I saw her eyes returning to her face, I looked down and quick begun me a doodle. Right then I had an idea. I drawed her face with the high forehead and all—the eyebrows that growed close because she never plucked them, I spose, the long, thin nose that looked like it might've been a little broke, the flat cheeks and square chin, the quiet mouth that got so big when it smiled, what by all rights din't deserve to be called anything but sad, mostly. I drawed all this, but I put a little of my personality in it. I left her eyes closed with hardly any lashes. And I give her a new hairdo, loose-like instead of flat, all pulled back in a bun, maybe. And since she were so nice to me that day, I left out the crow's feet. It weren't hard. Her face was usual-like smooth anyways, cept when she got out her eyes.

Then I drawed a picture of me and I'll be darned ifing the two faces weren't a lot alike.

She told me to keep that sketchpad and whenever I got the urge, I was to draw.

Me, I wondered on what urge she was talking about.

She sent me to bed up in her room after she showed me

some on how to play chess, what I wanted to play even though after a time she offered to switch to checkers. I kind of laid there in that bed thinking on how I liked that new game—it remembering me so much on billards what with the angles and all, the queen and the knight, my favorite ones to move—when I got to thinking on she'd probable-like be staying up to see ifing I done something crazy in my sleep again. I'd a little dream about me trying to ride home in the middle of the night without no light on my bike, but, far as I knowed, that's as weird as it got.

When in morning time I woke up with this big boner, I reached for my sketchpad and drawed a little, but I figured she wouldn't want me to draw on what I was drawing, so I give up and take me a trip to the bathroom. That made it a lot easier to swear off Helen and Peg. Whosever hand it was that morning in Sunday school must have thunk on I'd had a operation. I wished I could operate on my cue. But that would be like cutting off my hand.

I told her thanks and all, after I helped her clean up the breakfast dishes, but that I'd better ride into town and pick up the *Post* for Pop after Sunday school. She said I oughta concentrate on my studies and to come to her ifing I got ascared some more.

"I just have one more thing I must say to you, Charles."

"Yes Mam," I says.

"My radio is broken," she says.

"I swear I din't touch it."

"That's not what I mean, and I think you know it."

"Yes Mam," I had to admit.

"Are you afraid, Charles?" she up and asks.

"A little," I says.

"Do you hear it now?" she says.

"Yes," I says, "but it's only when I'm real close or something."

"Do you want to see the doctor about it?" she wants to know.

"No Mam, and please don't tell nobody," I says.

She said she wouldn't just as long as she thought I was all right. I was sure as one of my shots she'd be true to her word.

I knowed she din't want me to give up my friends just because I give up pool. She was real smart that way. She probable-like figured I'd be back in the barber shop come Thursdays ifing she told me I couldn't be talking to Nooner or nobody. Heck, that would be just like saying I couldn't talk to Pop.

Since I ain't seen Bob the Barber none since Wednesday last, I was starting to crave on his sarcasm a bit, so I figured Monday afternoon after school I'd get me some exercise and visit a old friend too. I din't hold it agin him none for giving the Schoolteacher the key to the shop, but he'd have knowed that, on account of he knowed I seen the Schoolteacher's eyes just like he done.

"Watchu got, Stick?" he said when I come in. I know by that he weren't mad at me for busting in. After all, it was him what met me up with the habit.

"I ain't shooting no pool. I swore off," I says.

"Watch this," he up and says and starts wiggling his ears witch was real easy to see on account of he wore this flat-top always trimmed neat as the cemetery lawn what was probable-like a advertisement. I use to always wonder how the Barber got barbered till I seen him doing it hisself. "You see these?" He pointed to his ears with both index fingers, then he points to his eyes. "Hath not a Jew eyes?" he up and wants to know. Bob the barber, he weren't no Jew, on account of I never laid eyes on one. I figured it was something the Schoolteacher use to say.

Finally I got what he was talking about. I looked at my sketch pad. "Oh you mean this," I says and hold it up.

He closed his eyes and nodded. When Bob the Barber done that, then you know you'd really been razzed on account of he had these Royal Crown bottles for glasses and his eyes was so far away you'd find yourself shouting at him to be heared, because he was sitting up in the upper atmosphere, he said hisself, even though he was on the same old chair in the same barber shop you was in.

"Well, I spect maybe you'd let me draw you sos I could have something to do." I din't want to tell him I felt naked riding into town without my stick.

"Well, you sposed right," he says. So me and the Barber, we just sat there, me penciling him in, us shooting the breeze about Termite-Town-Constable or Pyro or the Banker or whoever, waiting for closing time since what few locals and a couple of ginks from out of town, ceptings whoever happened to be in back, Bob the Barber sent on home because he says there weren't going to be no pool shooting exhibitions-like in town for awhile, anyways. What he said, it made me kind of sad. But I was sadder the last Friday morning when the Schoolteacher busted her ruler, so I din't say nothing to Bob. I just drawed.

Now that reminds me. I got to tell you on this. Wouldn't you know that in another couple days I had me a new income. It all started on Tuesday when Digger, bless him, give me a dollar for sketching him in the chair. I din't think much on it. I just ripped out the drawing and handed it to him. Pretty soon all the old ginks first, then ever body was giving me quarters and such to draw them. Not only was I getting rich, but I was getting good, dang near as good as the Schoolteacher.

But that ain't how I come to say "bless him" ever time I think on Digger. I guessed he felt kind of sorry for me, beings the Schoolteacher asked me to give up my God-given talent to make a income shooting pool and the fact he buried my Mom and Baby Sis and all. He told me next time there was teachers' institute of a Thursday for me to come to his office in the funeral home at one o'clock sharp, that he'd be waiting for me.

I wondered what it was all about.

"Never you mind," he says. "You just keep drawing."

I figured I owed it to him since he give me that dollar, so I said it back to him what I was to do of a future Thursday.

Now needless to say, I become as curious as the Schoolteacher. But I din't want to show no disrespect to the undertaker, figuring on how that could be bad luck, so ever time I seen him after that I pretended to pay him no mind cept the usual courtesy due a man of his profession. So I done what he said. I drawed. I waited.

One day in school I got to thinking on what it could all be about, beings Digger was always showing up in my drawings—not sos you could see him, but when I was drawing heads I kept picturing Digger's hung belly below the drawing, off the pad. I mean I din't want Digger making me no apprentice or nothing. And it sure weren't in my nature to draw dead people.

I told the Schoolteacher I was a little ascared, and because we was doing art, I guess she figured I'd taken me another stroll in the middle of a night or drawed or heared something, so we talk about it after school.

"Are you all right?" she says.

I told her I was fine, thank you, and then I tell her what Digger said.

She warned me not to worry, that she'd known Digger since he was a pup and he was in business to save lives as much as to smooth the way toward heaven, since that hearse was as much an ambulance as it was anything else.

I knowed that. But what she did was she pumped my tires up a bit. I could see myself come Thursday riding into town without a fret in my head.

I RUN UPSTAIRS above the funeral home to his office one o'clock sharp, about to give a knock, and I stopped short. I couldn't believe it, I looked at what I was holding. My stick. How could I've forgot my pad when Digger give me that dollar and all? I wanted to run back home, but he'd said *sharp*, and even though I'd begun to love Digger, bless him, I still din't want to show him no disrespect. So I leaned my cue in a corner, in a shadow by the door to Masonic Hall, across from the office. It felt funny, leaving go of my stick in a spot I ain't never been before, sort of like letting loose of Mom's hand in a department store in Lawless when I weren't no more than four, once. Still, the whole place felt familiar-like. I quick knocked.

Digger come to the door. "Wait," he says, a look on his face I couldn't read—happy or sad—and he turns for his desk, rooting under some papers. I says to myself I want to tell him I been waiting for this my *en*tire life, even though I knowed it was only a few weeks. I closed my eyes. About all I seen was my stick. I lifts my eyelids. Digger turned around and hands me this little envelope, yellow and stiff-like with a flap licked shut on one end, like something you ain't never seen but with a silver dollar in it on account of it was flat and hard, whatever was in it. Now that I think on it, it could've been a million dollars in it and it wouldn't've meant as much.

So I opened it because Digger, bless him, says I oughta. It was silver, all right, but it weren't no dollar. My heart starts beating sos I could notice.

"Some of the ginks in town wanted you to have this," Digger says. I looked down at it in my hand. I ain't never owned a key. What was the point of having one when you ain't got nothing worth stealing? Cept maybe your stick? And though I seen with my own eyes I ain't held this key in my palm for more than a few seconds, it felt as comfortable as my stick there, like I'd saw it before with all the silver plating worn off, witch couldn't be, I says to myself, on account of at this minute, for all I know, this key ain't nothing but pure silver and I ain't even heared tell of no silver plating, ever.

For a second I was ascared-like again. But then I just

pretend-felt the Schoolteacher's hand on my brow, like that Saturday morning, and I weren't shaky no more.

I turned around.

"Where you going?" Digger, bless him, says.

I turned back and hand him the envelope. The question was still on his face.

I couldn't've answered ifing I wanted. I weren't ascared no more, on account of I'd done this thousands of times. I turned away and grabbed my stick in the corner. "Please be true," I says under my breath. I looked at that key in the dim light of the hallway, held it there for a second, then I slips it in the lock of the door across from Digger's office. It fit. My hand was all rubber-like, my left hand, see, because I'm left handed, but my right hand, on account of it's my bridge hand, felt solid. Like I say, half of me knowed what I was doing.

I look back at Digger. Even though it was dim in that hallway, I figured his eyes was wide open because his mouth sure was.

"Who told you?" he said.

"No one sos you'd know them yet," I said.

At that, I felt and heared the click of the lock.

I should have kept my own dang mouth shut. All the older ginks was nervous with one another, convinced as they was one of them done spilled the beans. They wouldn't listen to me sos when finally they did believe me, they put me up on a pulpit-like wanting to know what I knowed. In other words, there weren't no chance they thunk it was chance what led me to that lock, that key zeroing in on it like a boner that knows where it belongs, Bob the Barber would've hisself said.

It wasn't something I could just make happen, the knowing, I mean. I never really known in my head what I already known, ifing you see what I mean. I always had to test it out. Like digging up them flagstone steps. Not till I counted them did I know. And like with Digger, bless him, me standing there in front of the Lodge hall, all I knowed was something told me what was behind that door. I din't know for sure until I seen it with my own two eyes and felt it with my own two hands, not that I believed what my hands and eyes were saying, sort of whispering to me like as ifing to wake me up from the most lonesome dream you had in your life.

I sort of spread my hands flat out on the surface, smooth as it was when I run my palms and fingers over it, because it had this give to it like the feel of a new crew cut, like you could feel the give but you couldn't see it, just like what you could feel under your hand ifing you was to run it down the sleeve of a Schoolteacher's suede coat as you passed through the cloak room on your way to the toilet. The surface was gray, but no gray you ever seen in your life cept the kind rich people's over-stuffed chairs was made out of in old time movies on the Barber's black and white Motorola. The surface was real hard too. You could knock your knuckles on it and afterwards you'd know any door you met in your life—wood, glass, metal—had give to it, not like this door what felt like the Vetern's monument in the park, like rock, like all the doors to the Earth, like a road paved by God for Jesus to walk, on account of this door was flat, not standing.

Once more, slow-like, I run my hands over the surface, like smoothing out a bedsheet, just to be sure it weren't no trick of the eye. Then I lift my hands and place my palms flat on the rail and hooked my fingers over the cushion. I close my eyes and walked my hands around the table, counting and crying inside at ever corner. The angles, they were right and they was four. My eyes hadn't lied, there weren't no pockets.

I looked up at Digger, standing in the doorway, his mouth still open. Today was the day of the test, the one I been studying on for longer than I was born, but not before I was born, my remembering always said. So what ifing I swore off pool? One look at this table and even the Schoolteacher would tell you this ain't no pool. This was to be, *was*, my chessboard. And I knowed she knowed it too. Otherwise I wouldn't be standing there. I wanted to take the test. Now.

"Lord Jesus, Digger, where's the chalk! The balls?" I couldn't believe how I'd said it to him, Digger, bless him. It's like sudden-like I am the boss and he's the butler.

He hurried to a drawer, tossed me a cube of chalk, rolled the cue ball my way, and set up the object balls.

"The lights, Digger, get the blessed lights!"

I chalked up, and got myself square, the lights come on, and I stroked one third full, sending that cue ball on its path, spinning sideways like a planet in a square orbit. I weren't worried whether I'd make the shot. The break shot, you see, is what they call a natural. For me missing a natural would be like a full-growed man wetting hisself. It just don't happen to a player in his prime. And me, I was in my prime.

What I was thinking was "shape," whether I'd leave myself with a clear second shot. And here come that cue ball off the third cushion like it were a ball bearing and the second object ball were the world's most powerful electromagnet. It was like I had me remote control. I shut off the juice when I had the cue ball on target and I seen it begun to slow down, deliberate-like, like seeing from a distance a car sliding on the ice down a hill and whoever's inside has got his brakes locked on account of there's another car stalled at the bottom and the Lord God has a plan for the meeting of all bodies and souls. My soul was in that cue ball, and I knowed I was about to get engaged. Me and my intended, we then come together with a kiss and I'm so shy and heckbent on having her we bump heads. Not great, I says to myself. But not bad neither. I made the second shot. The third. I quit counting only when I knowed it was real. Once, I glance up at Digger. His mouth was open.

I shot until I broke the tip off my stick. Digger din't say nothing. I din't even have to look at him. He reached in the drawer where the balls was and pulled out a repair kit.

I sat on a stool. We din't say nothing, Digger and me, bless him.

MONDAY MORNING I kept glancing up at the Schoolteacher to see ifing she'd be glancing back at me, but it were business as usual.

She stopped me on my way out after school.

"Yes Mam," I says.

"Your sketchpad, Charles," she says.

I'll be danged ifing that woman din't have a way! Of course it were what she don't say that give me the message. I knowed

I owed her big, so I just runned around and headed for my desk. I disremembered it, you see, what with billards always on the brain. I told her I was sorry and all.

She told on how the best way for me to tell her I was sorry was to not forget it again.

I din't. At least not sos I can remember, anyways, and cepting the time I disremembered it on purpose, what is another story, although it ain't really.

I had me this problem. How was I sposed to carry it and my stick? That afternoon I learned how to ride no hands.

Practicing in town around the square, I liked to killed myself. This car I ain't never seen before, I almost run into twice in two minutes. It was mostly of his fault, though, on account of I was on my side. I went to thumb my nose at him the second time—he gets me so ticked off—but there was glare offing the windshield, and for all I knowed it could've been a lady in there. Besides, how was I going to thumb my nose with my cue in one hand and sketchpad in the other?

I parked on the sidewalk in front of the shop because I seen Nooner's truck and I ain't sketched him none yet. Weren't nobody in there, though, ceptings Old Floyd and Cromangon Man. And Floyd—ifing he don't beat all—sitting up there on Bob's throne with his head half barbered, taking a snooze. I sits on the machine, across from Cromangon Man, and starts sketching him.

"Where'd ever body disappear to?" I asks him.

Now with Cromangon man, you're liable to get you an answer and you're liable not. "Fire," he says.

"Where?" I says.

When Cromangon Man don't say nothing, that can mean either of two things, either he don't know or he does know and he ain't about to waste precious words witch he don't own too many. I remembered him in school, him always being a lot older than me. He knowed a lot about the crick and the woods and making knifes and stuff.

So I ask of him what kind of fire.

He figured it weren't grass, beings it was a wet spring.

I asked him how come he don't join up with the fire department like the other ginks.

It was real easy to draw Cromangon Man what with his jaw always wired. So I close the pad and pull me out a Royal Crown from the machine and leave Bob the Barber an extra two cents on his register on account of I was taking the bottle out of the shop. I'll be, ifing I couldn't figure how I were going to carry it, my stick and my pad on my bike when I get outside, so I just walk across the square to the Masonic Hall.

Digger, bless him, weren't there neither, of course, him being second in command to Pyro. So I practiced some without him. When I come back to the shop, my bike, it weren't there, but all the old ginks was. I knowed what they was doing, because things was real quiet when I got in there.

"Where was the fire at?" I up and asked.

Ever body was straight-faced ceptings Floyd. He owned him the biggest grin you ever seen.

It was Nooner what spoke first. "Well, maybe you could tell *us*."

He made me real mad, but I figured the Schoolteacher would just say they was all jealous or mad at each other because they think somebody spilled the beans about the Hall key. I'd've rather had them jealous, so I just thought on how I could figure where they hid my bike. I put my empty bottle in the rack and got my two cents back off the register sos they'd all know I was ready to go home, but nobody said nothing.

I sat on the machine and opened my pad. Weren't no way I was about to draw me no gink, though, so I just drawed me a car like the new one I seen earlier and put a man in it. Sitting there all the while, just drawing, I had me a hunch where my bike was, and I quick-like jumped down and tore that picture out of the pad, disremembering there weren't no one in the room to give it to. So I just toss it in the wastebasket. Then I grabs my stick and run out and peeked in the back of Nooner's truck and seen my bike laying flat there. Then comes a big roar from the shop. It was like the Schoolteacher told me later, they was just jealous. So I got on my bike and rode on home, giving them something new to chew on.

COME THE WHOLE week, I'd be in the shop drawing me up a storm and them ginks sitting still for me, because they thunk I was going to tell them all on their fortunes.

Like a fool I played into their hands, me wanting to show off some. I couldn't seem to esplain it weren't something I could just up and do any old time I feel like it. It's like they wouldn't believe me none. So I tells Nooner after drawing him of a Friday that he'd be getting some nookie over the weekend, what I figured was a pretty safe bet. That put soda in all their noses, and they seem to slacken up on me some.

It weren't but a few hours, and there a lot of us were of a Saturday morning again, sitting in the shop, me taking a Royal Crown break from practicing when Nooner come in, a big smile all over his face. Bob the Barber got to razzing him about it were near on lunchtime and time for the noon whistle on the watertower to go off but that that wouldn't do Nooner no good because the kids was home from school today. Me being a farm boy, I knowed what Bob was talking about, all right. I thought I oughta tell you that just sos you'd know I'm normal as the next gink.

Anyways, we was just sitting there, cracking jokes and ever thing when I notice Bob the Barber's got this far-away look in his eyes, sitting up there in the crow's nest, looking out across the square. Then he starts to leaning forward a bit. Pretty soon he's got his hands on the armrest like he's about to spring up. We all got our eyes on him now, on account of there ain't no conversation coming from him, witch is like saying there ain't no manure what comes from a bull. Now we're all standing and gawking in front of the plate glass, and I sees Termite-Town-Constable at a distance running and waving something up high, looking like he just woke up and all, beings he had his undershirt on and was trying to hold up his pants with his free hand, what wasn't so unusual-like, I spose, on account of he were skinny and he slept mornings, beings he's the town constable what checks the locks at night. Then this bell like over at the high school goes off, real loud-like, and I think somebody must've dropped the atomic bomb on WGN because I can't hear it no more. Termite, he's still running across the square hard for the shop sos I figure there must be a fire, but none of the ginks is moving. Then I seen it. Termite's got his pistol in his hand, though you couldn't tell it none at first on account of it were still in the holster. He's yelling something about calling Lawless. He's in the middle of the square and Bob the Barber locks the front door. Halfway across the street now, Termite ain't shaved or nothing. His hair's all mussed. He's barefoot. Ever body and me in the shop starts backing away from the winda.

"Let me in!" he says, rattling the shop door.

"Not till you put that s.o.b. down," Bob the barber yells, and he points at the gun.

Old Termite, he just looked at Bob like he thought he was crazy and bolted down the street.

We all step outside and see Termite done ducked in the grocery store or the post office or something. The ring of the bell is so loud it rattles all the store windas.

"Must be the bank," the Barber says, and he runs in and locks his register.

Me, I disremembered all about lunch. I went up to the Masonic Hall. I practiced sos I wouldn't have to think on nothing else. You see, that bank is where Pop and me got all our money. I din't want to hear nothing about him and me having to move again ifing the robber got it all. I had me my table now, and I figured I was set up for life.

Finally the alarm stops ringing, and I'm here to tell you that was a relief, like maybe the Banker shut it off sos he could hear hisself think counting the money what was left. I mean I got to figuring robbers couldn't get it all what with money being so heavy. I seen Bob the Barber pull that box out of his machine a lot of times, him hauling it like it were a *ce*ment block, and all that were in there was dimes and a couple slugs.

It weren't but a couple of hours of me being up there practicing that I begun to lose my concentration and finally I get the notion to peek out the winda at the bank. Another thing is, I'm hungry. So I figure it does me no good practicing on a empty stomach, just like the Schoolteacher says. You can't really think without at least a little something in your belly, and ifing there's anything you need when you're practicing, it's the gumption to remember your worst shots. So I go back to the kitchenette and starts rummaging around, figuring the Masons won't mind ifing I was to eat on a little something, as long as I put it back. I find me some crackers in a tin and have me a regular old lunch with some cheese and bottle juice out of the refrigerator. There was some Falstaff in there too, but I figures that would be like stealing.

I sit up on a stool overlooking the square and I seen there sure enough was plenty of goings-on, what with the kids hollering cops and robbers around the Vetern's memorial in the square, some of the old ginks out on the bench in front of the shop, and people in bunches on the sidewalks, eyeballing the bank. There was something else, of course, something I ain't never seen all in one place before—county squad cars—three of them. They looked so plain and all next to Termite's Cadillac parked askance to them with his blue bubblegum machines on top revolving and flashing. You see, Termite's got him what we knowed around town as his problem with authority. His own authority. He ain't got none, so ever body said he up and bought this fast car and mail order accessories with some of the money his dead wife give him and put a mobile home on the vacant lot next to the implement store so that he could have some authority. What was like a sheep in a wolf's clothes, all the ginks said. Ever body knowed the town needed a night watchman, somebody to pick up the beer cans of a prom night—even though we was dry—not, Bob the Barber said, some crazy old coot thinking he's a cop. I heared tell he even bought hisself his own badge. He weren't really a bad sort, though. Like Nooner says, it takes all kinds, and what else are you going to do with a crazy old coot but let him play cop when he wants? I got a chuckle thinking on how today was maybe the biggest day of his widowered life, me sitting there, munching on crackers and taking another swig of orange juice what, though it smelled like Digger's office, bless him, weren't none too bad, I thought on, beings it was probable-like pretty old. Then I seen this strange car pull up. It must have been a Buick-like on account of it was big, a four door, like the Banker's only his weren't black like this, I remember. Three men got out. They had on suits with vests underneath like the Banker's, what was queer enough, and their shoes was as shiny as a salesman's. They was tall, and one had a pipe in his teeth. You just knowed it weren't no drug store pipe neither, even though you couldn't see it all that well. The three of them, they have sample cases too, and they walk up to the bank, closing and opening the door and looking around all at the same time like they owns the town but they never been here before.

All of the sudden I'm getting a little ascared and I stand up real quick-like, but sit down agin because I'm dizzy. I'm watching that door to the bank and looking back at that Buick for a reason that don't belong to me. The man with the pipe, I says to myself. I'm watching for the man to come out. I'm thirsty from the crackers, so I finish the juice. Now I'm sleepy, and I want to go home. But I don't want to go outside. I don't want the man with the pipe to see me.

At any other time, to me it would've been sack-religious, like standing on a grave, but I couldn't help it, not wanting to sleep on the floor. I sit the bottle down on the winda sill, close my eyes, feeling my way to the middle of the room. I laid down on the table.

SOMETHING WAKES ME up a lot later. It's a voice, a man's voice. My head feels like a basketball gone flat what somebody's trying to bounce. It's just the voice trying to shake me awake. It's got my shoulder. The grip is tight. I open my eyes and I'm looking at a cushion just like a cue ball sees it before it's about to carom off, and, like the cue ball, my brain must have a little English on it because it's spinning. I look up toward the ceiling and there is a man in a suit, but this sure as shoot ain't church.

"Charles Cousins?" the voice says.

I nod like I think so.

"My name is Mr. McMillion. I'm with the F.B.I. I'd like to talk with you about this," he says, and he holds up this sketch I done in the shop the day before.

I sits up on the edge of the table, holding my head, and

I guess a long time went by before I begun to answer him because when I goes to look at his face it weren't there. He'd moved over to the winda.

He picked up the juice bottle and smelled in it. He looked at me, still holding the bottle. "You're kind of young to be drinking screwdrivers, aren't you?"

Since I ain't never heared of swallering no screwdriver, just swords and stuff, I spose I din't say nothing.

He sits the bottle down and then sits hisself on the stool. I really din't know for sure who he was till he lit his pipe. "Can I ask you something?"

I say to him I guess so.

"How did you happen to draw this car?" he wants to know, holding up the sketch.

I tells him the ginks over in the shop was playing a trick on me yesterday and I weren't about to do their *por*traits.

"But why this particular car?" he up and says, real patient-like, on account of he must have knowed I were feeling a little sick and a little ascared.

"I seen it," I says.

"Do you know whose car it is?" he asks.

"No Sir," I says. And I told him how and when I about got runned over with it but I din't tell him why. I din't want to get arrested for riding no hands.

"Are you sure it was a Cor*vair*?"

"A what?" I says.

He looked at me funny-like. "This is a Corvair. A new kind of car."

I told him I din't know about that, but that's the car I

seen, all right.

"This is very good," he said. "Where'd you learn to draw like this?"

I says to him practice.

How long, he wants to know.

"Who wants to know?" I says.

He din't say nothing at first. Then he up and says it's him.

"Oh," I says.

"Well," he says.

"A couple weeks," I says to him.

He looks at me queer-like again.

"I ain't lyin'," I told him. I tell him I almost never lie.

He looked at me for a long time again. "I believe you," he said, but he looked like he still had his suspicions. Or maybe like the Schoolteacher, his *curiosity*, cept he din't have the eyes. Though the sun was behind him and I was fuzzy and all, I could see his face real good. He was thirty, maybe. Three times my age. Me, I was thirteen. "This car," he says. "Have you seen it before?"

"No Sir," I told him.

"How about the man in it?" he says.

"The man weren't in it," I said.

"What do you mean," he says.

"I mean that's just any old man. I din't see nobody."

He says, "You mean you saw a car without a driver?"

"No Sir," I says, "I mean that man is a woman for all I knowed."

He wants to know how come I put a man in the car then.

"Strangers is usually men," I said.

He looks at me. "How about that man over on the little table," he up and says. "Is he a stranger?"

All of the sudden I'm starting to get real ascared again. I look over slow-like at where the balls and cues are kept. I don't see nothing but the sketchpad and pencil. "What man?" I asks.

He walks to the table and brings me my pad, holding it up, square in my face.

By now I'm panting like a sun-baked pup. It was a man, all right. The best face I'd ever drawed, only I ain't drawed it. It was like with them clouds. Only this time the details was so sharp I could've told what color of hair he had, even though I done him in pencil and even though I ain't never seen nobody outside of Lawless with a beard. And so I never drawed that picture, though I knowed I had on account of it had some of my personality in it.

The F.B.I. man, he just closed the pad. He din't look at me queer-like or nothing because I din't look up, but I sposed the sigh that come from hisself meant I wasn't going to be getting in any more practice that afternoon.

"Charles," he said, "what do they call you? Charlie?"

I looked up. "I spose in town I go by 'Stick.'"

He took me over to the bank, and I just knowed all the ginks would be over there in the shop, gawking, even though I din't look across the square. I had me this real hollow feeling, like my privacy'd just been evaded, and there was the fear that what I was doing was taking the first few steps of a short trip to the loony bin in Lawless.

He took me in a little room and pulled out of his sample case this folder with squares on the pages—all kinds of different colors. I was awondering ifing this was how they figured out ifing you was crazy. I slow-like quit breathing hard when he asked me to pick out the color of the car I drawed. I turned some pages. It was easy, a silver gray.

"Stick," he says, "is there anything else you want to tell me?" He was leaned back in his chair, an elbow on the arm rest, holding his pipe in his teeth, looking right at me.

I looked down on account of I couldn't look at him no more. I told him maybe. But I had to talk to the Schoolteacher first. He got right up and left the room without saying nothing. I heared his voice talking to the Banker out in the lobby and then I heared it on the phone.

She come right away in her apron and all and, soon as she saw me, headed straight in the room, shutting the door in the F.B.I. man's face.

I started bawling when I seen that.

She come over, stood by me, and done with her hands what I knowed she'd do. She din't say nothing.

Then real sudden-like she says, "Charles! Have you been drinking?"

I told her that ifing I had I din't know it. But that my head'd been hurting bad.

I tried to esplain the rest, what for I was real ascared again because the F.B.I. man knowed I'd drawed a face I din't know I'd drawed.

"*Drawn*, Charles," she said.

"Yes Mam," I said.

She told me there weren't no ways I should be fearful of the F.B.I. Obvious-like I din't rob no bank and obvious I din't know who did.

She wanted me to show her the sketch, so I done it.

She picked up the pad and held it real delicate-like and sits down beside me. It was like I weren't in the room. And for certain the gink who drawed that picture sure enough weren't in the room unless he were invisible and owned a time machine. "It's simply incredible, Charles," she whispers. I knowed she weren't talking to me because I ain't never heared her lay praise like that on no gink drawing. And I knowed, too, then, there weren't anyone else who snuck in the Hall and done it for me.

"I just wish something, Mam," I says.

She finally looks at me, still holding the pad like she ain't done studying on it. "What's that, Charles?"

I tells her I just wished it wouldn't happen again.

And I told Agent McMillion ever thing I knowed, witch din't seem to please him all that much because the man who robbed the bank din't have a beard. Still, he asked me ifing he could keep the drawing. I ripped it right out and handed it to him, glad I was I wouldn't be seeing it no more.

The Schoolteacher, she took me home with my stick and my bike in her trunk, she waltzed me straight to my room like she already knowed where it was, and she had a real long heart-to-heart with Pop. At least, I figured that was what they was doing, them in the kitchen so long and me in my bed, my brain still doing summer salts.

I laid there awondering whether I hadn't oughta burn that sketchpad for all the trouble it could've got me into. But I owed it to the Schoolteacher, I owed it to Digger, bless him, to keep drawing. Besides, that weren't going to purge me of my dreams, ifing you could call them that. Weren't no way I could swear off sleep neither. Besides, I kind of come to like that old pad. It weren't as satisfying as my stick, but it give me something to do rather than all the time worry over my game. Anyways, a man's got to have a hobby, just like Nooner says. Maybe I could get real good at it like the Schoolteacher seen. I mean maybe I could make the lines come together like that when I weren't sleepwalking. Maybe my hobby could support my calling. I had to start thinking fast. Pretty soon I'd be a eighth-grade graduate, and all the local jobs was already taken up what with Digger, Bob the Barber, Nooner—him owning the dump—and crazy old coots like Termite and all. One thing sure enough, I says to myself, there ain't no way you're going to pay the rent playing three cushion. Ain't nobody to play you on account of there ain't nobody who can beat you. What's the difference, though? For me to bet on three cushion would be like the Schoolteacher chewing on gum in church.

I spose that heart-to-heart the Schoolteacher had with Pop done some good. I din't have to go trying to esplain nothing to him. But we was getting a slow divorce anyways. Maybe that's the way it had to be, especial-like since the Schoolteacher was more my old man than him most times lately. I din't want to hurt his feelings none, but, you see, I figured why talk to the preacher when you can talk to God hisself? I knowed he'd never really understand, even though he done said I oughta listen to the Schoolteacher. The problem was he never had her in school, beings he quit about the sixth grade, the same time she shows up in town. Pop and me, we was more like brothers after the funeral. And brothers who stay together is always queer. Not that he was going to wander off tomorrow or nothing. Pop, I think he knowed it why it was his duty to make a home for me till I was big enough to fend for myself. I spose that was what the Schoolteacher was bending his ear about. Anyways, we sure did go fishing a lot after that day. Mostly to the crick. And mostly there were silence. But that's how I later come to really know him. The quiet.

It was how I come to know about the critters too. But that will take some esplaining.

ME AND POP would be fishing of a Sunday afternoon, and we'd catch a glimpse of Cromangon Man off yonder. The Schoolteacher said Cromangon man was one of them people whose best friend was hisself. Now, *that* I begun to appreciate, beings that when summer come and I weren't up at the shop or bent over my table with my stick because it was too hot, it seemed natural-like to pick up my pole and head for the crick. I weren't much of a real fisherman, but I'd have my sketchpad and I'd draw me some nature for a change.

Now Cromangon Man, there was one gink who were a different breed of cat. He din't work none, beings he lived with his folks and went to the junior college in Lawless, though he never would tell me what he was studying on up there. He seemed he knowed all kinds of stuff nobody else knowed. He showed me how to catch small mouth when the only thing I ever got up to that point out of that crick was a sucker or a carp, cept nights, witch you'd catch bullheads. And Cromangon Man, he wouldn't use no pole. Just black thread and a spider lure he cut out of a old tire. But that weren't his secret. The secret was there weren't no bass what ever saw him coming until they was on the bank. Cromangon Man never walked to the crick. He crawled. Maybe that's why when me and Pop seen Cromangon Man off in the yonder, we never really seen him but the smoke from his fire instead. He near to lived on bass and cans of pork and beans. He'd catch one of them two pounders and he'd let out a war whoop the likes of witch you ain't heared since the last time you was standing by the water tower and the noon whistle went off. Then Cromangon man wouldn't say a word or even nod that you was there. He'd just head for the woods. It was all pasture on both sides of that spot, so it was easy for me to wade across and follow him into the trees.

The first few times I done it, I din't say nothing to him. He knowed I was there but he just cleaned on his fish like it weren't nobody's business. I could see he had hisself a regular place there, all set up with a log to sit on and rocks around the fire. The coals would by now be just right and he'd puncture a hole in that can of pork and beans, toss it in the fire, and fry that bass in something that looked like butter but din't smell none like it. He always cleaned up before he'd ate too, just like a Indian squaw, I come to find out.

He ain't said no word to me, never, until one day I follow him with my own bass. He don't even look up. He just pulls out two cans of pork and beans from his pack, punctures them both with his big old hunting knife, and throws them on the coals. Then he reaches over, pulls my bass off the stringer, and cleans it some. We're just squatting there, passing the plate, when finally Cromangon Man, he packs up, and he says, "Come on." Only this time we're headed the wrong direction, upstream, instead of down to the bridge where we always go our separate ways—me home and Lord knows where for Cromangon Man on account of while some claim he sleeps in town, nobody gets up early enough or goes to bed late enough to catch him coming and going.

I don't know that I'm all that keen on following him, so I keep a few strides behind, what weren't hard, him like a mule with a mission through the brambles and brush. All of the sudden I see up ahead that the crick, witch about a half mile back was to the left, now meanders up into the woods. We follow it forever, it seems, till I can't believe my eyes. Trees is laying ever witch way, and it looks like somebody's been at them with a axe.

Old Cromangon Man, he stops real sudden-like and he turns to me. He looks me square in the eye. He says, "They say you ain't told a lie in your life, Stick."

Well, I sure never heared that. And ifing they was voting—whoever "they" is—I spose I'd've elected to stay home on account of I never known what the truth is most times. But I din't say nothing back to him on account of I never could've thought on hearing anything quite so strange-like in the middle of the woods, especial-like from Cromangon Man's mouth.

"I want you to swear on your mother's grave you won't tell nobody what you're gonna see," he says, standing there, looking like a Neanderthal man more than a Cromangon. I oughta know. I drawed him.

So, I swears, what don't really mean much, I figure, even ifing I do lie, the Lord being merciful enough to know come judgement day that a promise don't mean a thing when there's the threat of a body's harm. Come to think on it, I might've told Cromangon Man anything he wanted, now that he had my curiosity up.

I FOLLOWED HIM up a little incline, away from the crick. We come to some tall grass, and I can see there's a path snaking through it wider than a man's walk. He tells me we're going to low crawl the rest of the way, so I sets my pole and pad down, but he tells me to bring along my pad.

As soon as I make it over this little knoll, I can see the crick through the trees and brush over the top of Cromangon's head, him leading the way. Then I seen the crick is real fat in this spot, but it weren't till we got to the bottom of the incline that I could see the lodge. "What is it?" I whispers to Cromangon Man, crawling up to his side, since the path was now wider and real worn, like he made hisself a blind what with a couple inches wide of grass between us and the crick.

"Critters," he says, and he slips this notepad and pencil out his breast pocket, looks at his watch, and starts making chicken scratches.

"I can't see nothing," I said.

Cromangon Man, he just looks kind of far away-like and then starts with more chicken scratches.

We must've laid there for a half hour and, still, I never seen a thing but a crow—and it flying real high.

We crawl back up the incline and then head back to the pasture.

"What is it, Cro? Beavers?" I ask him.

"Well, what do you spose it is?" he says, like he'd been taking lessons from Bob the Barber.

"I ain't ever heared of beavers around here, let alone seen none."

"But you seen the lodge, din't you?"

I told him I sposed I did.

So it turns out Old Cromangon Man let me in on his secret, though I ain't sure why till he tells me he wants me to draw them.

How can I draw them ifing I can't see them, I want to know.

He tells me he's got faith in me.

"Well, why do you want them drawed, anyways?"

"Does it look like I own a camera?" he says.

I tell him no but why would he want a picture?

He tells me those critters are his friends, and they won't be staying around long since beavers never do. He tells me that him and beavers, they are a lot alike.

"How?" I says, and I'll try to tell you what he says to me, using his voice and all, on account of Cromangon Man, his telling on it was kind of peculiar-like.

"Where you going to find yourself an Indian these days?" he says.

On a reservation, I spose.

"Yeah, and that ain't natural," Old Cro says. "Now think on that. For thousands of years Indians never had property and now they got property, ceptings that's a problem because they never wanted property in the first place. Indians is like beavers, mostly. Mostly they moved on, just like beavers."

"What's property got to do with you and beavers?" I up and told him.

"Nothing. Beings there ain't no such thing as property. That's just man made. Property, huh? Whose property is that where the lodge is? Ain't nobody's property, sure enough no human's."

"Heck it ain't," I says. "Ifing I ain't mistaken, we're standing on the Johnson farm."

"You don't get my point," he says. "I'm telling you there ain't really no such thing as real estate. Does anybody own land? It's the other way around. The land owns a man. People are all gonna be dead and buried in the land. You think dinosaurs owned any land?"

I told him that come to think on it, the dinosaurs *was* the land now.

"That's right," he says. "People try to make themself apart, when they actually is *part*. Ain't no beaver ever done something dumb like that."

Now I din't begrudge Cromangon Man of his thinking none, but it seemed to me here was one gink who was going to be one unhappy man. Ifing he really thought people was part of the land, then what's all the fuss about, I says to myself. When I looked across the crick and pasture and seen in the distance that place Pop and me rented, us squatting there permanent-like, I figured it was as much a part of the land as a tepee would be in its stead. I mean light bulbs is just as natural as making a fire. Both come out of somebody's head. But I din't crowd Cromangon Man none. I left him thinking on his own opinion. And I says to myself ifing that's the way he wants to live his life, so be it. The son doesn't have to follow the father's footsteps.

I still had one problem, though. How was I going to draw a critter I ain't never seen in my life? It seemed pretty important to him, though, so I guessed I oughta try. But ever thing I tried come up lame. The next day I told Cro it seemed I just couldn't draw what I ain't seen, and he told me he thought I always told the truth.

"What do you mean?" I says.

"Ever body knows you drawed that picture of that robber the F.B.I. man showed around town."

"That weren't no robber," I said. "The F.B.I. man said the robber din't have no beard."

"I don't care," Cromangon says. "I know ifing I never saw that face in Freeland, then you never saw it too."

There seemed to be a hole in Cro's figuring, but I couldn't see it. I told him, all right, I'd draw his dang beavers for him, but he had to understand that the stranger's face I done was because I'd accidental-like been drinking screwdrivers, that I still can't draw what I ain't seen or at least seen in my mind like in a dream or something and that ifing he still wanted me to sketch his dang beavers I'd have to see them.

So Cromangon and me, we spent most of the summer doing a low crawl along the crick. Far as I knowed there weren't no critters ceptings Cromangon Man and me laying there in that tall grass, listening to the birds, him making notes and me getting more and more tired of staring out onto the surface of the crick and at the lodge. I never got gumption enough to ask him whether he real-like saw them or ifing we was just on an old-fashioned snipe hunt. But I got my suspicions as to what the answer might've been. One Saturday morning I'm watching cartoons, and *Rocky and His Friends* comes on. So I drawed me a Rocky and show it to Cromangon Man that afternoon.

"See," he said, "I knowed you could do it!"

So I made Cromangon Man a whole bunch of Rockys. I left the goggles off, though. No matter how many I drawed, Cromangon Man, he had a name for ever one of them.

"Why, this must be Harold," he'd say, or "Esmerelda, you're a living doll," folding them pictures up neat-like and slipping them in his breast pocket. I spose I did draw each of them a little different.

I mean to tell you that was a load off my mind. Cromangon Man, he seemed to be satisfied when I tell him I must have sketched the whole family. I told him too I thought it was getting time for me to retire my pole, that I'd be bringing it out of storage probable-like of a Sunday only with Pop. I was having some trouble with my stroke, I said, and I thought that pole was throwing me off a bit, what was the truth. I spose that's why the Bear would come to say he never wanted me handling no ball but a basketball, him thinking other sports would throw my shot off.

Anyways, I'd got to worrying on what Cromangon Man had said about Agent McMillion showing around town that drawing what I din't but did do. Old Cro, he tells me one day when we're laying by the crick that the ginks was all amazed at how when you looked at that picture you seen red, though it was lead pencil. The ginks also said it was funny how goosey the Banker had got, that he'd jump ever time he seen him a redhead in his bank, no matter ifing it were man, woman or little girl.

Me, I hadn't got ascared again for a long time, but I begun to worry on the Banker a bit. I mean I din't want something I'd made by hand to wreck somebody for their *whole* life. One afternoon it'd been about a week since I seen the Schoolteacher and I moseyed on out to the graveyard on my bike since I had me some time on account of my game seemed to be back, and she were glad to see me, you could tell, maybe on account of I come to visit when I weren't ascared. She was trimming around the stones with clippers, so I give her a rest, careful-like to not step on no graves. We both knowed this was going to be my last year in the schoolhouse, but neither says it.

I showed her my pad, and she was right pleased, I could tell. There was a lot of nature in there, hardly any heads atall since what faces I'd been drawing I sold and since I ain't been up to the shop all that much what with all the fishing I'd been doing. The Schoolteacher, she named a couple of the spots along the crick, what kind of surprised me and all, her being tied down to the parsonage and me never picturing her on hikes. She wondered how me and Cromangon Man was getting along, and I tell her that sometimes I thought we din't see eye to eye, but mostly I like it all summer, it being so peaceful and quiet out on the crick where there weren't no radios or nothing. She din't say nothing. She knowed when to hold her tongue, the Schoolteacher.

But not me. Sometimes I just up and say dumb things. Like that very afternoon, although I don't think I knowed at the time how dumb it was.

"I been wondering," I says to her.

"What, Charles?"

"What's going to happen when they close the school?"

There was a long pause. "I'll manage," she says.

"Maybe you could teach at the new grade school when they get it built," I says to her.

"Possibly," she says.

Possibly.

I hated it when she'd say that.

Anarchtopia, she'd come to call it, like it were a continent all to itself when she knowed it weren't more than a little town what happened to be there, beings before there was the town, there was railroad tracks and the richest dirt you ever did see. Freeland, we called it, because that was its name.

I ain't up on local history much, and I figure that's a good thing on account of you wouldn't want to hear it. To tell you the truth, I weren't much interested in the future neither ever since I'd been sleepwalking. I'd rather be telling you on *now*, what is kind of funny, because it's already history by me just telling on it.

Some ginks say you can't live in the past. Well, they oughta said you can't live in the future, too. The funny thing is you can't live now neither, beings now it is already gone. So I figures there are two ways to look at it. Either we was all dead in Freeland or we was living in another dimension. Ever time I walked away from that graveyard I knowed we weren't dead. There ain't no dead thing what can ache in itself like that. So I knowed we was all alive and living in another dimension. I knowed so after I traded my billards book back for some science fiction up in Lawless.

Nooner, he wanted to know on the way home what it is that possesses a man to stay in Freeland when he was all growed up with a pack of kids of his own. I sposed he wasn't talking to me, but since I was the only other soul in the truck, I said wanderlust sure enough weren't in *this* gink's nature. Nooner, he just nodded.

Who's he kidding, I think. He knows dang well he loves that dump of his for the freedom it gives him to come and go. That's why Nooner give up on farming long ago and let the place return to its natural self. What a way to have hisself an income! Sell a few acres, buy a bulldozer, dig a hole, have the people pay you to help you fill it. Heck, you only got to crank up that dozer once a week on Tuesdays to cover the coffee grounds. So what ifing there are a few flies? The hole ain't near the house none, beings it's on the other side of the ridge and down wind. Hog farmers got it just as worse, what with the stench your nose gets used to anyways.

But Nooner, he was just mumbling like any other man, even though he were a gink. You got to have a want ifing you want to stay alive, I figure. Me, I got my want. My table. And I sposed Nooner's wife knowed that Nooner had him his. I weren't a farm boy for nothing.

Anyways, I'm reading me this science fiction book on the way back from Lawless to have something to do because Nooner, he never talked in the truck sos to be talking to someone but hisself. I spose that's how I come to be trapped in science fiction. I mean when I took *that* book back, I picked up another one to have something to do on the way home again. It just went on and on like that, repeating itself, like I were in some kind of time warp or hall of mirrors, what I ain't never seen but on TV on account of the carnivals what come to Freeland is *one*, during the Centennial, and even it were kind of cheap-like, beings the carnies must've knowed that all the men and ginks would just stand around watching the rides go round and round and not wanting to buy their sweethearts or kids or selfs no ticket to nowhere, what is where they are ifing we is living in another dimension.

So there Freeland is, a hundred years old. I'm fourteen, the summer before the eighth grade, and her, the Schoolteacher, is maybe forty, though she don't look her age on account of ain't nobody in Freeland looks their age because you figure that ifing they ain't gone to heaven like Mom and Baby Sis, then they got to be at least a hundred years old being Freeland ain't changed and never will. What's my backyard is my backyard and it ain't never going to be your backyard, even ifing you're going to buy the property what's behind it.

Let me try and esplain what I mean, and I'll save us both some time sos you can know the history on Freeland without having to hear it.

Take Bob the Barber up on his throne. One day he is all in a huff beings the place behind Old Floyd's place what Floyd's daddy owned too was up for sale sos Floyd—with his folks long gone to the hereafter and all—could have him some more income what to live on sos the Banker wouldn't send him to live in the loony bin up in Lawless.

Now, Bob the Barber, beings he were the sarcastic kind of gink he were, was also good hearted, what you can tell because he give me my stick and my name and my encouragement. Well, he loved Floyd too, not that you could tell it all the time. Still, what he done was help Floyd out. They was going to sell that house behind Floyd's house, but some lawyer from Lawless said they couldn't do it till they had the property surveyed, what weren't no cheap operation.

Well, Bob the Barber, sitting on his throne, said that was about the craziest g.d. thing he ever heared. And I knowed he was mad because he used another bad word too I ain't about to say on.

"Why on Earth does some hot shot with a telescope got to come down here to tell us what's your backyard and what's mine when any idiot can look at the blasted lilac bushes separating the two and tell you the difference?" he says.

Now that I think on it, I can say what Bob the Barber's want was. He wanted to be left alone, what was pretty much the way any man or gink in Freeland wanted it, ceptings for the Banker witch he din't count beings he weren't no gink nor local born anyhow. He was from outer space, Bob said. That was one fact I could sure enough agree on, beings I'd been reading science fiction when I weren't practicing or drawing. Still, he were a human being and goosey too, ever since I drawed that face I give to the F.B.I. man. I weren't about to suggest we should throw him out of Freeland, especial-like when I looked around me there in the shop and seen some other faces what could be used on the cover of the story book in my lap.

Old Pyro was in the shop too, that day, him waiting for a trim. Nobody called him Pyro, though—leastwise not to his face. His name was Chauncy, what seemed to sound right, beings he was always working this farmer's match in his teeth like he were too lazy to tear the toothpick package when he come out of the coffee shop and his cheeks was always smeared with Vasoline, beings they was fat and always windburned to sunburn or something. Pyro din't have no kind words for the Banker neither, cept it was probable-like on account of he din't want his second-in-command, Digger, bless him, to know ever what he was thinking on, said Bob the Barber when Pyro left.

"How come?" I asked Bob.

"Well, it's like this. You know how Termite's got his problem with authority?"

"Yeah."

"So does Pyro."

"Well, how come you don't all elect Digger the chief?"

"There ain't a gink alive who ever wanted to be boss of anything ceptings maybe hisself," Bob says.

There he stands, cutting hair, twenty-some years on him,

with the Schoolteacher's hooks still in him. How I knowed that was because cept for drawing in my sleep I were the boss of myself, now that I had me my name and my table to practice.

I had to laugh on that some. I begun thinking on how there was degrees to being the boss of yourself. Now take the Schoolteacher. Now there was the boss of herself, ceptings that now that I was on the edge of earning me a eighth grade diploma, I could see she din't have no problem with authority. It weren't her idea to buy herself no badge or to wear a firechief's hat. She just wanted to do what she done best, be the Schoolteacher. I knowed now she hated it when she had to bust the ruler over my bumper, and it weren't on account of she were cheap. Why she would get so angry was that she hated I made her have to do it. I remembered on her telling me knowledge is power. But I figured she were talking about a kind of power Termite and Pyro knowed nothing about.

Then, on the other hand, you had Floyd, who couldn't wipe his nose unless Bob the Barber done it for him. Still, you were sure that had nature been more kind to him sos he din't own that big head and all, he would've been just a regular old gink instead of the adopted old gink he was. I mean it's like he had to've been half-raised by the Schoolteacher like the rest of us ginks but that God, seeing the mistake He made as to what womb He put him in and when He put him in it, give him this problem with water on the brain sos Bob the Barber, being the latter gets a big heart planted in his chest, could help Floyd become the boss of hisself and stay out of the loony bin. I knowed this beings there was talk at the shop that most of the people in the loony bin is voluntary members, what was a big surprise to me.

And then, sitting there on the machine, I thought on Nooner. With having his own business what with land he bought from his old man with a loan from the Banker, he was the boss of hisself, mostly. At least, like Bob the Barber says, ginks don't want to be the boss of anybody else, and Nooner made it, as far as the bank felt. And then there's the Banker, who weren't the boss over hisself but the boss over ever body else, I heared tell when listening to my old man. Of course the Banker don't then own the bank none, I know now—Termite and Pyro owning the bigger part of it—but the Banker din't own hisself neither, beings that a man could get so goosey ever time he saw a redhead.

But it's all like I says earlier. People is the boss of themselfs in degrees. The Schoolteacher was the boss of herself. So was Bob the Barber in a way, what made it possible for Floyd to be his own boss, who was a notch up on even the Banker and his board of directors. I figures Nooner fit somewhere in the middle, seeing it was summertime and only a hour ago with his older kids off playing in the woods and him and me on our way back to the shop from Lawless that he got the urge to stop by his place and take care of some business while I stayed in the truck. Like I said, I weren't a farm boy for nothing.

So I'm just sitting there in the truck, reading me some science fiction and brushing off a few flies when I hear "Daddy's home!" in a voice I knowed, and I looked out through the windshield and here come the oldest girls, all four of them, running towards me out of the woods near the dump, their hair flying and them puffing. I made real still-like because I figure they couldn't see me none, beings there was probable-like glare off the windshield and on account of I din't want to scare them none. The biggest one, Becky—I knowed her good for four years, ever since she started first grade—is in the lead, and she stops short when she's even with me, and I'm looking right at her out the passenger's-side winda. They was all in a line when they was running, and it was real comical seeing them all pile up on one another sort of like the train wreck what was to happen in town.

"Chucky!" Becky says to me. All them little kids at school called me that because I could throw them a softball real good sos they could hit it.

"Hi," I says, real cheerful-like. It give me a little flutter in my chest when they called me that, beings I knowed I was the closest they knowed to a big brother. Little girls give you that feeling that you're growed up, even when you're fourteen. And these was so sweet that sometimes I just wanted to squeeze all four of them at once. Not that they couldn't be little Devils, too, especial-like when they started acquiring their womanly parts, but they're always so doll-like when they're little.

They wanted to know what I was doing there, and I figure I was about to become the babysitter, so I tells them that their daddy and mommy was busy with business and I was here to watch them for a while and Becky said, "Oh."

I run them back into the woods, me being a pretend boogie man and all, scaring them and all, when we come up to where we can see the crick, so I says we should go skip stones or something. The littlest, Martha, gets real serious-like and says they ain't allowed to go by the crick and besides that's where the troll lives, so I take them back up to the house, figuring on us playing baseball or something. Little kids, I says to myself, now they are the boss of themselfs.

Pretty soon Nooner come out of his house, and all four of the girls go running up to him, and he gives them a big hug and hands Becky a roll of Life Savers.

"I told you Daddy told Mommy he had to get dynamite," Little Martha says.

Becky says to her that the Schoolteacher was going to be mad at her because she forgot ever thing she learned over the summer, beings *dynamite* starts with a "d" not a "l." Besides, she says, holding up the roll, "Do you see a fuse here?"

Nooner din't say nothing. He just smiled and shook his head, me and him climbing back in the truck. Nooner, I thought on how it was good the Lord made him a pretty good daddy, on account of, like the Barber said, the Devil made him so horny.

THAT AFTERNOON IT got hot. Hotter than a two-peckered billygoat, Bob the Barber says, him having worked hisself up a terrible sweat trying to keep the machine stocked. Digger come in and said it was too hot in his office, so the four of us, him, me, Nooner, and Bob the Barber and Old Floyd—cept Floyd din't count none, him with his head boiling and all, what was the Barber's comment what got soda in all our noses, even Floyd's—played Euchre in the back what with the Barber having no customers on account of ifing he did they'd probable-like have a Lawless lawyer on his behind suing him for handcrafting flat tops with the sun being as hot as it was and folks passing out on the sidewalk and all.

Digger, bless him, he changes the subject sos he's talking on the winter time and how miserable it is fighting fires with your hands and feet freezing but leaves hisself open to a line from the Barber on how you can always put more clothes on but you can't take enough off. Pretty soon the two of them is in a stew, Nooner putting in his two cents worth too, saying the both of them is the most contrary sons of bitches. I sposed there was no way to fathom how the local volunteers managed to smother so much as a grass fire ifing they bickered like that, and it weren't till latter in my experience I come to know that Freeland firefighters was much better at containing fires than they was at putting them out. It was sort of like what went on at that Euchre table. Digger and me, we'd always be partners agin Nooner and the Barber in the winter time when it were too cold in Digger's office, too cold for the schools to be open, too cold for a crewcut, and too cold to copulate, the Barber'd say. Floyd, he din't care how hot or cold it was so long as Bob the Barber let him keep score. We'd be sitting there, one of them getting grumpy and all, on account of there ain't no gink what doesn't love to win at Euchre, especial-like when you're playing for your pride. Ever body but me and Floyd would be real hot at one another until they left the table, then they was the best of friends, because, I spose, they remembered on then that Lady Luck, she done dealt them all equal hands like she were the helper to the Schoolteacher. Ginks knowed there weren't no losers among them because there weren't no winners neither. Digger and me, we'd win one time, and the Barber and Nooner would win the next. What got to me, though, was I couldn't understand why they got so riled during the games. You knowed they liked to play, just like you. But then they'd get hot. I figures it was like Bob the Barber said, "Heck, Stick here probable-like knows what's in our hands before we play them." I sposed he was right, cepting not in the way he was thinking. I knowed that what they had in their hands din't amount to a hill of beans compared to what a gink has got in his head and heart. Besides, when you're thinking on what Lady Luck just dealt you and you're on that only, you're neglecting her boss, what is the Law of Averages. Now the Law of Averages might have the Lady deal you both bowers, two trumps on the side and an ace kicker all afternoon, but the next day you're going to find all your hands look more like feet. The Law of Averages is like God. It's always been there, even when the dinosaurs was sitting here instead of us. Lady Luck is more like Jesus, who done come and went. I sposed Cromangon Man was right about some things, and when I looked at Floyd, I was happy as heck just to be holding a hand. Leastways I had something to play, even ifing it weren't no pat loner.

But the Earth needs scorekeepers. I'd peek at Floyd, and sometimes I just knowed he was thinking on the Law of Averages too. And for a fact he'd wink at me when the other ginks was getting hot. Old Floyd, he seemed to know that Lady Luck left him for a time but that she'd be back. Or maybe it was the other way around, beings there was probable-like a lot of dead people what wished they lived as long as Floyd even ifing they was just a scorekeeper, even ifing it were a hundred degrees in the shade, what is a lot closer to ninety-eight point six than where they was.

One thing for sure about Floyd is there was no way he couldn't even steal a ticket to hell, not when you ain't got Free Will, the Schoolteacher would come to say. And Floyd, I figure he was about the closest thing we had to a real prisoner in Freeland. And of the ginks sitting there at that Euchre table, me, I had, ifing not a ticket to heaven, at least the money for it in my pocket. I had me my table what was going to keep me on the straight and narrow. The only thing worrying me was whether that would be enough to get me past them gates or whether I'd have to stand around outside, just waving to those inside, but never—like in a bad dream—never able to touch them. Lady Luck was on my side all right. But what about the Law of Averages? It'd been a long time since I drawed in my sleep. It'd been a long time since I'd been in trouble. I figured I was about due. I sometimes wonder ifing it's the figuring that brings it on or ifing that it's about to happen that brings the figuring on. Up till this point I ain't drawed in my sleep enough to know. But after the Euchre game busted up, I decided to mosey on home and ride back to practice in the evening when it'd be cooler. Though I been sipping on soda, my mouth is dry as chalk, so I stops in the drug store for some Life Savers. I felt guilty chewing the whole roll, thinking on how Becky and Little Martha probable-like only got a couple apiece, beings they had to share their roll with their sisters. But, like the Barber says, "Age has got its privilidge, unless you're Floyd."

I fixed me up some cold pork and beans for supper, just reaching for the can in the cupboard like I already knowed what I was to eat, beings mostly because it was too hot to heat anything. Pretty soon I open my pad and I'm doodling, sitting there at the kitchen table, eating my beans and drinking some milk. Before I knowed it, I looked up at the clock and I been doodling for two hours straight. I know it's time to go to practice, but it don't feel like it none, beings it's so hot and all, ceptings that's not the real reason. I wanted to doodle some more.

I just keep doodling, it being not such a crazy thing, I says to myself, beings it keeps my mind off the heat. Now I'm in the bathroom, getting ready for bed, and it takes me a hour on account of ever stroke of my toothbrush, it seems like, I've to stop and doodle some more.

I doodle in the hall between the bathroom and my room. I doodle with my pad on the chest of drawers. I get hot, so I go to the living room where there's a little breeze, and I doodle. When final-like I'm in bed, I look down on the floor and see this trail of doodles I've teared out of my pad that followed me, I figure, all over the house. But for some reason it don't bother me none. It just seems natural-like that there oughta be that trail, just as natural as flagstone steps out in the front yard seemed now. And when I thought on that, it even seemed natural that the flagstones should now seem natural-like, beings they was all along. It was just that the future ain't caught up with them there yet. Or the past. But that's another story, although it ain't really.

So I'm doodling, laying on my back in bed, and the next

thing I knowed there was Pop, standing over me. He wants to know what's going on. "I come home from work," he says, "my back aching from pushing a mop all night, and what do I see but more to mop."

I sit on the edge of my bed.

Pop's talking but I don't hear him none.

I get out of bed and pick it all up. "Sorry, Pop," I says, "I don't know what got into me."

"You want I should call the Schoolteacher?"

"What for?" I asks.

"On account of that's what she told me to ask you ifing you was acting strange-like again," he says.

I told him no, and my pop and me, we had some Hydrox cookies and milk.

I looked up at the clock. "Pop?"

"Yes Sir," he says.

"You know, Pop, I weren't no farm boy for nothing."

"Whatchu mean?"

"I mean it don't take three hours to drive here from the plant."

"Oh," he says.

Like I already says, Pop and me was getting us a slow divorce.

I SPOSED I'D slept all I was about to sleep that night what with it still so hot and all. I laid in my bed, thinking on those doodles, how I din't even know I was doodling when I was doodling. I flipped on the light and shuffled through the stack of them, beings what else does a gink do when he can't sleep of a summer night at four o'clock in the morning when the Lord ain't seen fit to make it anything but hot and dark.

The next thing I knowed the sun is coming in through the winda what I left the blind pulled up sos to be able to breathe. I roll over, and I hear this crack like the sound of a piece of plastic snapping under me. The very second I knowed what it was I jumped out of bed and spun around to look at the wall. You see, I was real used to seeing that wallpaper with them big flowers that nobody ever seen in Freeland or even Lawless, and I'd study on them big things when I was laying in bed with nothing else to think on, but now the flowers was gone. In their stead was my doodles, all twenty pages, all neat-like taped on the wall and all flush with one another and together like a big rectangle or the drive-in screen on the way to Lawless or the general shape what you see when you're thinking on the bed of your billiard table.

I kind of cuss myself first, thinking on how I'd be buying me a new sketchpad, being it weren't like no six gun on TV what never runs out of bullets. Then I glance down at my bed and see the Scotch tape holder all broke. I'm thinking on how this mess puts a terrible bite in my income for the week, standing there, counting the pages, wondering on what a miracle it were that the number come out an even twenty, witch to you maybe seems like a little thing, beings the big miracle was it's amazing I done that in my sleep atall. But to me walking in my sleep weren't so crazy any more. What was nutty was the number of pieces of paper. I remembered stepping down from the chair in the shop one time and how ever other gink but me must think I look different-like what with my hair gone to crewcut from flattop. But me, I din't look different to me beings I watched the Barber shear it off in the mirror. What I'm saying is I watched myself make them doodles. And when a man makes so many doodles I figure there's a purpose besides excaping the heat, especial-like when he could be up at the Masonic Hall practicing his Godgiven ability. But why should a man make twenty pages of doodles sos when he goes to hang them up in a room what he become a man in, on account of it was there he had him his first wet dream, they should come together flush so as to let the man know they was actually parts of a big picture? I knowed, I thought, why there was thirteen stones in the front yard. But something told me I hadn't oughta know why I'd drawed my twenty pages of doodles, unless I wanted to get ascared again.

I WAS FIBBING to myself, but I din't know it. You see, I guess I just pretended the reason there was thirteen steps was because then I was thirteen. The Law of Averages says that there could've been a even dozen, but I figured that God din't want me counting no dozen stones what with that not being bad luck and all and Him not wanting me to get the big head or so terrible ascared because of all the time he seen me count-ing the dozen heads in that picture the Schoolteacher done of

The Last Supper hanging in the church basement. But on the other hand, God works in mysterious ways. Both the School-teacher and the Barber seen that. I guess He wanted me to think of them twenty pages because ifing I din't, Digger, bless him, beings that he's the coroner, would never've been able to bury Cromangon Man, not that he ever did.

As soon as I asked who I knowed was about to be twenty, I started reaching for my pants, even though I din't have the answer. I look up at the wall, and sudden-like I seen it. Instead of all them big flowers, it was one terrible big one about to bloom in my brain. It were a map there on the wall, like a world map of a tiny acre but a map like you ain't never seen sos the spot of land you was looking on, you was seeing from all directions at once, sos the map was more like a sculpture than picture, beings it weren't just two dimensions, but three, sos you could turn it over and over in your head and feel the surface of it, even though it were still a flat map.

I was tying my shoes, my eyes still glued to the map. You could tell the crick was running through it, but it weren't near our place. It was upstream. I knowed beings I could see the dump up in the corner of the map. Up there I followed the crick downstream to where it got fat. I seen the toppled trees. I seen the dam from the front. I seen the home of the critters. And there was a big roll of Life Savers sticking out. And tunnels, two of them, running under water. Then there was the trail of matted grass what was empty. And there weren't no blind no more. Then there was the glint off the tinfoil, what were a illusion, I come to find out, on account of there was sparks.

I busted into Pop's bedroom and shook him awake. He looked up at me like he was surprised the world was still here, witch I was surprised too, knowing as I done that very second that we really was living in a different dimension, but mine more differenter than his.

"Pop, I ain't got time to esplain," I says. I says, "Call the firehouse. Tell them it's Nooner Johnson's," and grabbed his car key and run for the back door.

Now I'm coming on to Nooner's just as fast as I dare when I see there's a car ahead of me turning into the drive. When I pull up to the house, what I seen with my own eyes is as strange as ifing I'd just dreamed it—the Schoolteacher banging on Nooner's door in her robe what was blue like her dress. I set the brake and jump out of Pop's car. For the first time I can hear the fire whistle way off. The Schoolteacher, she's still banging on the door, but the way she looks at me she knows I know she knowed. Then she looks to the woods quick-like and looks back at me. She ain't pleading or nothing. One of us has got to go into them woods and fast.

"Nooner!" I yells and starts racing for the crick. Then I was close, real close, so close I could see the lodge and the sparks. Then the hand of God what come to be Nooner's hand reached up out of the ground, trips me, and I'm still on my feet but stumbling till I can't keep my balance no longer, down an *in*cline, sliding into a stump, one cheek pressed flat agin it. I don't hear the blast. All I know is the air done hit me like a wet bail dropped from the loft. Then there's this rain, the sharpest this body's ever felt, since it ain't just water but mud and stones and sticks, too. When the rain passes, I see something flapping out of the corner of my eye, and I look back and what do I see but the biggest bass any gink laid eyes on, his head about halfway blowed off. And though I can't hear the flapping none, I knowed it's got the worst pain a fish ever felt, so I jump up, me beings a farm boy and all, and starts beating this bass on the head with a stick. Something grabs me from behind, and I turn around with the stick half-cocked and it's Nooner. He's got red in his face, his eyes all narrowed to a pair of slits, and he grabs me by the T-shirt with one hand while he's shaking his finger at me with the other, his jaws doing ninety miles per hour, though I can't hear him none, thinking on that it's like we was under water.

Nooner, final-like I think he's got the message I can't hear none. He grabs me by the arm and starts leading me up the *in*cline. Final-like we're about halfway out of the woods and Nooner stops short. I look up and here come the Schoolteacher running. As soon as I seen her I thought on Cromangon Man, and I starts sobbing-like, I guess. I just knowed he was in that lodge, though I never really knowed it, because nobody ever seen the body or his clothes or nothing, not even Digger, bless him, seen it, although we all seen with our own eyes the memorial service in the funeral home.

It weren't long before Nooner's place is crawling with volunteers, and even Pop, he'd come on my bike. Old Pyro, he had his firechief's hat on, wondering where's the fire. The Schoolteacher, she done whisked me off to her car and motioned

Digger over. I told him I knowed Cromangon Man was in that beaver lodge, not sure as to whether he could hear me, on account of I couldn't hear myself thinking, let alone talking.

"How do you know?" he writ down on a scrap of paper from the glove compartment.

"Don't tell no one," I asks him. "I drawed it."

That seemed good enough for Digger, bless him.

I seen Becky and some of her sisters looking out a winda at me when we pulled out of the drive, and I waved and seen the smile on her face when she waved back. We drive by the parsonage, the Schoolteacher quick puts on some clothes to go to Lawless in, and she drives me up to the hospital.

I weren't there more than a day, just enough to see my name in the paper what I din't like seeing atall. "Freeland Man Missing After Blast" was the headline, though it fortunate-like weren't no front page news. Lucky, too, there weren't no mention of it by Wally Phillips or nobody else on WGN what I could hear real loud till my hearing come back.

The Schoolteacher, she picked me up the next day with Pop having to go to work and all, and we had hamburgers at a new place in Lawless they called McDonald's. I don't like it much because it reminded me on the Agent what I had no hankering to meet up with again. But the hamburgers and fresh-fries was good, although they don't sell no Royal Crown there.

I told the Schoolteacher what had been on my mind what with her driving to Nooner's place in her robe and knowing what I knowed and all.

She told me that just like I had a secret with her about

my radio, she had a secret with her so she couldn't tell me how she knowed.

Now that really got my curiosity up, and I don't mind telling you none I was a little jealous-like. On the way I bust out with, "Well, am I *ever* going to know how you knowed?"

"Perhaps," she says.

Here I am, fourteen, and her, she's forty-four, and she's got to go and say "perhaps." Lord Jesus, how I hated it when she'd say that.

Then I got to thinking on something. I weren't the only one who saw her at Nooner's in her robe. Maybe them others would start asking questions too, although it were a cinch they weren't going to be asking *her* no questions, leastways not no gink, what with her eyes burning holes clear through them.

Pop, he was gone to work by the time we got home, so I ask her to come in, what worked out nice since she had something she wanted to give me just like they do on the soap operas when you been in the hospital and all.

A new sketchpad she'd wrapped fancy-like in blue tissue. I told her it was a good thing she done it on account of I near run out of paper and I told her about the doodles. She wants to see them. So she's standing there in the doorway of my room, looking at the opposite wall, slow-like shaking her head, and I go back out to the kitchen, seeing it's not right for me to be in the same room where there's a bed, especial-like when it ain't made.

She's there in the hall for a real long time. I'm getting fidgety, and final-like I look up and she come walking slow-like into the kitchen, eyes staring straight ahead, like somebody sent her remote control. She stops, and then she looks right at me, but there ain't no worry on her brow when she says, "You've never even heard of Cubism, have you, Charles?"

Since I knowed she weren't no friend of the Russians *or* Castro, I said I ain't, what was the truth.

Now, the Schoolteacher, she din't say nothing. She just sits down at the kitchen table like I asked her sos I could draw her and break-in my new pad. Besides, I wanted to show her how proud-like I was she give it to me then.

"Mam?" I says. "About Cromangon Man," I says.

"You mean Theodore."

I bite my tongue-like. I knowed she never liked ginks calling one another by their names. "Yes Mam," I said.

"What about him?" she said.

It was easier asking her questions when you was drawing her because you din't have to look up all the time. "You liked him a lot?" I says, keeping my eyes on my business.

She din't say nothing for a second. Final-like she says, "Yes, a lot."

"How come?" I up and asked.

"Because in many ways he's a lot like you."

I'll be danged ifing the tears din't start welling up in both of us, after a big silence.

"Was he like you too?" I said.

She din't say a thing. She just got up and come over and put her hands on my forehead and the back of my neck, and I drawed. I drawed and I drawed.

You see, it was like *this*. When you had the Schoolteacher in your kitchen it weren't like she was the Schoolteacher no more. What I mean is she knowed you weren't ready for no big answers unless you had big questions. And me, I was inheriting my share of the Old Curiosity she owned, but it weren't right that I should be asking the questions yet on account of I'd never get the answers. The Schoolteacher, she knowed how to teach you, all right. She'd take you just so far and then she wouldn't answer nothing, what made you come up with more questions. Sometimes the questions was the answers. But mostly she just knowed that ifing she give you the answers then you ain't going to remember on them like when you make up your own answers. It weren't no picnic. But how else is a gink to know about living and dying? Especial-like when Digger, bless him, done buried his only mother and baby sister.

In school it was different. By the time she was through with you, she'd done did a dance on your head you ain't had time to ask no fancy questions on unless they was facts. I spose that's how I got all "A's" in geometry at the high school. I mean the next year she'd drilled me in all the algebra them teachers in the high school would ever know sos come October they pushed me on into geometry. It would help me with my drawing, she said, though I knowed she figured it would help me with my Godgiven talent on my table too. Besides, the Barber said, with the way I rambled on and talked when I did talk, they had to have some evidence I din't belong in the loony bin in Lawless.

I spose he was right. After all, it were the Bear what taught me geometry as good as basketball. And it were him who come to understand I din't belong in the loony bin, even though he had the most to lose by what I done, me being tall and lanky for my age with a good eye, a soft shot, and my anticipation. But I can't tell you about that right now, because ifing I did, even you would say they oughta bought me a one way ticket to Lawless.

Of course the ginks weren't mad at me none, cept maybe for Bob the Barber a little bit, him beings my biggest fan and all and the one what give me my name. Ginks just don't get mad at one another when they're growed up, unless they're playing Euchre or maybe attending a memorial service for one of their own.

THE WHOLE TOWN showed up. You see, it ain't often in Freeland what somebody gets blowed up sos Digger, bless him, couldn't find none of the pieces. Some was even wondering why he signed the death certificate, even, when there weren't nothing to bury. Well, Old Digger, I figures he done it for Cromangon Man's folks. They was real old, you see, moved off the farm. There was no way Digger was to avoid two more funerals on his hands unless he stopped the worry. And like Digger said, it's a lot easier to plant them even when there ain't nothing to plant than trying to find them when there ain't nothing there to find. Anyways, Digger believed me when I told him Cromangon Man was sleeping with them critters, sposing the critters was actually *there*, beings you couldn't prove it by me even though I drawed them.

It was the Schoolteacher what delivered the speech. She said all them good things about Cromangon Man. Like he was his own best friend and was still with his Maker, what I knowed were possible ifing God were more than a man with a long beard and powerful hands sitting on his throne. Ifing God were all, like the Bible said, then, yes, it were likely because then God'd also be the dirt and the dinosaurs. But the Schoolteacher din't stop just there. You could tell she really wanted to put this fuss ever body made to rest maybe sos Cromangon Man's folks could get some rest themselfs. She talked on how she had seen him in the woods a lot of times—what was news to me because to see somebody in Nooner's woods from where she lived you'd have to be able to see *through* the woods—and that-there was where he felt most free, witch meant closer to his Maker, I sposed. She told it were a pair of beavers, male and female, what made Cromangon Man come to see the woods as a Eden where the Lord hisself might walk. And that the beavers'd made a family what Cromangon Man become a member of, ifing only through his being there. His gift was that he was a naturalist-like. When it was clear to him there was no longer anything for him to learn remaining apart from them, he become part of them.

Finally, here come the shocker. She said she seen him enter the lodge through the chimney in the top on the morning of the blast.

There weren't a soul in that funeral home nor among the bodies spilling out of the entryway onto the sidewalk that din't believe ever word she said what with her eyes having looked into your eyes. There weren't nobody who thought to raise their hand and ask her what she was doing there of early morning in her robe neither and how come Nooner din't see her none.

But even the Schoolteacher, for all her ways, couldn't nip in the bud what she must've seen coming. People just din't want to leave. For a fact, that memorial service turned into a sort of town meeting with Nooner getting blamed by Termite for blowing up a beaver dam with no permint and me getting blamed by Pyro for turning in a false alarm. Even the Banker got in on it what with him losing money on the loan he give to Cromangon Man to buy the car Cro used to travel to the junior college when he weren't living with the critters.

Now me, I had it all pretty well figured in my head what'd happened, beings I was privy to some facts and beings that I'd drawed the critters what weren't. But other town folks, not knowing the whole story, couldn't figure out why, of an August morning, Nooner blowed up the dam.

Well, Nooner, he told them, and he told them good. In the first place he din't blow up no beaver dam. He blowed up a lodge what ifing they want to see the dam witch is still there, they was welcome to it. He blowed up the lodge because the beavers all done left and how was he to know Cromangon Man done turned into a beaver hisself? The dam he ain't blowed yet, on account of ifing he blowed the dam first then it would be more dangerous blowing the lodge with the lodge more out of the water and all.

Now Bob the Barber, beings that emotions was running so high and all, for some queer reason started to take Termite's side and wanted to know how come Nooner wanted to blow up the dam in the first place, beings it was beavers and all, witch is a lot like humans.

Because for two reasons, Nooner says. He said he din't

want his kids drowning in no crick, what got the whole funeral home real quiet-like sos any other man or gink like myself would've had tears in his eyes after he was done saying or hearing on that.

Then he said the water was working its way towards the dump, it being so wet and all last spring, and he knowed then he had to do something about it sometime.

"Well, for Christsakes," Bob the Barber says, "How come you never told nobody?"

Nooner, he just put his face in his hands, and right there, in front of the Schoolteacher and ever body, he broke down crying. Now it ain't *just* quiet. You can't hear no breathing, not even your own—cept Nooner's. Then he composes hisself-like and looks up and with this pleading-like wore on his face he says, "Because I din't want nobody—leastways my kids—to think I blowed up a family of beavers."

Nobody moves or makes a sound. Then the Schoolteacher, she comes over and she puts her hands on Nooner like she done me so many times and just stands there, looking down at the carpet in the center aisle, but not sos you can't see her eyes.

There weren't nobody what was about to have another piece to say when she done that. Real slow-like, all the people, men and ginks alike, begun to get up, the Barber first, then all the ginks laying a hand on Nooner's shoulder on their way out. Even me.

I t was a pitiful sight what with the whole clan of ginks, some folks I ain't even told you on, moping around for the next week in the shop with two of their kind always missing—Cromangon Man and Nooner. Me, I'd go and practice some, and then I'd come back and sketch these long, drawed-out faces sos my income was cut on account of there weren't nobody who wanted to remember those times beings it was clear that trust had been busted some.

But some people begun to realize they wasn't perfect, and you just knowed it wouldn't be long before there were only one of what was missing, although it weren't so bad for him, him being in a pretty good place, I figured, with Mom and Baby Sis already there.

Wouldn't you know, though, it would take something like an act of the Lord to get Nooner back in the fold.

There hadn't been a real fire since the day before the bank robbery, and that weren't no big one, just the old outhouse what is still standing at the rest stop on the highway south of town. Nobody could figure how it got started, sitting there for a hundred years never having had the notion to burn up before. When one of the ginks in the shop thought maybe the robber might've started it so as to draw the eyes out of town sos he could case the joint, I slipped over to the Masonic Hall and worked some more on my stroke till I knowed all that talk would've died down. Otherwise, I knowed they'd get around to talking about the Banker and how goosey he was all because of me. But that's another story, although it ain't really.

Well, Nooner, he had his old truck with the floorboards full of holes, you know, and the body just full of cancer sos a lawyer from Lawless couldn't tell you what year nor model. I spose the Lord decided to put it out of its misery beings one early morning when it was real hot-like, so hot you just know when the sun peeks over the horizon that to look at it in the face is going to scorch the insides of your eyeballs, Nooner, he's eating his breakfast, and he smells something what he knowed he hadn't oughta be smelling since he ain't burned trash for a week. He takes a long look out the kitchen winda and what he had was this kind of Christmasy feeling, staring on the windshield of his truck as ifing it was the glass doors on the fireplace at Pyro's house during the annual Fireman's Holiday Celebration Night, he said. But Nooner, he knowed it weren't December, so he calls in the alarm, it seeming funny-like the flames was on the driver's-side, because Nooner, he don't smoke. He got his family away from the house in case she blew, and by that time there weren't nothing Nooner nor nobody near could do to stop that truck from burning.

Me, I din't have no dream about it. Leastways I don't think I did, on account of I checked my pad later, but I heared the fire whistle, and when I stepped out of the house to see ifing I could spot some smoke, I smelled, from over a mile away at my place, what I ain't never smelled but in Nooner's truck, so I hop on my bike.

I gets there just in time to see the rear winda pop. Pretty soon, here come the fire truck, and Nooner's truck is so far gone, they think, that what Pyro tells them to do is spray the house first, beings it was so close. Nooner, he gets real mad because, I spose, that truck, it were as much his home as his house, and he tells Pyro there weren't nothing but an ignoramus what wouldn't've first sprayed the truck, given she could've blew. Poor Old Pyro has got all the ginks there but me yelling in his ear, him just chewing on that farmer's match of his, adjusting his firechief's hat over and over, acting like he was the boss of hisself when it were clear he sure weren't the boss of no gink. Then, real sudden-like, and for what seems no purpose, the fire, she just stopped. There weren't no flames, no smoke, no nothing. Just a ticking noise coming from under the hood as ifing that old bomb had been out for a joy ride on its lonesome. Nobody said nothing. And when the ticking noise cooled down to where it was as quiet as the second hand on that new-fangled electric watch in the drug store, there weren't nothing what could be heared over it but the sounds of doors slamming on the vehicles of the volunteers, men and ginks alike, what was arriving, saying, "Where's the fire?" When final-like Nooner's truck quit glowing sos you could stand beside it without your eyebrows getting singed off, Nooner, he walked up to it like it might bite others but not him, and he peeked in through the driver's side winda what had blowed too. What he saw is I spose what ever gink saw and was for the next week the talk at the shop when Nooner and another gink what was giving him a ride to Lawless to hunt for another truck was there. It were a lucky thing, the ginks said, and me, I had to agree, that Nooner weren't in his old truck when it caught afire. On account of there weren't nothing what burned but the outline of a man behind the wheel.

Now what the ginks was talking about the entire week when Nooner weren't in the shop was the Banker. Come nine-fifteen the morning Nooner's truck'd decided to go to truck heaven and pass through hell on the way, the Freeland National Bank employees what was three local ladies was still standing outside on the sidewalk waiting for the Banker to open up shop. Well, needless to say, a Banker what ain't there at nine o'clock in the morning what with a new loan to write up sos Nooner can get hisself another truck is a Banker what ain't going to be there at nine-thirty neither, since he normal-like, Bob the Barber said, gets there at eight-thirty, probable-like so he can count the cash three times before he hands it out to the teller ladies.

So the ladies what is probable-like worried about their jobs and all, one of them, come nine-twenty, wanders over to Termite's trailer and knocks on the door, wondering ifing Termite heared any rumors about the Banker being sick that day, the same Termite who ain't even heared any rumors about Nooner's truck what with him only responding to one alarm in town, that being a bell not a siren. So Termite, he calls the Banker twice and gets no answer—once at home and once at the bank, maybe thinking on the possibility the Banker's heart give out final-like with him being so goosey and all lately, and Termite maybe knowing he wouldn't be surprised none ifing that was the case since his own heart skipped a couple beats before he rung-up the F.B.I., they says.

Me, when I seen them three ladies out of the corner of my eye, I'd already pedaled straight to the Masonic Hall. I practiced right through lunch, and I weren't hungry a bit neither, leastways not hungry enough to be rummaging through cupboards in the kitchenette. But this powerful thirst was coming on, I says to myself, like it hadn't been hot that day, and final-like I were so dry I knowed I had to have something out of the Barber's machine ifing I din't want to pass out none, and there was one thing I know for sure, I weren't interested in passing out that afternoon, not with me and my sketch pad in the same room.

So I lay my cue on the table, pick up my pad, lope across the square, I magine, to the shop like I'm a parched giraffe and I got blinders on, knowing full well who's over at the bank and who probable-like ain't. I heared my name, and I don't like it one bit. Why in the world din't you just get you a drink from the facucet I says to myself, but then again I knowed it din't make no difference. I stopped right at the Vetern's monument in the middle of the square and turned to see him walking my way, thinking on how it don't matter where I run to, he's going to be there too. Heck, hiding in Freeland would be like the Devil trying to hide from the Lord Hisself.

He'd changed a bit, maybe thinner or maybe just the fact he had on a different suit, beings it was sort of an off-white and there weren't no vest. I ain't never seen nobody with more than one suit, cept Digger, bless him, him what owns three on account of it's his business to wear suits, and that there, I thought, was probable-like the reason I din't want to talk to Mr. McMillion none, him seeming a little strange to me again, even though I knowed him now pretty good even though he kind of slowed-up his gait while he got closer to me and pulled out of his breast pocket his pouch and reached for his pipe in a side pocket. What would've made me real happy is ifing the pipe had been the same as before because I knowed it better than I knowed his face, pipes not changing much like human beings and it being the thing I'd stare on when he listened and I talked. But this was a different pipe too, black instead of brown, and I ain't never seen a man what owned more than one pipe at once.

So I says to him, "You lose your other pipe?"

He looks at me a bit. He smiles. "Witch one?"

Now I knowed these F.B.I. men was high class, what with him owning as many pipes as Digger, bless him, owned suits. And I knowed they was smart, too, what with him stopping short of me about three yards sos I wouldn't feel like no critter about to be somebody's fur coat.

The agent, he lites his pipe now, and neither of us don't say nothing.

Final-like, I can't take it no more, beings it's so hot and all, me standing there in the middle of the square what with there being no shade in my spot sos I've to move a little closer to him where he'd found some shade.

I says to him, "Did you catch him yet?"

"Who?" he says.

Now, I want to tell you, I never figured on such a silly

question in my life so I just up and says, me being kind of ornery because of how terrible thirsty I was, "Who else?"

He just looks at me, and then he says, "Stick," he says, "would you like a Coke?"

Now me, I was brung up just like you, and I knowed I shouldn't be taking no candy from strangers, but Agent McMillion, he weren't really no stanger no more, even though I were only fourteen and he was thirty-four, maybe, beings he was with the F.B.I. Lord forgive me, but I lied.

"Well," he says, "how about some ice cream?"

"No. Thank you," I says, and then something just comes over me and I turns around, and I'm running.

I'll be danged ifing the next thing I knowed I ain't looking at the ceiling fan whirling around in the shop what's telling me I'm laying in the Barber's throne. What's more is I got my pad in my lap, and when I take a look at it, I seen this half-baked drawing with all these funny looking boards on it, like the side of a house. For some reason I'm thinking it must be Nooner's place and I look over to my left and there's Floyd's grin.

"You passed out from the heat," a voice says.

I look to my right and there's the Barber. Digger is standing at my feet, and behind him, just a bit to his right is Agent McMillion.

I closed my eyes. "I done drawed in my sleep, din't I?"

I opened my eyes again, and they all had grins on like Floyd's, ceptings Agent McMillion. He was puffing on that pipe, looking toward the winda.

"It was real comical," I heared the Barber's voice say.

"Yeah," Digger said, "Who would have knowed it was possible with your eyes closed like that?"

"Stick?" I hear the agent say and I look at him, but he ain't looking at me, beings he's still studying on something, still puffing.

"Yes Sir," I says.

"You know there's been another robbery, don't you."

I told him I sposed there was.

He looks at me. "You know that it's more serious than that."

I said I sposed I did what with the Banker being so goosey and all after he seen the face I drawed.

"Mr. Renolds," what is the Banker's name, "is missing," he says. "Did you know that?"

I tell him I don't, what was the truth.

He takes his pipe out of his mouth. He comes real close and he looks me in the eyes sos I can't look away ifing I want to. "Will you help me?" he says.

Dang. I'd've rather been laying in one of Digger's coffins, bless him, I says to myself, with the lid closed, cept I figured while they might be able to get my stick in there without busting it, shooting three cushion in a foot locker would sure enough cramp your stroke. So I kind of tuned Agent McMillion out and jacked up the volume on WGN a bit. But the F.B.I. man, he weren't no F.B.I. man for nothing. He was going to have it his way, and since there weren't no way he was going to have it any way but his, and because there weren't nowhere else for me to look but in his face, what by now was pretty familiar-like, I asked of him what did he want me to do.

He tells me I have to go slow, beings I passed out, but this is important enough sos it had to be done now. He wants the ginks to come along since he figures I'll feel more at ease. So Bob the Barber, he done closes up shop without his usual hesitation, he figuring, I spose, that though the Banker could be low down since he weren't never the boss of hisself, he were still a human being, even ifing he were from outer space. But me, I figure the Barber has got no choice with the money gone from his customers and all. How's he going to keep this throne room of his otherwise.

AGENT MCMILLION BRUNG his car over to the Shop, and we all get in, and it's so new-smelling and cool I begin awondering whether the Agent has got a block of ice up front under the hood melting, so cool I ain't felt since the last time I stuck my head in the Barber's machine.

The Agent, he drives us to the Banker's house, and I'm feeling kind of guilty and all, holding onto this glass of lemonade the Banker's wife give me, her looking so sad and ascared and in shock and all. I says to myself she knowed it was me what drawed the picture what made the Banker goosey.

The Agent, he asked her to please sit down by me and describe the man that kidnapped her husband in the middle of the dawn.

"Charlie," she says.

"Yes Mam," I says.

"It was him," she said. "The man you sketched."

Now, I spose you think I'm going to tell you I dropped my lemonade. Well, I din't. I just nodded some and said I was sorry, what I was, her not being from outer space, I knowed on account of she were local born.

Agent McMillion, he asked ifing he could talk with me alone and I just sort of stands up like one of them zombies on TV late at night. I knowed my soul's no longer my own, him taking me in the Banker's den.

"Are you all right, Stick?" he says.

I tell him yes.

"You know how it is on the TV when someone is kidnapped?"

I said yes.

"Well, this time there won't be any ransom."

"Oh," I said.

"We have to find Mr. Renolds fast."

I figured they did.

"Are you receiving any impressions?"

That's what he said exact. I remember because I started to get ascared on that question on account of I thought maybe he was talking on he knowed I had a built-in antenna. "Whatchu mean?" I says.

"This is where Mr. Renolds spends a lot of his time. Does it tell you anything?"

I looked around. "I spose not," I says to him.

The Agent, he just looks at me a bit, then he looks to my lap. "Let's take your pad back in the living room," he says.

I spose when we bust in on the conversation in the next

room they'd been talking pretty serious-like, since Floyd's grin were gone. The Banker's wife, I don't know her name then beings the only time I ever heared it, I remember, I'm tuned in on one of them knee slappers on the Wally Phillips show a long time ago. Anyways, she knowed my name because there ain't no Freeland citizen what don't know a gink's name, beings ginks is often the butt of jokes, Bob the Barber said what with the Schoolteacher being the boss of herself.

Well, on account of we was low class and the Banker's wife was high class, the ginks weren't talking like no ginks I ever knowed, though it could've been because she were a woman too. Digger, he weren't married none and din't know how to act around no lady unless she be the Schoolteacher or a new wida or some other whose relation just up and croaked. And Bob the Barber, he ain't found no women what would have him neither, what din't matter one bit, beings he was married to the shop and his self-took responsibility of looking after Old Floyd. And Nooner, him being the biggest gink of all, beings he was the only gink what had a wife, but not really, beings they weren't married by no preacher or judge, Bob the Barber said, but the horniness what drove them to cohabitation. But, Nooner, he weren't at the Banker's, and Floyd, he don't count, he being the gink what the clan of them adopted before I come along.

Anyways, the Banker's wife told Agent McMillion she thought she had to lay down now, her head splitting with worry, I spose, because she were a human being. I seen the grin start to return on Floyd's face when he heared that, but it fades when Agent McMillion tells her he understood but would she mind one more question. Then he up and asks me to show her them boards I done sketched when I had my stroke in the sun. He wants to know from her ifing it's got any meaning. You could tell she was real interested, beings she knowed I was the one what drawed the face what made the Banker goosey. She looks at my pad real hard and sort of tilts her head in one direction and then another.

"I've seen this," she says. "What is it, Charles?"

"I'll be danged ifing I know, what with me hardly ever traveling south of town," I up and says to her.

Now all of the sudden, the Banker's wife, the Agent, and the ginks is looking at me real weird-like.

"What did you say?" the Agent says.

I told him I said I din't know what them boards were.

"No," the Agent says, "what did you say about south of Freeland?"

I told him I recollected I din't say nothing about Freeland, witch were the truth.

"No," the Agent says again. "That's not what you said. You said—"

"Excuse me," the Banker's wife says, "I've got to lie down before I collapse."

Agent McMillion, him being the gentleman and all, says yes, of course, and he takes her by the arm and leads her to the staircase door.

I look over at Floyd, and I seen his grin's coming back.

The Agent, he closes the door and turns around. "Stick," he says, "sit down."

So I sits down.

The Agent, he starts talking in this real low voice. He says to us all he don't want to frighten the Banker's wife none but that it's real important-like for us to figure out what I said.

Well, it was real clear them ginks understood, since you could just tell in their eyes, even Floyd's eyes, that they knowed I own a power I din't know I own, on account of I were me, even though the only time I was absolute sure I were the boss of myself was when I was practicing on my table.

"Now let's think back," the Agent says. "Exactly what was it Stick said?"

All of the sudden there was this voice in the room what sounds like me but it weren't me. Ever body but Floyd is looking at Floyd. Me, I look at Floyd too, and he's just about to finish the sentence.

"... what with me hardly ever traveling south of town," Floyd says, him glowing like a twenty watt bulb, maybe.

"That's it!" the Agent says.

Floyd, he just grinned some more.

Bob the Barber tells Floyd to stop congratulating hisself before he gets the big head, but there weren't nobody in the mood to get soda in their noses on that one, especial-like since we was all drinking lemonade.

Well, it weren't but a second we're all serious-like again, the Agent asking me what I mean by me never traveling south of town.

"I really said that?" I says.

All the ginks nod.

"Stick," the Agent says, "you must concentrate on that drawing," pointing to it where it now lays on the coffee table.

"What is it, part of a barn?"

I looked at that sketch real hard, about as long as you could hold your breath under water, and when I come up, my mind was just as empty as when I went under. I looked up at the Agent and I shaked my head.

"Damn," the Agent said, "I wish we had a hypnotist."

Now I want to tell you, hearing him talk on that there, it made me ascared, because I din't want nobody putting me to sleep and me accidental-like talking in the voice of Wally Phillips, since I seen me enough on the TV to know that the hypnotist the Agent brung in would be the same what is the boss in the loony bin in Lawless, so I got to thinking fast and hard on what it were I thought on about that drawing when I woke up laying in the Barber's throne.

Then I up and says, "I think I thunk on something I ain't told on yet."

The Agent, he got a look on his face as curious as the Schoolteacher's.

"You know them boards?" I says.

He just nodded, Agent McMillion.

"I was thinking on how they must've been on Nooner's house."

"Who's Nooner?"

For a second I din't know what to say. It never dawned on me there would be folks in this world what never knowed Nooner sos I'd have to say a speech.

Bob the Barber busted in. "His place is north, where the fire was this morning."

The Agent was interested, you could tell.

Now I busted in. "You know how them boards is looking kind of funny-like?"

Digger, bless him, says, "Yeah, it's like they was scorched or something."

"That's what I seen, too," I says.

Agent McMillion seemed to think we was on to something. "What do you think, Stick?" he says.

Now there I am, about to shrug my shoulders, when all of the sudden there's that voice again what is my voice about to come out, but it ain't me what said a thing.

All the heads, cepting Floyd's witch don't engage in much activity no-how turn to Floyd.

"Did he say 'no'?" the Agent says.

"No," Bob the Barber says, "he said 'nope!'"

The Agent says, "Why did you say 'no,' Floyd—that is your name, isn't it?"

"Yep," Floyd says.

"Why did you say 'no'?" the Agent says.

"You can't ask him like that," Digger says.

The Agent, he looks at Digger a little cross-like, and you could tell, Digger, bless him, he just shut up sos the F.B.I. man could find out for hisself.

"Why did you say 'no'?" Agent McMillion says again, leaning in Floyd's direction.

Floyd don't say nothing.

The Agent, he's thinking on something, you could tell. Then he says, "Why did you say 'nope,' Floyd?"

Again, Floyd don't say nothing.

Bob the Barber says, "Digger's right. You can't ask him

like that."

The Agent, he sits up straight in his chair. "Well, what do you mean?"

Bob the Barber turns to Floyd. "Floyd," he says, "is that sketch part of Nooner's house?"

"Nope," Floyd says.

The Agent leans forward again,"How do you know?" he says.

Floyd just looks at him, that grin of his like he just had a first taste of something he liked.

The Barber looks at Agent McMillion again. Then he says, "You went to school to get your job—right?"

The Agent just looks at the Barber.

"Well," the Barber says, "believe me, I been to school sos I can talk to Floyd. Just let me ask the questions, OK?"

The Agent, he nodded.

"Floyd," the Barber says, "are them boards from around here?"

"Yep."

"Do you know where?"

"Nope."

It was like Agent McMillion would never learn. I says to myself, this is one F.B.I. man what now is not the boss of hisself, beings he's more of a stranger than I thought. But then I knowed he weren't from outer space nor Lawless neither. I figured he were a human being and a good one at that. It's just that to talk with Floyd you got to know the code. But there the Agent goes again, blurting in on the interrogation-like. He says to Floyd, "But how can you know the boards are from around here when you don't know where they are?"

Floyd grinned at him some more.

Now me, I knowed the answer to that, beings I knowed where the Banker was from, though I din't know where he was. And Floyd, he knowed them boards was in his head, even though he din't know where they are. I figured the Agent could use a few lessons from the Schoolteacher.

Well, the Barber, real calm-like, he said, "Jesus Christ, McMillion, will you let the man talk?"

The Agent looked at the floor, sighed, and shook his head. I spose he was frustated.

"Now, Floyd," the Barber says, "what can you... no, I mean, are the boards in Freeland?"

"Nope."

The Barber looked square at me and said, "The boards, are they south of town?"

"Yep," Floyd says.

Agent McMillion looked up.

The Barber says, "Are these boards so that you'd remember them ifing you'd seen them?"

"Yep."

"Are they laying down or are they standing?"

Floyd don't say nothing.

The Agent sudden-like says, "Are the boards laying down, Floyd?"

"Nope."

The Agent, you could tell he done broke the code, on account of real excited-like he says, "Are they standing?"

Floyd tells him yep.

"Is it a house or a barn?" Digger says.

"Nope."

"Is it a house?" the Barber says.

"Nope."

"Can you tell us where it is?" Agent McMillion blurts out.

"Nope."

I thought the Agent was going to have a stroke on that one, him dang near falling off his chair, but he weren't laughing none.

And Floyd, he weren't laughing none neither, but he sure were agrinning. You see, with ginks, you got to have patience, even when Floyd weren't no real gink, cepting by adoption by a man what was one, even though the Barber were young enough to be Floyd's grandson, maybe.

Digger, he never gives up on no gink, because that would be like giving up on hisself, bless him. Old Digger, I spose he had one more question what was his trump card, so he asked of it to Floyd, "Floyd," he says, "are those boards scorched?"

Now all of the sudden Floyd ain't saying nothing, and his grin's starting to sag a little. You could tell Floyd had something like a headache coming on, and believe you me, that would be some ache, what would've been Bob the Barber's comment ifing he were thinking on it, but Bob the Barber, he were just looking at Digger, like Digger, bless him, just reminded him of something.

Well, I turn WGN down so I can hear what Digger is mumbling to hisself, and Digger, bless him, sighs, "Trouble it don't happen but what it happens in threes," and I thought on what I knowed was going on in Digger's head, beings he just played his last trump card he thinks, and he's probable-like thinking there's going to have to be another memorial service soon, this one for the Banker, and since there's two memorial services the Law of Averages says there's to be a third.

But Digger, bless him, he ain't a quitter like the whole town—cept ginks and the Bear—would one day call me, and Digger, he just looks to Floyd, and Floyd looks back at him like he knows his headache is about to get better, a hint of that grin of his coming to life again, and Digger says, "Are those boards at the rest stop?"

"Yep."

All of the sudden Bob the Barber jumps up out of his chair and done a little jig. "I knew it!" he says.

Digger turns to Agent McMillion and says loud-like, "Well, there's your boards!"

"Where?" the Agent says.

"Where?" I says.

"The outhouse," Digger says.

"The fire before the first robbery!" Agent McMillion says.

"Oh," I says.

Floyd, he don't say nothing but what his grin says.

ME AND DIGGER rode in his hearse, and Floyd come along with us too because he likes the siren. I knowed Old Pyro would be real mad, but Digger, bless him, beings he was second in command, took it on hisself to turn in the alarm sos we'd have a search party for the Banker, though I got to thinking later it were more like a surprise party than a search party with the F.B.I. man opening up that old outhouse what was propped shut, showing the Banker—sweaty, bug-eyed, gagged, and all tied up, sitting in there with his pants down around his ankles.

Now the Banker, he weren't goosey no more, but just in case, Red Sullivan, a gink volunteer what I ain't told you about, kept his painter's cap on, and Pyro left his hat in the truck. And that's how folks come to know it weren't redheads what made the Banker run and hide with a case of the crazies, but it were me. The Banker, all the ginks said, he got one look at me there with my pad and he run and vaulted the fence for the corn, saying he wouldn't come out till I was gone. Digger, bless him, figuring the Banker wouldn't be needing his hearse, drived me and him back to the funeral home. Me, I picked up my stick and rode on home on my bike, not feeling so well, what with the heat and all, but mostly because I knowed I drawed with my own hand what give another human being a case of the crazies, though the Schoolteacher and the ginks all come to see it another way.

"Why, the Banker would still be sitting out there on that shitter ifing it weren't for you, Stick," Bob the Barber said. "Ain't I right, Floyd?"

"Yep," Floyd said.

Nooner, he put his two cents in too. He figures I save two lifes, both the Banker's and Nooner's what with the Banker back in business and able to borrow Nooner the money he needed to get hisself a new truck. But the things what Nooner couldn't figure was two. Sposing the fires was related, how was it the robber was a redhead with a beard the second time, beings he weren't red the first time? And how come Floyd knowed the boards was *them* boards?

Well, me, I knowed the answer to the first, but the answer to the second would be like pulling teeth.

That robber the second time would be what was the robber the first time, beings the two was related. Funny thing is the answers to Nooner's questions is related too.

It were the Barber what asked of Floyd the day after Floyd become a hero and all what Floyd had in the sack, the Barber thinking on Floyd having made hisself a trip to the counter in the drug store and was probable-like sucking hardcandy. Of course, Floyd din't answer none because the Barber ain't on purpose asked him right. So this goes on and on the whole day, Floyd just sitting and agrinning with the top of this little sack all twisted and blooming out of his fist like a petunia what took sick, him never looking inside.

The way it turns out, Old Floyd, beings he'd seen *Dragnet* aplenty, spotted that sack in the Banker's driveway, and must have knowed it'd have evidence in it. After about three days of Floyd clutching that sack, the Barber just up and took it from him, what din't seem to bother Floyd none, beings he just kept agrinning. The Barber, he looked inside of that sack, and him being the smartest Barber you ever seen outside of Lawless, he put two and two together, mainly on account of the code.

"You cut yourself, Floyd?" he says.

"Nope."

You see, what the Barber found inside was band-aids. Not your regular band-aids in packages neither, but they was open and they was the kind that had iodine already on them. Now Bob the Barber, beings he was the one what adopted Floyd the most, knowed Old Floyd had something to say or else he wouldn't've been carrying around those band-aids for near on three days. So, the Barber just give out a big sigh and set hisself on his throne because he knowed he was going to get to play twenty questions again, only with Floyd the game might be twenty thousand. But the Barber, beings he's so good at putting two and two together, it took him only about twenty minutes. I knowed because I was there.

Me and the Barber, we had this notion what we told Agent McMillion, and it become the very one we was telling on to Nooner now. Here it be.

The robber what got away twice was the same man. When he knowed what easy pickings the Freeland Bank were, what with only Termite guarding it and *him* asleep, he growed hisself a beard and tinted it all by smearing iodine on sos anybody what would see him would think he was just a stranger and not a robber, what with him having a different car, the Banker seen, on account of he got kidnapped in it. And before Nooner asked how I knowed the robber was going to disguise hisself a redhead, I told him it weren't me what in the first place said you could see red in that sketch.

Well, Nooner, he wants to know why, ifing the robber disguised hisself the second time, how come he don't do it the first time?

I says to Nooner maybe he did. I says when I study on the sights in Freeland I keep coming up with the same picture. Men and ginks what don't wear beards, what is all of them, wears a disguise. Maybe the robber shaved just for when he come the first time. Ifing so, he might stir up trouble again, only this time natural-like without no clean-shaved face and without no iodine in his beard on account of trouble there ain't but what it don't come in threes. And ifing he don't believe me, he can ask Digger.

As to how Floyd knowed that them boards I drawed was of the outhouse, that's another story, although it ain't really.

The Barber and me, we had it figured that Floyd, beings he had such a big head and all, must have a big brain inside of that head too. In other words, maybe it weren't just water in there, but more brains. Maybe Floyd had what the Barber said was called a photographic remembering. So we did us a experiment. The Barber and me had Floyd close his eyes.

I said to Floyd, "Is there a machine in this barber shop?"

"Yep," he said.

"Is there Royal Crown in the machine?"

"Yep."

Bob the Barber busted in. "For Christsakes, Stick," he says, "that ain't a question to be asking no Einstein." He turns to Floyd. "Is my chair red and white?"

"Nope," Floyd says, his eyes still shut.

Well, Old Floyd, he could've fooled me, because when I closed my eyes what I seen was red and white.

"Is my chair red and white and silver?" the Barber says.

"Yep."

Sure enough. Me, I forgot on the chrome. And with me reading all that science fiction, too.

Now the Barber must've figured that was just a warm

up, because he asked Old Floyd a real hard one then. "Has my chair got a guarantee stamped on it you seen when we installed it?"

"Yep."

"Is my chair good for the life of the purchaser?"

"Nope."

Well, I guessed Old Floyd blowed the theory right there, ceptings to say maybe Floyd had read it wrong. Me, I din't know what to think. I mean I figured that the idea of a gink who drawed in his sleep knowing somebody in the same town what had photographic remembering was agin the Law of Averages. But then I got to thinking on how it would be agin the Law of Averages ifing there were *no* town where there weren't both, especial-like in outer space. Maybe we was all living in another dimension. Maybe we was living on a world in outer space and the Banker was from the real Earth. Me, I din't know what to think. The way it would turn out, though, Old Floyd, he did have him his photographic remembering. It's just it were only with words and boards and faces and such.

The Barber told Floyd he could open his eyes, and sudden-like a peculiar thing happened. Old Floyd, he just kept his eyes shut, his grin gone, like he was taking a nap with his chin still up. It being closing time, me and the Barber din't say much about it, even when he din't wake up none until we got him out the door. But the next day he still weren't agrinning none, and his eyes was still closed. But he could hear you all right. You knowed because when Nooner come in and they all seen how sorry I was about giving another human being a case of the crazies, like I says, Floyd said the Barber was right when the Barber asked of him ifing it weren't for me the Banker would still be in the outhouse.

Well, ifing it weren't for Floyd, nobody would've knowed what I drawed, not even me. But you know how sometimes you kind of get the big head—not like Floyd's—I mean so you forget to give the other credit where credit is due. Well, that's sort of the way we all was with Floyd. Now take the barber shop, for a fact. Old Floyd started to open his eyes again, all right, but he'd always have them closed when he come in the door or when Bob the Barber was talking to him. Otherwise he wouldn't open them until he got situated facing the winda first. What we done was knowed Old Floyd was giving us a signal, but since he's always been about a thirty-minute ride from the loony bin in Lawless, nobody, not even the Barber, cared much about what Floyd din't want to see, or seen. When crazy things was happening in Freeland nobody seemed too worried about what'd happened or what's going to happen. Everthing sort of run together anyways. When I'm thinking on this whole story I'm telling you, I says to myself who's to say the end is any differenter from the beginning when the middle is all part of the beginning and the end anyways? A man what is born in Freeland dies in Freeland or somewhere just like it beings we all live on the same planet, even the ones what is from outer space. Now take a man what ain't born in Freeland but dies in it instead. Who's to say he weren't living in Freeland all along when you go splitting hairs, trying to separate when he lived from when he was born. I mean when he was born he was living then too. And when he died he was living. You divide a man up into his birth, his life, and his death and you got trouble. You talk about Freeland's past, its present, and its future and you got trouble. And now ifing I was to go and tell you this story has got a middle what is different from the end or the beginning you'd have trouble on account of a lie is made out of trouble. And trouble, it don't happen but what it happens in threes. Just ask Floyd. Ask Nooner who knows what happens when you go splitting a beaver lodge up into stick and mud and stones. Ask Cromangon Man who knows what happens when you go splitting the land up into his and yours and mine.

It weren't of yet I heared her call it Anarchtopia, but I bet you my new stick she'd thought on it. How could a person not when they been seeing it from her viewpoint? For one thing, she become our live-in preacher. I was as surprised as anybody else to hear she done missonary work on a bunch of reservations what we was hearing about in her sermons. There was even talk she'd married and buried a Indian medicine man. Well, I don't know about that, but what I do know is I started attending church as regular as Sunday school what with Indians to hear about instead of sweetness and light what the circuit preacher who wore a flower and said it in his squeaky voice talked about. Funny thing was, I weren't the only local what begun to show up in church. They was in them wood folding chairs to match the pews in the aisles too, and it weren't even Easter. You'd look around you and you'd just knowed you was seeing the closest thing there'd ever be to a convention of ginks. But there was others too, like Termite and Pyro, what was fine with me, beings I figured they needed a little education, but it weren't fine with the other ginks, I could tell, them being a little more protective maybe, since the Schoolteacher, she was looking younger ever Sunday, and one warm September morning you could see she had a white dress on under that black robe. And her shoes was differenter too. They was heels, all right, but skinnier and taller with no bows. I ain't saying there was nothing to worry about, but the ginks, they trusted Termite and Pyro about like you'd trust a bare lectric wire under a rug. The ginks, they was so conditioned to giving the Schoolteacher respect what she earned that they was a little nervous the way you might be ifing you owned a purebred bitch for hunting with and two old mutts who could barely work up a boner come sniffing around, even though you had her in a cage.

But she was the same Schoolteacher across the road. She drilled me in algebra and made me double up on my science fiction, beings it was good for my vocabulary. History were a big thing with her too, but no bigger than anything else, science fiction included, though she never heared of the books I was checking out. Nooner, he never heared of them neither, but he was too busy to notice I was checking out two books at a time, him with all the dials on his new dashboard to watch. The trouble was the rides was getting more boring, beings I couldn't concentrate on my science fiction what with that radio in the new truck, even though it weren't hardly ever turned on, ceptings for storm reports.

What reminds me. I ain't told you on the storm cellar in the schoolyard yet. Witch is a good thing since it weren't time on account of it's a different story, although it ain't really, beings it's the story of how I become a mother and a healer. It's how I knowed I could be more than the best at billiards ifing I wanted, witch I din't. It's how I come to know about the Vision of the Flock. And it's the story what ain't got no beginning nor end since who can know for sure the first or last time he'd seen a bird, a crow?

Me, I'd be laying in the front yard of a October day when I din't feel like practicing or drawing none, just looking up at the trees and such what was turning, and there'd be the clouds all white agin that neon blue and I'd think on those clouds while I was laying on the flagstone what I dug and what was warmed by the sun, you could feel, beings part of you was on the ground, witch weren't damp none, but cold like it oughta be damp. And me, I wouldn't want to get up off them stones, and I wouldn't ceptings for once when I got to thinking on Helen and Peg and go to the bathroom for to get them off my mind because they was evading my private thoughts on how nice it'd be to just go lay on Mom and Baby Sis's stones, feel them all warm as the stones I was on, knowing that though their bodies was cold and decayed, their visible memory was them stones made warm and all by the sun. And though I knowed the dark and the winter what'd make them cold was coming on, I also knowed the light and the summer was coming on. I knowed as long as I'd be there the sun what was actual a star would always be there. And even ifing it weren't, I wouldn't have me no worries, no ache what I felt when I walked away in the graveyard, no suffering like what an animal don't have to suffer, beings he can't see beyond his nose and know there'll be more to suffer. And I thought on that bass I killed when the lodge got blowed up and says to myself, though it din't make no difference since that fish were as good as dead anyways, it was dumb to kill it since the only suffering it could know was pain, not a human being's pain what is grieving what goes on.

Then I'd see it, a flash of it, I mean, the sun, coming off the back of a crow, beings there was a whole flock what lived in the woods, them what lived all over the world, I come to find out, cepting New Zealand next to Australia. And I'd hear that *rcaw, rcaw,* and *rcaw,* and I'd know it were the sun talking, just like I knowed it were the night talking too, because what we call the sun ain't nothing special about it, beings it's a actual star. That's how I come to know each of us was hooked up with ever body else in Freeland, on account of the sun was hooked up with the stars, on account of the sun—ifing it was related to the stars, them being so far away—there's no way no man nor gink alive nor dead ain't hooked up with the rest of his kind, beings he ain't nearly as far away from his kind as the sun is from its kind.

All of this I'm telling you I'm telling sos you'll understand how I become a mother and a healer and how I come to name my pet, what I kept in the storm shelter and weren't tame atall, Old Crow.

I'm laying on the front yard on them little clouds of a October afternoon and I heared this huge squawking coming from the tops of the trees along the fence line. It's the crows and they got themselfs a owl, I figures, after I read up on it, or maybe the owl has them. Anyways, I seen this black flash by the fence line out the corner of my eye, and I just knowed what it was. This crow, he was crippled, all right, flapping and hopping around the yard like a fly that big old horned owl had tried to swat but only dazed. Now it were the distance what made me think of him as a fly, but when I come up close to him and see his suffering, he ain't as common as a fly no more, he's like a piece of ever thing, the day and the night, what fell from space and is still alive. So, Old Crow, I took him in.

I took him to school. I din't have no cage at home, so I took him to school the next morning and I put him in the storm shelter and fed him baloney ever morning early before any little girls and ginks shows up, and I closed the door so he could heal before something made a meal of him. I din't tell a solitary soul, not even Becky.

Believe it or not, it was how I come to learn about the Schoolteacher and her secret.

The Schoolteacher, I asked her that first morning I sneaked Old Crow in the storm shelter whether she might own a book on birds on account of Nooner and me, we'd just been to the Lawless library, I says, and I needed it now. She looks at me kind of strange-like, but she says yes, she's got several books on birds. It never dawned on me she weren't seeing me when she was talking to me. Heck, I never seen she was sick till Sunday morning when she was preaching and you could tell she done something like black out. Old Termite and Pyro about run over each other racing for the pulpit, but by the time they got there, she'd got better. Boy, did they look dumb. Anyways, I run down to the basement and got her a glass of water, since I'd seen her get that look in her eyes a couple of times during the week, only she was sitting down then, and she'd asked me, because of me being the biggest, I spose, to get her some water, please.

But I din't have to get her no glass of water when I ask her about the bird books, beings the Schoolteacher, her curiosity had to be stronger than any thirst. She wants to know why I say I need the book. Well, I tell her I don't really need it. It's just I want to read up on crows, what was the truth, me being so dumb to've thought I din't need to see a book on birds when poor Old Crow, he'd sit in the dark of that storm shelter for near on a week without nothing but the water in the baloney to help his thirst.

Well, the Schoolteacher, she done something different when I told her I wanted to know about Crows. She slow-like got this smile on her face like you just remembered the Lord finally answered one of your old prayers, and she sent me right away across the road to pull a book off her shelfs, something I ain't never seen her do before. Now that book, it was fat, and it was all about crows. She had me studying on it off and on the whole week. Now that's the Schoolteacher for you. You got you a touch of the Old Curiosity and sudden-like you ain't got it anymore because you done been buried under the facts. Then something else takes over in your brain, and it ain't so plain as to be called curiosity. It done took over your body too. You was hungry and thirsty and questions and answers was the only thing that would fill you up or wet you down. The problem was you'd get hungrier and thirstier on account of she made you harvest your own grain and dig your own well before she'd let you eat or drink.

So it weren't that book what give me a glimpse at the Vision of the Flock, even though it were as fat as it was. The things, they was two. First, I seen I weren't bringing her no more water when I was bringing Old Crow water. Second, the morning I come to school and was to feel like a mother what just give birth and a healer too was the morning Old Crow, as soon as I opened the storm cellar door, flapped right out and lazy-like flew off, the same morning the Schoolteacher quit having them blackouts.

Later it hits me like a shot. Her secret. It was with herself. Lord Jesus, I cry to myself, sitting at my desk, there was three of us. There was me. There was Floyd. There was her. How on Earth could the Law of Averages've both cursed and blessed us so?

Maybe we din't all belong in the loony bin in Lawless after all. Maybe there was more of us. I sure hope so, knowing as I did that trouble it don't come but what it comes in threes. But I knowed she weren't crazy. And *I* sure weren't crazy. And Floyd, that weren't craziness in his head, the Barber and I knowed, but the biggest brain you ever did see. And the Agent, he seemed to know something too, like he's seen it all before. Otherwise he might've called up a cattle car and shipped the lot of us to Lawless.

So maybe God was having Him some fun with the Law

of Averages. Maybe there was some reason on her seeing what the crows see, me drawing in my sleep, and Floyd with his photographic remembering. And then maybe there weren't. Maybe it were the Devil what done it to us and Bird Dog Benson were right. Maybe she were a witch.

I never believed it for a minute. I was only testing the water some, though I did say to myself once that I wondered what would happen ifing I asked her for a book on witchcraft, beings ever body knows you've got your bad witches and you've got your good ones. But the key weren't in witches. It was Indians. I'd've bet my stick on it.

Well, now that I knowed her secret, why she showed up at Nooner's place in her robe and all, I had to know whether I should tell her on it, because there I was, about to bust with my own secret. I studied on what I oughta do that night over my table, and I'll be danged ifing I din't miss a natural, that's how wrapped up I was in whether I should oughta talk with her. Final-like, I decided on I din't need to tell her I knowed. It was enough to know I weren't crazy just because my tuner was broke on WGN, when there was people—well, one, at least—what had in their brains a built-in crow's nest. Besides, there was a chance I was wrong about what Old Crow and the rest of the evidence made me believe. And I sure enough din't want to know I was wrong, beings even she might then see to it that my table and me gets a permanent divorce, beings in all my dreams I ain't seen no three cushion in the loony bin.

IT WAS HARD that school year, what she and I knowed was
going to be my last with her, to not just up and tell her I
knowed the secret. But you never can tell about the Schoolteacher. Maybe she already knowed I knowed. I sort of thought
so in church when I'd see them eyes what I was certain ain't
looked at any other eyes but mine for the entire sermon so that
them and that harsh voice of hers would lift you above the
pews, above the steeple even, so high you could see all Freeland and the way God seen it, it being kind of a joke what with
Termite and Pyro being the bosses of ever body but themselfs,
the Barber playing the fool when there ain't no king to play
for, Nooner running back and forth in his new truck, Digger
in his suit with nobody to bury on account of Freeland ain't
changed in a hundred years, ceptings when Mom and Baby
Sis left, and there ain't nobody what dies, really, anyways, and
me bent over my table, ascared to look up on account of I
knowed He knows my secret and ifing there was any one who
ever owned the power to quarantine me from my table, it were
Him, and final-like, Floyd, him being the easiest to spot.

But I found something out at the shop during Christmas
vacation what made me real jealous and probable-like led me
to hint to her I come to know her secret. All the ginks, they
was talking on how the Schoolteacher done made the holiday
the best they ever had, her knowing the right things to say and
all sos they was appreciating their lifes much as any afterlife
anybody ever dreamed up, when the discussion got on how it
was she was good at it. Well, they was talking on how she was
the boss of herself. They was talking on how she were different, too, up at that pulpit than when she was in that school-

room. Witch I knowed, but I ain't really thought on, and how I knowed was I knowed crows was curious too, the smartest bird that ever lived, and they could change real fast to new places just like a *human* being. Not only can they talk, but they can laugh, beings you don't split their tongues none like ever body says you oughta, beings then they'll just bleed to death. And ever body in Freeland knowed now the Schoolteacher could laugh, although you only heared it about as often as you hear a crow laugh.

But that ain't what made me jealous, cepting that, in a way, it is. I mean here I was, the only gink what would ever know her secret, on account of me, I aimed to keep it, and sudden-like one of the other ginks says the reason the Schoolteacher's got his attention in church the way she does is because it's like he just knows that she's looking right at him and nobody else.

Now I knowed what all the other ginks was saying, even though I weren't hearing them. They was saying the same things happens to them. God hisself could've just stepped on me and I wouldn't've felt more squashed.

I want to tell you it put some distance between I and her. But then, on the other hand, it din't, because that spring in school I was getting the eyes from her more than ever. Not that she had to bust anymore rulers, but I started to do something dumb what was to hurt her by accident. I begun leaving my pad at home, and bringing my stick, what was real dumb, on account of I had to pass by my house after school on my way to the Masonic Hall anyways.

But the cruelest thing I done was out on the ball diamond when I was pitching to Becky and all the other little ones. I said for Becky to knock a homer so far into the corn that Old Evil Eye couldn't even find it. Now pretty soon all them little kids is talking Evil Eye, and you know how it is with them little ones. When they get a taste of something they like on their tongues, that's all they say for about as long as it takes them to get tired of a new toy, what, in the case of little kids is considerable-like, beings their own folks never owned a whole lot, especial-like money enough to spend on toys. Anyways, I don't think they called her it to her face, beings there ain't no gink quite that dumb, but I knowed she could hear it while she graded papers. She couldn't miss it with it excaping from the mouths of them all at least once a recess for a week. And I knowed she knowed I was the instigator.

All that friction between her and I had to come to a halt, me now feeling worse than jealous, so what I done was, I let her in on a secret about a week after I quit hauling my cue to school and took up with my pad again. I told her on Old Crow. I said I'd been dreaming on him a lot, ever since I knowed I become a mother and a healer. I told her it was account of me that they was saying Old Evil Eye and I was sorry because she knowed I seen her like a natural mother. I knowed it was her what was giving me my encouragement what was as important as the woman what give me my life. I told her I was jealous when I heared in the shop how much more ever body come to like her after she become our live-in preacher. I said I knowed that was dumb because I knowed what she was about to do, because I drawed it in my sleep, what was the truth, something I ain't seen her do with no gink before in school, even though she done it to me times when I needed it, and that, I knowed, was about to patch ever thing up. I said I was about as sorry as a gink could be. And then, before I'm even done talking, me sitting there in my desk, she gets up from her desk and she comes over to me and she does with her hands what they had to do, and she done it in front of all the kids sos they are crying real soft-like and coming over and touching me too.

"Stick," she finally says.

When she were done on saying that, I couldn't answer none. I just looked up as ifing to say, "Yes Mam?"

"Now finish your lesson."

"Yes Mam," I says.

Well, from then on I was fourteen and part of her was fourteen too. Or maybe she was forty-four and part of me was forty-four. Whatever it be, we got along real good. I begun to draw her at home from remembering on her. But one thing I knowed was I din't have no brain like Floyd's. I'd think on the drawing I'd done the night before, but when I'd come to the schoolhouse of a early morning, no matter ifing the weather was the same as it were last night, and no matter she were wearing the same color blue with that polka-dot scarf around her neck, she'd be different than what I drawed. And it weren't that I couldn't capture her none. You could look at all them sketches I had on my wall through a magnifying glass, and you'd still know it was her, though I might've made her hair, what was per usual pulled back tight in real life, into wings what was either flying or still as Old Crow's—what I come to call in my head ever crow I seen— when he's sitting on a fencepost, him being the lookout with that wary-like look in his eye.

What I knowed now was I ain't learned to draw like no ordinary artist, not that I'm a artist but a billiard player by trade. What I mean is, while I never had the details in my head, they just come out of their own. I always seen the big picture before I seen the pictures what made it up, and that begun to eat on me a bit, knowing Floyd owned the photographic remembering and him and me were half and not whole. And I knowed the sketches of her on the wall weren't drawings any more, really, but they become modern art, I knowed, because Lawless had a book on it I checked out, beings I was inheriting a share of the Old Curiosity. You see, what I figured out about all the modern art artists was they had to learn how to draw before they done them masterpieces. Now me, the best drawings I done I was walking in my sleep, while them drawings up at the shop weren't really no more than sketches, and I figured them modern masters spent a real long time at it, not like me what had only been at it a while. What I knowed was I had to be able to draw real good before I could make me some real modern art, but there I was doing it all backwards. And I knowed what I had on paper weren't the truth.

So I goes to see the seer, what is like talking to a crystal ball, ceptings the crystal, it's got a bigger word choice.

"Can you draw them outhouse boards like I done?" I says to Floyd.

"Nope," he says.

"How come?"

Floyd, he don't say a thing.

I got real mad at myself. Here I am, a gink what knows

the code as good as any gink but Bob the Barber, and I break Old Floyd's concentration on whatever he keeps looking at out the shop winda.

"Floyd," I says, "Would you like to draw on my pad?"

Floyd, he looks at me, and he gets this grin what is unusual ever since he's been closing his eyes when he come into the shop.

"Yep," he says.

So I sits down with Floyd and right away Floyd starts drawing these pictures of naked ladies.

Now I sit there and take about all I can take, hoping that Floyd will change on his subject some. But it ain't going to happen. Floyd, when he's done with one, just up and draws another one. They was real crude, too. Like he ain't never seen a naked lady but his own doodles, maybe, what probable-like ain't a far cry from the truth.

"Floyd," I says. "Can you draw me?"

"Nope," he says.

I sort of figured it. "Just naked ladies?"

"Yep."

So I drawed him a picture of Bob the Barber in his chair, ceptings I din't tell Floyd what I was drawing beings I wanted it to be a surprise. And while I was at it, I asked me some questions of him, using the code, of course, what made it like pulling teeth sos to figure what you could about photographic remembering.

What I found out was, Old Floyd, he had hisself a power of remembering what was near equal to the size of his head. First off, I says the Lord's prayer and he says it too. But me,

I just figured that was like a warm up exercise sort of like the pledge of allegiance what the Schoolteacher had us do ever morning to get our brains in second gear witch probable-like weren't a necessity in Floyd's case since his brain was already stuck in second, albeit in another dimension too, and for that he had to travel at the speed of light, I knowed, because I don't read science fiction for nothing. Besides, there ain't no parrot or parakeet what I ain't seen on TV couldn't handle the same job. Floyd's specialty was when he done it, it sounded just like the Schoolteacher saying it using my voice because I was trying to say it in the Schoolteacher's voice what was real powerful-like and raspy when she said it. But, Old Floyd, you could say him a list of words what made no sense, you could read him the headlines of the *Post Dispatch* backwards—all the headlines—what I done while I was sketching the Barber reading them editorials in his chair, and he could spit them right back at you, and it don't matter how many words.

Then, "Floyd," I says.

Floyd don't say a thing.

"Floyd," I says, "is there four bolts holding the plaque on the Vetern's memorial?"

"Nope," he says, and he could've fooled me.

"Floyd," I says, "is there six bolts holding the plaque on the Vetern's memorial?"

"Nope," he says.

Now, I want to tell you, as much as I looked at that plaque on my trip back and forth from the Masonic Hall to the shop, I was sure as a Lawless lawyer there was four bolts on that plaque, so I drop my pad and step outside and take a look, but it weren't to be. So I come back and sits down, and I look to Floyd and I says, "Floyd," I says, real confident-like because I'm sure as a Lawless lawyer again Floyd's about to tell on another miracle since I seen with my own two eyes there weren't but three bolts holding that plaque on account of one falled out, and I says, "Floyd, say I was to count backwards from twenty. Can you tell me how many bolts is on that plaque when I get to the number?"

"Yep," he says.

Well, I'm counting and it's doing my heart some good to see Floyd's grin back on his face all the way, and I get down around ten sos his grin, ifing I ain't mistaken, is starting to fade some again, and by the time I count five it's gone, and when I count four, Floyd shuts his eyes, and on three he's shaking his head, so I just keep counting, "two, one, zero, blast off," and Floyd repeats with "two, one, zero, blast off," holding his head and shaking it real wild-like back and forth. Then, sudden-like, there's nothing—just Old Floyd sitting there, calm and peaceful-like, with his eyes still shut.

"Floyd," I says, "is there three bolts holding the plaque on the Vetern's memorial?"

Floyd, he don't say nothing, his eyes still shut.

Well, I figured Old Floyd was sending me a signal, all right, but it's just that I din't take to the message, thinking on as I was that he wanted me to change the subject. So I ask Floyd about other things around town I knowed and some what I din't know. Come to find out, Floyd, he did have his photographic remembering about words, bolts and boards and stuff like that, but why I'm telling you on this is another story, although it ain't really.

You see, I'm finishing off my surprise for Floyd, what is the pains-*taking* sketch of Bob the Barber I made of him in his chair, and I hold it up to Floyd sos I can coax him out of the dimension where he'd got hisself locked in witch is his trance with his eyes closed and not grinning, and sudden-like he opens his eyes and you could see the pupils witch was real wide at first shrinking to pinpoints and staying there, and Floyd, he shouts "*Fire!*"

That's how it come to be that the path I made in the grass in the square between the Masonic Hall and the shop had a low road and a high road. But that's another story, although it ain't really. You see, never in his life did the Barber ever heared Old Floyd get so emotional, he'd come to say, what was a good thing beings not only did Floyd rock me back on my heels when he shouted, but he done shook the Barber so, beings Bob was a volunteer fireman, that all I could see was flapping wings what was the *Post Dispatch* returning to Earth from the dimension the Barber finds hisself in when he was studying on that editorial page and he got rose from the dead, standing there next to his throne with a look in his face I ain't seen since I seen it in Nooner's face when he had me by the collar after the lodge blowed up.

But the Barber, he ain't just hot, him looking at the both of us like he could kill us, but he's on fire. And I don't mean mad. I mean fire, the real thing.

I LOOK TO the cushion of his chair and I see me these flames. And like the fool the Barber hisself said he was, he looks down at that throne and he tries beating those flames out with his hands. It was then I could see Bob the Barber, the gink what give me my name and my encouragement, what had become Floyd's adopted daddy even though he weren't old enough, was in big trouble because the seat of his pants and his smock was afire too.

So I drop my pad and I dive and tackle the Barber, and Floyd comes over and with the funny papers there on top, smothers the fire with the *Post Dispatch*. And now I'm about sick to my stomach because all that was on my mind was the smell of burning hair, and I forget all about the Barber's throne till I feel the heat of it, the red cushions now a even brighter red and some orange and black too since the flames from it are near-like on the ceiling.

Floyd and me, we get the Barber outside, or maybe it were more like the Barber got us outside. You couldn't tell who the hero was, the three of us tumbling over the other but mostly because the Barber was cussing us for not having helped him save his throne.

"But you was afire, Bob!" I shouts at him.

"Oh, bullhockey!" he says.

"You was too!" I says. "Weren't he?" I says, and I turn to Floyd, but Floyd is running as fast as a hydrocephalic can run, holding his head, in the direction of his house.

Somebody—we never knowed who—turned in the alarm, but it was too late. It just weren't in the cards that that barber's chair was to look like a throne no more. I mean what you'd come to think of was the cockpit of a space ship what got hit by the biggest ray gun in the galaxy, them cushions and even the foot rest all melted and charred before the ginks could get at it, not that they did get it put out, since the water they poured on wouldn't stop the flames no-how but that they just up and quit of their own accord.

Now ever thing happened so quick-like what with Digger there to help me convince the Barber he was afire since it were plain as day with his smock and the seat of his pants what were white and tan looked like a T-shirt you accidental-like left a hot iron laying on while you answered the phone. And with Pyro barking orders about hosing ever thing down. And this smell like burnt rubber what I smelled was coming from inside the shop but what I seen was really the soles of the Barber's shoes smoldering because his feet was on the footrest when he caught on fire. The Barber, when he seen that, he started stripping right there on the town square, and we could see these blisters on his back and his butt and his feet, but the Barber, he din't have no pain.

Well, like I say, what with ever thing happening so quick-like, I ain't had time to wonder on the miracle of it all, but me, I put two and two together and it come up three, and that's how, like I says, there come to be both a low road and a high road to that path I'd made between my practicing and my drawing for my income, although ifing you was to look at it now, the path, I mean, you'd never know there was a high road what was the path I made steering clear of the Vetern's monument. No. Ifing you was to look at it today you'd see the high road is all growed over again. But on the other hand, there wouldn't be no Vetern's monument there to steer clear of neither, ifing you was to look on it today. Old Floyd, he seen it coming. Just like he seen the trouble what was coming to the Barber's throne.

The Barber, he got hisself all healed. I come to look at him different after he did, too. Not only was he the boss of hisself, I figured, but he might be President too, what with him having felt no pain when you could see as plain as the hand in front of your face that Digger knowed there oughta've been pain. As for his throne room, mixed with the lilac water, the powder, and the Bay Rum, there is always—as far as this gink's nose is concerned—this hint of the smell of burnt hair. And I spose other noses smell it too. Otherwise I doubt the Barber would sink so much capital in the *per*fume bottles witch is the only real change what come about in the throne room cept a new chair next to the old one, beings the Barber couldn't part with the first one, and besides, the old one made its self the best conversation piece of its day, although there weren't nobody what would sit in it again unless they belong in the loony bin in Lawless, and that was proof enough for me that Floyd weren't crazy, beings he was able to open his eyes when he come into the shop too, though the Barber had to think on getting him a lead dog when he was out on the street on account of not only would he always situate hisself with his back to the winda, but his eyes was shut to all the goings-on in the square. And only I really knowed why.

As for me, beings I'd drawed the Barber in his chair, I figured it was lucky for him I done so when I did. Instead of giving another human being a case of the crazies like I done the Banker, with the help of Floyd I'd saved the life of a man, even though he wouldn't've had no pain when he burned up.

Maybe it was just me, but I thought on how all the ginks and little girls at school always seemed to be looking up at me now when I was looking down at them, beings I become a hero. And that made me feel even taller. And though I knowed I was outgrowing my clothes, there weren't no way I was going to outgrow the likes of Becky and her sisters. A gink what gets a taste of being a hero like I done is going to make it a habit, ifing at all possible. Little kids, they need somebody who's growed but not all growed sos they can feel safe, I spose. So the closer it come to graduation, the sadder I got. I knowed that Helen and Peg what was in my class just couldn't wait to get over in that new high school where there'd be somebody to appreciate their womanly parts. But me, not only did I have no desires on them, but I sure as heck wanted nothing to do with that new building or them people what was to know I were a gink what had no normal upbringing, beings ginks was the adopted souls of the Schoolteacher what was strange and powerful so to make ginks strange on account of when they come out from under her wing they still is ginks hellbent on being nothing but the boss of themselfs, just like the Barber would say.

Me, I got to thinking on why it were the girls always come out from the nest with their wings already spread, and I decided it was natural-like for them to be a mother and a healer, while ginks, they had it learned in them. It seemed to me the one best way for a man to become boss of hisself were to make in his brain what a woman had in her heart. Now Helen and

Peg, their problem was they just ain't become growed yet. They was girls, not women. They still had a touch of gink in them. I knowed they'd be all right once their womanly parts become as natural-like to them as what they had in their hearts. The Schoolteacher, she had her womanly parts. I could see them in my drawings. They was what made her the Schoolteacher what was the boss of herself, you could tell, because she din't have to use them to make her a woman, beings she kept them hid the way she dressed so plain and all. And like I said, it weren't until she become our live-in preacher she was looking younger, like maybe she knowed she already was and maybe she knowed the congregation needed that, beings they was mostly ginks and the families of ginks what had to know her in another way for her to get the new message across.

And even ifing Pyro and Termite might have heared her old message, I've to say I doubt on it they could've understood the new one. You could tell they was fake when they'd shake her hand after church, telling on what a fine sermon it was. What they was thinking, you thought, was what a fine, eligible woman she was becoming, and how fine it would be ifing one of them with their money what they inherited could buy them a wife what was about to retire from her schoolteaching—because ever body knowed the schoolhouse was doomed—sos they could satisfy their problem with authority.

Now I figured I knowed what she was up to, beings she was civil to them, her trying to set a example and all because they was still human beings, but why was it, I says to myself, that she's encouraging them by making herself up to look younger ever week? You see, none of us knowed her new message yet sos I had no way of knowing it was her way of preparing us sos we could believe what we was to see with our own eyes someday sos somebody like me what knowed her good enough to know even her secret could tell you, ifing he wanted to, that the Father what art in heaven ain't really there atall, and there ain't no reason to fret on it none.

WELL, I DONE graduated, and I want to tell you it were the second most saddest day of my life but, like most lonesome things what I figure happens to a body in its life, it don't mean much in a whole life. I mean, you stub your toe or something while you're practicing on your table or dancing to one of them great old tunes on WGN and it hurts like heck at first, beings the pains just got born, but after a while you almost forgot it was there, and then in a week, unless you happen to wiggle your foot or stub the same toe, the pain done died and went to hell where it can make itself useful. And ifing I hadn't graduated natural-like, then I'd've graduated that same year unnatural, like poor Becky and Little Martha done and all the other ginks and girls done that June, ceptings Helen and Peg, beings they was in my eighth grade class, because, you see, Nooner's bulldozer graduated Becky and her four sisters and ever body else along with Helen and Peg and me.

I knowed it was a job that would be done no matter what, but I sure had me a hard time figuring on how Nooner could do it with a clear conscious, not that he ever was to feel proud about it. But then I thunk on it. Maybe it was better that a gink done it, just like it were better ifing you had a sick cow to go to the shed for your own sledge hammer rather than have the Vet put her down with his. Though Nooner won't never say nothing on it, I've suspicioned ever since that it were the School-teacher what talked Nooner into being the one what done it. After all, he was the one come of late to populate it most. But I don't know that the Schoolteacher had to go begging him or nothing. Word was, up around the shop, Nooner picked up a good check from Pyro and Termite to level the place, what ain't so unreasonable I spose since Nooner has the monopoly on bulldozers and Pyro wouldn't use the place for practice for the volunteers since this was one fire department what was a lot better at containing fires than putting them out, what probable-like means they din't trust themselfs much when it come to containment neither and there was good materials in that schoolhouse what was worth something, what to Pyro and Termite would be like setting afire to a dollar bill, the first, the Barber said, they ever owned between the two of them and the very one they still owned beings they was chickens of the same feather who done all their investments together, and final-like, there weren't nobody in the mood besides Pyro and Termite—who wouldn't've done it anywise on account of they *was* chicken—to take a trip up to Lawless for some dynamite because of what bad luck done to Cromangon Man, they fig-ures.

I spose you're wondering on the Schoolteacher, how it probable-like bothered her a lot to see the schoolhouse get tore down when she couldn't look the other way ifing she wanted what with her place of residence across the road and, even ifing she'd've gone into town, the Vision of the Flock.

Well, it weren't to be like that. What ain't so surprising when you think on it. I mean she knowed it was coming. Even us younger ginks knowed it was coming what with the need for to pay money for the new grade school they was building attached to the high school. What surprised us the most was it weren't no dirt farmer what bought the land but Pyro and Termite at the auction. And what was weird-like was them two rented that land to the farmer on the west what was trying to buy it sos he could put it all in corn. And what was *weirder*-like was Nooner had orders to leave the storm shelter alone, what weren't so weird, beings its hard to knock down a hole in the ground, but the farmer, he weren't allowed to plow over it, what wouldn't've been likely no-how since it were a structure like a small quonset what stuck halfway out of the ground and were made of real thick steel, and the farmer, he was made to leave a lane from the shelter to the road witch din't make him none too happy since there ain't nothing what gets under the skin of a grain farmer more than obstacles what he can't plow through when he's got crops to plant, him with that look in his eye when he come up to a fence row sos even the roads, ifing he had it his way, would be all in corn. But like the School-teacher taught me, there ain't just *weird* and *weirder*. There's *weirdest* too, what all makes plain old horse sense when you think on what you know when I'm done telling on this and because trouble it don't come but what it comes in threes. The weirdest thing was Old Pyro and Termite done had a power line running from the road to the shelter and a lectric fence all around the shelter what no gink dared go near with the way it hummed, especial-like me—such a terrible static I heared so that Wally Phillips sounded like he'd decided to do his broadcast from Mars, what surprised me some when I thought on how I knowed I weren't nowhere near a radio when I'd sneak up that lane through the corn on my bike days I'd visit Mom and Baby Sis and the Schoolteacher, days I knowed Pyro and Termite wouldn't be there.

She was weeding in her garden one day when I come by to ask of her ifing she could borrow me a new pad till I got to Lawless, me not wanting to take no money from her on account of I knowed she'd lost her job and all. But she wanted I should take it, and she told me she knowed what was on my mind but I din't have to worry none.

I looks at her hands with that black soil under one of her nails and I seen they was beautiful. Not only for what they could do and done for me, but like herself, her hands was getting younger ever day too. "Watchu mean I don't have to worry?" I says.

"You know what I mean. You're wondering how I'll manage," she said.

I told her I had to admit on that.

"I have money," she says.

"You mean your pop was rich?" I says.

She just smiled. "Charles, people don't ask questions like that in polite society." She went back to her weeding. "No," she said. "And I have to tell you I won't be teaching in Freeland, either."

All of the sudden I couldn't help it. I just started bawling. She stood up and took my face in her hands and made me look in her eyes what weren't her eyes. "I'm not leaving you," she says.

Well, that. That just makes me bawl some more. "But how will you live?"

"Listen to me, Charles," she says. "I'm going to tell you, but you can't tell anyone."

"What?" I says.

"The books," she says.

"What books?"

"My books," she says. "They'll see me through."

"You don't eat books," I says to her, thinking it sounded real growed up.

But dumb me. I couldn't figure on what she were talking about. Them books wasn't just books. They was a collection. The kind of fancy collection you'd read about maybe in the *Post* of a Sunday. Well, I sposed her secret was safe with me even ifing I was to blab, because there ain't no local born what could've imagined, even ifing you'd've showed them a picture of it, that a stack of books could be worth the kind of money she was talking.

"But your books," I say to her. I had to close my eyes. "I can't see you without them."

She tells me books are only books. She tells me she'll always own them, even when she sells them. She says she'll sell them off one at a time.

"But you're the Schoolteacher," I remember pleading, my eyes still closed, her hands still on my face.

"Charles," she says. "Look at me."

I look.

"What is my name?"

To be honest, I had to think on it for a second, beings I ain't to this day heared no gink call her anything but Mam or the Schoolteacher, cepting in school, but there it was mostly Teacher and only one time Old Evil Eye. I was saying to myself I wished I had Floyd's photographic remembering sos I could see the church bulletin. Then it come to me, what I'd heared some folks talking in line after church. "Miss Luda," I says.

"Yes, Charles," she says. "You see, I was someone before I was the Schoolteacher and I'm still that someone."

I've got to tell you, she was making me real nervous-like, beings she still had her hands on my face, beings it felt like she'd something more to tell me, something I weren't about to like.

"Only, Charles—"

"What?" I says.

"Luda is my first name."

My hunch was right. I was beginning on getting ascared.

"What is my last name?" she says.

Well, by then I knowed I was right, but I weren't about to say it none, beings ifing she were to tell me I was right I'd've known there was dead people walking this world what was bad enough knowing there was people probable-like from outer space too. But I knowed it not because I knowed who'd lived and died in Freeland or who'd wandered off or who got kidnapped. I knowed it just like I knowed when Digger, bless him, give me that key to the Masonic Hall that I done held it a thousand times before. I closed my eyes again.

"Charles," she said. "You see your mother in me."

How could I lie? I opened my eyes.

"There's something more."

"What?" I says.

"Your mother can see you too."

I knowed that she meant it, and she weren't talking about no telescope in heaven, neither. But me, I had a telescope so big it was like all this happened on another planet so far away and so long ago sos it was just now coming into view, being now was the future, and the present was in the middle between the two planets. The Schoolteacher, her name was Luda Corvus, and she were the mother of my mother's mother, the one what run away after she bore her baby girl at a real young age, the one I ain't even sposed to be telling you on yet beings she ain't told a soul until her last sermon, until she final-like got about as young as she could get and still be the live-in preacher, when she give us her new message. And I knowed it now. I knowed why I had me my table. I knowed why she give me my pad. But none of what I knowed made me any less ascared. She pulled my forehead down on hers and right then and there I cried.

Now I don't mind telling you straight out there was a thing what was eating on me some. It ain't I din't trust her to tell me the truth, and it ain't I din't believe what I knowed in my heart, but ifing Miss Luda Corvus were the same what bore Mom's mother, how come Pop never told on it? Well, I got to thinking on it some, and then I knowed there weren't no way he could've laid eyes on her, on account of he come from the south, beings he weren't local born and beings he weren't born at all yet when Miss Luda Corvus what was my great grandmother was alive and living in the house what me and Pop adopted. But so what, I says to myself. There's other ginks and folks what was born when she was around, and they would've knowed the Schoolteacher were the same what was my mother twice removed. How come nobody knowed but me?

So I put the question to Pop. "Was I adopted sos no body in town would know I was?"

"If ing you was adopted," Pop said, "then the midwife done brung you in her suitcase. Whatever would give you a fool's notion like that?"

"Pop," I says, "was Mom a Corvus?"

"No, she were a Smith," he says, "But I recollect she had some Corvus in her."

Now I could see I weren't about to get me nowhere with Pop, and I were saying to myself it was too bad there weren't no picture of the Corvus what bore my grandma, and without even thinking about it, I'm on my bike for the shop to see the Photographer, but he ain't there sos I have to catch him at his house.

"Floyd," I says, and you could tell Old Floyd was real glad I come to see him, beings he had his grin on and all, "did you ever see the Corvus woman what bore my Mom's grandmother?"

"Yep," he says.

"Was her name Luda Corvus?"

"Yep."

"Were she the same woman what is the Schoolteacher?"

"Nope," he said.

Well, it weren't that my heart stopped or nothing when he said that, and it weren't I din't trust him none. It was just that I got to thinking on how maybe Old Floyd's lenses was a bit rusty maybe, so I had me one more idea. The next time I hitched me a ride with Nooner to return some science fiction, I asked them at the library how I would find me a real old story about somebody who got lost sos they'd never find her. Well, they was kind of nice to me and all because they knowed me, and it weren't but a few weeks of trips there that I found what I needed in the *Lawless Letter,* and it were a story about this young girl who was lost and her name was Luda Corvus and she were from rural Freeland. But the thing what told me Floyd was right was the picture they had of her in the paper. Now, me, I drawed me a copy of that picture, even though I knowed it weren't the Schoolteacher what I was drawing, although there was something familiar-like about the way I could feel the lead coming off my pencil. But I could've drawed me a zillion copies of that picture, and there weren't no way, ifing I were true to my eyes, it was going to be the same girl what become the Schoolteacher.

I takes the sketch to Floyd. "Is this the same Luda Corvus what become lost?" I says to him.

"Yep."

"Is this the same Luda Corvus what teaches and is the live-in preacher?"

"Nope," he says.

Later, I says to Pop, "Ain't it strange-like that there would be a Luda Corvus what was lost in Freeland and a Luda Corvus what was found to be the Schoolteacher?"

I remember exact-like what he said. He said, "Stranger things has happened, and stranger things will happen." Now, I'm here to tell you that that's the smartest thing you'd ever hear from your old man, because I knowed with the eyes in my heart what din't have no eyes that both that girl and the Schoolteacher shared the same insides. As for Old Floyd, it turns out he was wrong and he was right. He had him his photographic remembering, all right, but he was sort of like me, beings he weren't too much up on history what he couldn't see. It were the future what was our specialty.

I SPOSE THERE'S something in the Law of Averages what says a brain can't know it all unless you was born like a Floyd was born with a head like a melon you'd enter in a contest, the Barber might've said hisself. Me, I had no manner of figuring on what Pyro and Termite was up to with that storm shelter and neither did Jewels, the gink what built them the fence and strung the lectricity. It were such a curious sight, though, sos I found when I was drawing or even practicing on my table my mind'd mosey on out there and before you knowed it I'd be studying on it again.

I told to the Barber what on Earth did he think they was doing, and he said it din't matter none, beings they was the *craziest* pair you'd ever see outside of Lawless, and it weren't them what was worrying him none, but, speaking of a case of the crazies, it were the Banker what they oughta reserve a rubber room for up in Lawless, beings he seemed to be hanging around them some lately, beyond banker's hours even, what is a considerable amount of time to hang around in.

Well, I tell him I'm surprised, beings the Banker is high class, even though he may've falled to low class in witch case I wouldn't know because I ain't laid eyes on the Banker since I seen him heading for the corn, with Pop making my deposits for me, what is probable-like the way the Banker wants it, and, by the way, has there been any news I missed from Agent McMillion?

No, he says, not that that oughta surprised nobody none, what with the Barber doubting whether the F.B.I.'d be dropping by for a shave and a trim—or anybody, for a fact—when the Law of Averages says that Freeland has got to be the only spot in the universe where your barber's chair catches afire of its own accord, you got a Banker with a case of the crazies, ginks what draw in their sleep and shoot immaculate three cushion when they ain't even been taught, and—and the Barber, he looks up now from his *Post* out the winda—and the one person in the world with the answers to all the sixty-four-thousand dollar questions you could dream up, ifing only you knowed the code sos he could talk—stumbling and feeling around outside for the door handle when all he's got to do is open his eyes.

Old Floyd, he come in then and situated hisself sos his back was to the winda. Me, I knowed why he were acting so crazy-like, but I figured on the Barber thinking on I belonged in the loony bin ifing I was to tell him there was something like a bolt of lightning what was to catch the Vetern's monument afire. I mean the padding on a barber's throne is one thing, but a boulder with a metal plaque on it burning up is something wholly contrary to nature.

I asked of Digger, bless him—who come in now to use the machine—how come Freeland has got a Vetern's monument in the square when there ain't but one name on it anyhow, and him I never heared of, beings there weren't no man nor gink with a name what I din't pronounce some.

Digger, he just looked at me dumb-like with his mouth open.

About then, Bob the Barber up and wants to know ifing the Devil done took Digger's tongue or whether he's got his mouth open because it's fly season. "Tell the gink," the Barber says.

Well, Digger, bless him, and me, we switched places, on account of it had to be me with my mouth open after he was done telling on it. That Vetern's monument out there was the only memory of the soldier what come back from the first World War in a box car on the train. Nobody seen him before, but he knowed all manners of healing, and since Freeland never had and never will have no Doctor in town, he set up shop, even ifing he was shell shocked they all say, on account of there weren't nobody what died in the time he was here, cepting maybe this little girl who were about my age, but nobody knowed for sure beings they never found her or nothing, and that little girl—and Digger, bless him, he looks to the Barber and back at me, all misty-eyed, and sort of swallers and says— "and that little girl was the mother of your grandmother."

And how I remember exact-like what he said is I hear an

echo and I look over, and Floyd's got his grin on and he's saying, "and that little girl was the mother of your grandmother."

Now I knowed they wasn't talking about Pop's grandmother, because as far back as he knowed, he din't have one. And when I got to thinking on Mom never knowing her grandmother, it sudden-like got me kind of misty-eyed too sos I din't like talking or nothing with my curiosity all balled up in my throat.

"Stick?" the Barber says in such a way he's about to drop another bomb on me.

I look up.

"Stick, there's folks what says you are the spitting image of him, you being the first male born of his seed, on account of they say he was your great grandaddy."

"—because they say he was your great grandaddy," Floyd says.

"That's part of why ever body wants to do for you," Digger says. "Because he done a lot for locals, healing them and all."

"Then why do they say he was shell shocked?" I manage to say, my heart pounding so loud-like I can't hardly make out the echo no more.

"It's the way and how he died," the Barber says. "Ginks say they seen him a few times walking on the crick, making his circuit. Other locals say he drowned, witch ain't likely, ginks says. There wasn't never a body."

"You mean the crick was froze over," I says.

The Barber, he looks at Digger, then he looks at me. "No," the Barber says. "Stick, locals don't think ginks alone is crazy. They think your great grandaddy was crazy too, even though he had him his powers of healing."

"—even though he had him his powers of healing," is the echo what lingers.

All of the sudden, me, I can't take it no more sos I'm up and running out the door because I want to read me the name I looked at a hundred times and I heared a hundred more and I want to go up and touch it, to run my finger over the letters, but I don't dare, on account of I see now there's another bolt gone from the plaque, and now I'm standing in front of it, and I'm looking at it for a long, long time, and I says it plain as day and I hear it coming from behind me sos I spin around and there's Floyd and him with his grin and his shut eyes and saying in my voice, "Nazareth. Jay Nazareth." And suddenly I knowed, I just knowed that the only thing what was to keep me from volunteering for the loony bin in Lawless was I was ascared in my heart for that little girl, the kind of ascared no crazy man could feel. What meant, I sposed, I'm ascared for the Schoolteacher.

But I couldn't tell no gink. I couldn't tell no local born. I couldn't tell Pop even when he weren't local born. I couldn't even tell her neither, because she took one look at me, after closing the door on that black sedan of hers, parked like she was in the middle of the road to her place, and she come running my way, me pedaling hard as I can straight for her, and the next thing I knowed I was looking up in her face what was worried and beautiful and I could feel the blacktop what was sticky-like and hot under me, and I knowed my head were in her lap because I looked over and seen my bike laying flat and her hands was on my forehead and neck.

She took me to my house and led me to bed. When I waked up she was still there. I knowed there was nothing more she had to tell me now, not that she would always. Me, I just asked of her questions not about herself or her new message what I wasn't sposed to know on yet, but knowed, or else I wouldn't've been me.

"When it's over," I says, "am I still going to have me my table?"

"You can have only what is possible," she says.

"What do you mean?" I says.

"You have to be brave. The gift is within you—not outside of you," she says.

But that weren't her new message, though it weren't really her old message neither. I figured on what she was telling me was I had to learn on not to be ascared ifing I was to know whether the Earth would allow me to use the talent it seen fit to give me. I knowed her new message about the same way you know about dreams. I mean sometimes you just can't remember them. Other times you can see them but they don't come out right sos it's sort of like watching TV from another room with the door shut, beings all you get is the music and the words. Now ifing dreams was words and music only, I figured I would've had me plenty of practice to listen on her new message, what with my inner ear on the radio band with the dial stuck. But dreams is more pictures than sound. That meant that while I knowed there was a new message sort of like when you go by a front winda at night and you know the TV is playing inside that place, I only knowed it was there, not what channel was playing, let alone what show. So her new message, when I did see it, it were sort of like watching a show with the sound turned way down. What I figure on she was telling me is I got to get up in that dark room and go over and jack up the volume. But I just ain't mustered the courage yet, beings I knowed ifing I was to stay real still any strangers what would look through the winda from outside would pass on by when I din't answer the back door, beings they couldn't even see I was there, and for all they knowed, the TV just got left on and there ain't nobody home. And even ifing I was to pull the shades so nobody could look in, what were my usual habit anyways, it was safer to stay still in my chair sos I wouldn't draw the attention of whatever ghosts might be in the house.

Now I want to tell you I don't believe in ghosts none, unless they are the kind what haunts in your head like Mom and Baby Sis, but there was one thing I'd to ask the Schoolteacher then and there, whether it were a ghost whispered in my ear I should draw me them flagstone steps what was all growed over in the front lawn. All she would tell me—and now that I thunk on it, that was probable-like all she needed to tell me sos I wouldn't be ascared of living in that house—was it was her what laid them there, her being a Corvus. But me, I read her mind. Or maybe I was reading my mind. I just knowed it was him, the Vetern, what told her to put them stones there and I could hear him saying it just as good as I'd hear Wally Phillips on a clear day when I were near a radio what weren't near the storm shelter, what meant, these days, in town, on account of the old Corvus place what were the adopted home of me and my Pop was just too close of late, beings there had to be more powerful goings-on than that hum of that fence.

And I knowed that the Schoolteacher, she laid thirteen stones, beings she was thirteen years old, and I knowed that the reason I could hear his voice was my grandma what I ain't never laid eyes on because I ain't laid eyes on a grandmother of mine, had ears like my mom who weren't conceived yet, she had ears and that the Schoolteacher was carrying her child inside of her, the child what would carry my mom.

Me, I only wished I knowed what else the Vetern might've told her, but it weren't to be, beings maybe I'd the power to read minds only when they was up close sort of like I could read a radio's mind when there weren't all that static and only when it was up close. Me, my head was spinning so bad there weren't no way I was about to get me a fix on that channel, and since the Schoolteacher probable-like din't want my curiosity to be worrying me no more, knowing I'd my practicing to do and my education to learn in the next few years, she weren't about to weight my head with history what is dead and buried, I figured, and asking me ifing I'd be all right, she took off soon. I made up my mind before I fall asleep that I'd draw me something for in the morning. That was the closest I knowed how to be brave. And Lord Jesus did I draw! You'd've sworn the Vision of the Flock passed through her hands into my head, me laying there, calm and pretty much healed, even though I could feel the heat coming on outside, what was strange, I says to myself, beings it was getting near on sundown. But it weren't the Vision of the Flock what made me draw like that, because, per usual, what I drawed, it ain't happened yet.

It were Sunday next she calls it all Anarchtopia, and not from the pulpit but in the funeral home. I begun feeling a little guilty during the service at what I last drawed, on account of I was thinking on maybe ifing I ain't drawed it, it wouldn't've happened none, but I knowed too that that was a crazy way of thinking since there ain't no human being but a Jesus what could've created the miracle what was to start the ball rolling sos to set us free in Freeland, not that we was in a prison or nothing before it all happened, but because I knowed we was living in a different dimension. Funny thing is, though, I got to thinking on, that when you come out of one dimension there ain't nowhere to go but another dimension. You take your prisoners in jail, for a fact. They step outside, and they think ever thing is all right now, beings they must feel so high-like that they are in heaven. But once they been out for a while, things don't look quite so handsome, beings they know they are in a town what is in a country what is a part of the Earth and there ain't no scientist what is smart enough to build them a rocket ship to another solar system, let alone heaven. And what rocket ship could take a soul to heaven unless the soul was in a body? Like I says, the only time you are really free is when you're between dimensions, what really don't exist, because once you're out of one dimension you're in another, beings they're like soap bubbles stuck together. Well, you can see, freedom ain't nothing but a state of mind on account of it ain't something what is in the universe what itself is a big jail cell beings the cell door is the pearly gates.

Now all this I figured on because, like I says before, I ain't really heared her new message yet. I ain't heared it at the funeral neither. I only knowed it'd come. But what I knowed, because I heared her tell it, was we was all about to enjoy ourselfs our qualified freedom and there weren't no reason for us to think Freeland wouldn't be a better place to live, though it weren't quite as populated as it used to be.

Now the things what I drawed was three, and they was in a style the Schoolteacher never seen, so you can figure on it, I can't tell you on the form, but I can tell what they was about. They was about rock, they was about rock and metal, and they was about metal.

But when I wake up I don't find them three drawings what slipped to the floor, and even ifing I had I couldn't hardly concentrate on them none what with the static in my inner ear like the WGN tower become the source of all lightning on the planet. I get dressed, ready to head south into town for some relief when I seen outside I must've slept right through the storm what with branches and the undersides of leaves littering the lawn and even the road.

I ride into the square, the static about gone now, cepting I could still hear it some, this crackling and all underneath my brain in my sinus like I had a bad cold and I just blowed my nose.

And ifing that town square weren't a sight to see! What caught my eye first, I spose, was I seen Nooner's new truck parked on a side street before I even get into the square, and then I seen there weren't no pickups nor cars neither parked in the square, like it were a late afternoon of a Sunday. But I knowed it were even more deserted than that, and sudden-like, I seen it, or for a fact, I din't see it. The Vetern's monument, it weren't there no more.

I stop in front of the shop and ever thing is dead in the square, you could tell, because your eyes was drawn to Bob the Barber's lectric barber pole, what you never paid any attention to before in your life since you was about Becky's size, the magic in the first time you really seen it back in your brain, beings it was something raising out of nothing and there was limits to it, you could tell, as you stood there watching it screwing up out of itself, beings you thought on how it were like a person could fool hisself into believing his life would go on and on ifing while he stared at it he never looked below it nor above it sos to see there's nothing what his life sprung out of nor where it's going, like time *ain't* really. The red stripes on that pole, they was like part of her new message, like blood running up hill, like flames flaming up, always changing but never changing. Ifing you was to look at them like they was your life then your life would never end neither while you was looking at them. But ifing your mind wandered, then you'd get ascared because you'd be thinking on how there weren't nothing above and nothing below or maybe how it was getting near closing time and God, like the Barber, was about to pull the plug. But the difference was there were a Barber while there weren't no Father what art in heaven. Not the kind ever body else is talking on.

Real sudden-like I hear this wail coming from the shop sos I turn my head and see through the winda Floyd in there and he's pointing at me and he's got his eyes open, what is real novel, beings I ain't seen him looking through the winda since the day the Barber's throne caught afire. And the Barber, he's standing in the doorway yelling at me to get inside *now* and bring my bike with me before Old Floyd has him a *can*iption fit. So I hands the Barber my stick and my pad and wheels my bike in the shop.

"What in tarnation is going on?" I says to the Barber.

Well, the Barber, he takes me into the back room, beings we left Floyd staring out the winda with this real ascared look in his eye and sweat all over his brow, what in the case of Floyd is like a bucketful of sweat, the Barber might've said, and there is Nooner and Digger in the back, talking in whispers.

"Where's the Vetern's memorial?" I says.

Well, the Barber tells me they figure a tornado done got it of the middle of the night, and Floyd, he don't understand tornadoes none, him figuring as he does that what goes up must come down and him being afraid that boulder is about to crush somebody or something ifing they or it is out on the square. And Floyd, he just now up and volunteered hisself for the loony bin in Lawless beings all the cars and people had to be cleared from the streets before they could get him calm and Nooner and Digger and the Barber was all in a pow wow about whether they should oblige Floyd's wishes and run him up there this morning and do I want to be in on the decision on account of Floyd and me seemed to be of one mind of late like Siamese twins joined at the brain.

Me, I tell the Barber that ifing the decision is going to be *no*, then, yes, I want to be in on it, but ifing the decision is going to be *yes* I din't want no part in it. Well, the Barber, he sposed my vote was no, and that made it a tie, Digger and me agin it and the Barber and Nooner for it. What we needed was somebody to break the tie and we couldn't have Floyd vote because that would be like him voting for hisself in a *humble* contest. So what the Barber decides is we take him to the Schoolteacher and let her decide. The Barber, he could've called her on the phone, but he figures we'd best get Old Floyd out of there anyways and, besides, the Schoolteacher would probable-like want to take a look at him. So Digger, he sneaks out the back door and gets his hearse and pulls it up out back, and before you knowed it, we sweep Old Floyd up and then five of us is on our way to the parsonage, beings the Barber din't spect much business this morning anyways.

The farther we get out of town, the more Floyd is like his old self, until finally he's got this big grin on and he reaches over the seat in front of Digger and turns the siren on, what is a relief to me, beings it drowned out the static in my inner ear, beings it drowned out Wally Phillips too.

It ain't but a minute or two we can see the spire sticking up, beings these days the church, the parsonage, and the grave-yard is like a little continent in a parted sea of corn, cepting it sits on a crossroads. Digger, he shuts the siren off sos not to scare the Schoolteacher none, and real sudden-like the world is so quiet it's almost like Wally Phillips is broadcasting from another planet. I can't believe I can't hear the hum, beings we were practically on top of the storm shelter. Nobody notices when other ginks what is three and a adopted gink goes up to the front porch of the parsonage that I'm lagging behind, and the Old Curiosity I inherited from the Schoolteacher done pulled me like a magnet across the road and through the corn to the storm shelter, beings the lane weren't accessible from the church side of the field and I din't want the ginks to see me heading for the corner to get to it.

Now what I seen though I don't know it yet was the second of the three things what I last drawed, beings the first thing I drawed—rock—was something what was happening while I slept, the flying Vetern's monument what I drawed from above like I was in heaven and seeing Dorothy's house when the storm come in *The Wizard of Oz* on TV. That's what I drawed first, I figure. And what I drawed second I was looking at, but from another angle, beings I was on the ground and not up in the air like Old Crow when I drawed it. There was a hole in the middle of the top of the storm shelter, and when I climbed over the lectric fence, beings the power line was broke, and crawled up on top and peeked in, I seen the rock and I seen squashed underneath the rock a ton of metal what was steel, copper, and chrome.

Me, I just laid there on top of that storm shelter, working the Old Curiosity with the facts what I had before me like a man might work his teeth with a toothpick, when I hears this car slowing down out on the asphalt, and I figure to myself here come Pyro and Termite sos I jump over the fence off the top of the storm shelter and land in the corn. And who should be driving up towards the shelter in the lane with his blue bubblegum machines on top of his Cadillac but Old Termite.

Well, the rest of what I seen out there peeking through the corn weren't a pretty sight at all, and I want to tell you that you never saw anything quite so pathetic in your life till you've seen the man what were the night watchman of Freeland and has his problem with authority, beings he weren't the boss of hisself and never would be, stand over that hole, looking down at the mess what was once his Perpetual Motion Machine, what would give him some authority and what he had all his dead wife's money tied up in, all broke up—as ifing he was standing over his own coffin—and pull out his mail order revolver and shoot hisself in the head and miss.

Maybe he done run out of bullets with that shot, I don't know, but he made me so ascared I couldn't move none even when I knowed I should've had the sense to run. But I watched, and I seen him dazed-like fall off the storm shelter and slow-like pick hisself up, get into his Cadillac and back out of the lane without him ever looking over his shoulder.

He backs onto the blacktop without stopping and I says to myself it were a lucky thing nothing was coming, and then I heared my name in the voice of a gink coming from the parsonage like I just got woke out of a dream, and sudden-like I remember it. I remember I drawed in my sleep and I remember I drawed rock, rock and metal, and metal. And I seen the third thing I drawed and I get real sad, beings it would've been a lucky thing for Termite ifing he would've got rear ended on the blacktop, beings it would've been better than getting hit broadside by a train.

Well, as it turns out, the Schoolteacher, she casts a wasted vote on account of the Barber and Nooner changed their minds when I told them ginks, all out of breath like I was and not shot, that Floyd was right, because he knowed what goes up must come down, and ifing they don't believe me they can ask the Vetern's monument what landed but a hundred yards from here.

It weren't that the ginks din't believe me none, but they had inherited a little of the Old Curiosity too, and when I tell them about the metal I seen inside the shelter I knowed that with ginks first things is first and they weren't about to worry over no train wreck what ain't happened yet. So there's the lot of us, standing on the roof of that old storm shelter that all of us between us but Floyd proable-like played about a million hours of Iwo Jima on, a hole blowed in it by God's artillery.

"Watchu spose all that metal is—the makings of a space ship?" I says to Nooner.

Nooner, he don't answer, but the Barber says, "No, but it's too bad it weren't. Maybe we could fix it so them two loonies would fly back to the moon."

Well, it was the suicide letter what come to lead us to believe what Pyro and Termite was cooking up was the world's first Perpetual Motion Machine, but it weren't Termite's suicide letter, beings he din't have time to write one, beings it was the ten thirteen what hits him and his bubblegum machines broadside about the same time the lot of us ginks was speculating on the roof of the storm shelter, and such a terrible mess it was when you seen it, too. Somehow three of them boxcars behind the engine derailed and the way they ended up we had us a new monument what was the most weirdest metal statue you've laid eyes on, beings a good portion of it were the twisted metal trailer what housed Termite and got swept from its spot on the lot next to the implement store and landed ahead of the cars in the square.

We was amazed when we pulled up in Digger's hearse that this second tornado-like what come and gone ain't taken out any of the buildings with it. I jump out of the hearse, and since I weren't no volunteer having to stick around for the fire whistle what is now blowing and will blow forever-like on account of ever body then disremembers to shut it off, I quick take the stairs three at a time and check on my table, only to remember on I ain't got my stick with me anyways, being it's left in the shop, and only to figure that was about the most selfish thing I done in my life, knowing as I done that Termite was dead and squashed in his Cadillac somewhere along the tracks like a spider when you opened up a rumpled up Kleenex to see ifing you got it. And poor Digger, bless him, you just knowed how he hated them scoop shovel jobs, what with the accidents he sometimes cleaned up after out on the main highway and was the talk at the shop. Bless him, even after the mess what Termite made, nobody could've dreamed the trouble Digger would come to see.

THERE WEREN'T MUCH activity down on the square from my viewpoint what was a winda of the Masonic Hall, because, I suspicioned, the volunteers would be looking for the Termite what'd be dead and caught in his Cadillac like a piece of meat you can't pick out of your teeth. But I seen the Banker stick his head out the door of his fort, looking for me, I says to myself, and since the coast must've seemed clear to him, he moseys on out and inspects the new monument, talking with other folks who's standing around. One time I took my eye off him, and then I seen him looking up my way, but he ain't seen me because of the reflection—I know—or he'd be with a case of the crazies.

So there I was trapped till the Banker makes up his mind he's got his curiosity satisfied. And there I am thinking on the third thing I drawed what was the new memorial that would be there only for a couple of days on account of the railroad, it sent in a crew to clean it up real fast sos they was arriving by the time the Banker got his ears filled, I figured, beings when I look for him to see ifing I was still trapped, I din't see him none.

Well, as it turns out, there was a lot of folks what would come to say it was his nerves what made him disappear again till the Agent and his men counted the money and come up short. All I could think on then was I hoped there was enough left sos those ladies what worked in the bank could get their pay and Pop and me wouldn't have to leave on account of we'd be out of our income what was still stored in that bank to pay for the rent and groceries. But I never even brought it up to Pop, not wanting to give him any ideas.

It turns out there weren't no reason for me to be upset none. The Agent knowed the robber ain't come back, and the way he knowed it was the suicide letter the Banker left his wife what really weren't a suicide letter but a disguise for the Banker to leave town in. The funny thing is, though, that that suicide letter real-like *was* a suicide letter-like beings once Pyro caught up with the Banker, the Banker were a dead man anyhow. And Pyro, he never real-like caught up with the Banker, although he did, on account of the Agent says the Banker's death was measured as being from natural causes what was the Banker's fright that Pyro might catch up with him, the Barber said. And that's why all the ginks at the shop called the letter what weren't a suicide letter a suicide letter anyways. And that's how it were possible for Old Pyro to pull the trigger on the Banker when he din't own no gun and even ifing he had, it wouldn't've done him no good because the Banker were already dead.

Them three, according to the ginks at the shop, was building themselfs something like a Perpetual Motion Machine sos Termite and Pyro could get them their authority and the Banker could get him his fortune. What they done, though, was they spent all their money on a fool's notion. And I spose that ifing I was to tell this like it would get told in a TV show, you'd be especting me to say Pyro done poured gas all over hisself and lit his farmer's match on his teeth when he finds out the Vetern's monument had squashed his invention and the Banker had took off with what was left of his cash. But not Old Pyro. What he done was, the railroad, being it was back on the track so fast, the ginks guessed, he just waited for a fast train of the middle of a night and laid his neck on a rail. Poor

Digger, bless him, had to get out his scoop shovel once more after Floyd come and got him, the same Floyd what instead of a ascared look on his face had a grin and took Digger to show him what he found on his way to the shop, the body and the head what Digger was to haul to Lawless because it was Pyro's will he be creamated.

Me, I'm sitting there staring at that jar flanked on both sides by coffins of a Sunday afternoon, wondering what Digger, bless him, is going to do with Pyro's ashes. I ain't never been to no triple header, what was the Barber's words for it, cepting he said it was actual-like a double header, and he said he figured the way Pyro done hisself in, beings it were so gruesome and all, was pretty shrewd, him giving Digger, his second-in-command what had more authority than the chief because he was the boss of hisself and Pyro weren't, something to dream about for the rest of his natural life and him taking out a little insurance that he'd have his wishes to be creamated come true, what with his head so squashed there weren't no needle and thread fancy enough sos Digger could get the head back on the body. And what was weirder, sitting there in that funeral home, was one of the caskets was closed and one was open, and what was weirdest was the Banker's wife wouldn't come to the funeral home, but it were her wish that Digger play only one song on his record player—"Rock of Ages"—and he was to play it for the whole service, over and over again, and that is what he done, standing off in a corner, and he done it admirable-like too, without scratching the record much, and turning down the volume just right sos we could hear the Schoolteacher and what she was to have to say about a Freeland what she would call Anarchtopia.

Me, I was real happy the Banker's wife weren't at the funeral none, what with me being the one what give another human being a case of the crazies, but the Schoolteacher, she made it real clear-like that it weren't nobody's fault but their own, what happened to them three. Though it weren't in words like what I'm telling you, she said that them three wasn't and never would be the boss of themselfs. And the way she knowed it was because them three was after her for her knowledge sos to iron out the details on their invention.

Well, you might've knowed that the Schoolteacher, she weren't about to help them none, even ifing she would've knowed witch screw to tighten on that machine to make it work, ceptings she would've told them the answer was within themselfs and not some fool contraption, ifing they was really interested in being the boss of themselfs. But what they was interested in was being the boss of ever body else.

Now I got to thinking on how this weren't like a funeral so much as it was a lesson, ceptings I thought on how I'd learned me lessons at the two funerals I been to, too, although I weren't sure Cromangon Man's memorial service was what you'd call a regular funeral. I sure enough knowed that the service for Mom and Baby Sis were a funeral, though, beings I figure there weren't nothing but a funeral what could make you that hurt. And I spose the lessons I'd learned was all one big lesson, beings what I was finding out was I weren't quite as sad at this funeral and maybe there was good reason why.

It weren't that the Schoolteacher wanted you to feel happy or nothing when you come out of there. I mean she was talking about three human beings, even though one of them *were* from outer space. And even though the Banker weren't Freeland born, he at least knowed a good thing when he seen it and stuck, just like the Vetern, I figured. That's what the Schooteacher up and told, anyways.

Well, you know me. You know I put two and two together and it come up to three, beings what I were thinking was that was why the Schoolteacher hung around too. Because she knowed a good thing when she seen it. And that's why I weren't about to get me no job in Lawless, what with my table just a few stairs from where I was sitting and me with the chance of becoming the boss of myself, on account of like she said, there was two paths we could now travel, beings, I figured to myself, they were kind of like the low road and the high road I wore down on my trip back and forth from the shop to the Masonic Hall. The paths, one was to be ascared and the other was to be brave. Maybe the town of Freeland din't have any leaders any more. Maybe they was about to be buried, ceptings in the case of one what was about to be blown to the winds. Maybe what Freeland needed, just like what ever place needs, is leaders in ever one. You could tell by the time she was done that what she thought we should do, men and ginks alike, was to be our own police and firemen, what was pretty much the case anyways, and to start our own bank. Now there was a stalk of straw to chew on! You could tell the ginks liked that idea real good.

But the Schoolteacher, besides boosting up our courage like she done, she give us a lesson to think on too. She said that when she was fixing up the eulogy she was to give that afternoon, she come across a little fact in her mind, beings *eu* means good and when you add it to *ology* what it means is good words. Well, I knowed that right enough, beings how many times she done quizzed us ginks in them Latin and Greek roots. But what I couldn't figure on was how she got to *Anarchtopia* from there, what was her next fancy word she laid out for us. Well, the way it turns out, there's a word in the middle what got her there—*utopia*. You see, it's the sound of the first syllable in *eulogy* and *utopia*. But she knowed *utopia* weren't the right word for Freeland, because when you hear on it, beings *utopia* means a place, utopia is both a good place and no place, since "u" spelled with a "u" means *no* too. So what she done was she thought up her own word, *Anarchtopia*, what to most people would be a bad place beings they could hear *anarchy* in it. But it din't *have* to be a bad place, she said. Me, I knowed what she meant, just like ever other gink in the funeral home. *An* means without. *Arch* means ruler. And ifing you've got a whole bunch of people what is the boss of themselfs, you sure don't need one what wants to be the boss of themselfs and ever body else.

Well, cept for the fact that the Schoolteacher was the live-in preacher, we had us a little of the old Anarchtopia right there in Freeland, I figure. The problem was, was we going to take the low road or the high road? Was we going to be brave or ascared?

I happened to look over at Floyd, him with his head busting at the seams and his grin on.

I don't mean to say with none of my talk the Schoolteacher wandered from the subject of the three what we was there to remember on account of they was human beings. The School-teacher, she was real kind to them I thought, beings they had such hard lives because they was rich. And it weren't that the Schoolteacher thought it was a sin to be rich, you could tell. And who's to say who's rich and who ain't anyways? I looked around me in that funeral parlor, and I come up with the one person who was the richest, beings I knowed he owned three pipes, but I says to myself, so what? He knowed as well as I knowed he couldn't smoke them three pipes at the same time. And even ifing he could he weren't real-like no differenter than us, even ifing he were a stranger, because he can't be smoking them all the time just like the ginks what come to the funeral without a chew in their cheeks because there are times when a man has got to show some respect. And I figure that at a funeral what a man is doing is showing respect for his own life as much as for the dead, especial-like when the dead is the likes of Pyro, Termite, and the Banker. I mean a funeral makes a man stop and take notice, beings there ain't no place where you can get the smell of a flower like at a funeral. Maybe they would've come to like themselfs better. Maybe they would've seen like I knowed the Agent was seeing we're all in the same solar system, beings living is what we got in common, even ifing you own three more pipes than the gink what is sitting next to you.

But I got to wondering on the Agent, whether he was there only to pay his respects. Then I thought on how that bank robber must be eating on him some, since the last I heared they ain't yet caught him. I started feeling sorry for the Banker, knowing in my heart that part of what killed him was his fright over what I drawed in my sleep. I knowed it weren't my fault. But that din't make me any less sorry. Come to find out, the F.B.I. man, he was at the service because he was feeling a little guilty too. I knowed because he told me. You see, Digger, bless him, had to make three trips out to the cemetery, beings he couldn't fit two caskets at once in his meat wagon, what the Barber calls it, and it just din't seem right to make only two trips, on account of it were Pyro's will that his ashes be buried. So Digger, he saves the easiest for last, the ashes I mean, because he's so tired and all from digging three graves, even though he brung in a backhoe from Lawless. So the Agent and me, we had a long talk because we weren't pall bearers like ginks what knowed Termite and the Banker better. But our talk, it got cut short, you can see why, ifing I was to tell you about the thing what happened. But that's another story, although it ain't really beings it's how there come to be the second of three empty graves in that cemetery, beings the first were Cromangon Man's. Digger, bless him, opens up his door on the back of that hearse on the third trip to the graveyard and there come a gust of wind what tipped over the jar Digger had been so careful-like with sos all us ginks out at the cemetery about sent out a scout to see ifing Digger got lost, beings he drove that jar so slow-like to be buried. Well, them ashes, they come out of the back of that hearse like a swarm out of a hive what was set on stinging their keeper, and then they just up and vanished but not before they leave poor Digger, bless him, with a sneezing fit.

Me, I figured there'd be three of us feeling guilty. But the Schoolteacher weren't about to have none of it. She just marched over to that jar, screwed its lid back on, and set it in the grave, what was real shallow, beings Digger saw no necessity to waste money on a six foot hole when one bite of a backhoe'd be enough to hold them ashes for eternity, not like Termite's body what got so squashed there weren't no way, the Barber said, Digger could've pickled him, and, unlike the Banker's body—what even though Digger done him up right for his widowed wife, smoothing out the look of fright in his brow and mouth—it don't make no difference, I knowed, because we're all going to be creamated one day when the sun gets so big the world disappears like spit on a griddle.

Me, I don't read science fiction for nothing. The Banker, I knowed, would someday return to outer space where he come from.

Well, anyways, up till the time the Agent and my long talk got cut short, I was hearing what all the ears at the shop'd need to hear, ifing there was to be more talk about us starting our own bank. The Agent, he had one of his own artists use what I drawed to copy sketches of the robber, one without a beard and one with a beard sos when you looked at it you din't see red. Well, there was people in Lawless what said they'd seen the robber, so the Agent, he figured the trail was hotter than it's been.

"Stick," he says.

There were something in his voice I din't like. "Yes Sir?"

He looks at me for a long time, I could tell, because I—me—I was looking at his pipe in his teeth what he'd keep there between Digger's deliveries and what he hadn't lit, I suspicioned, to show his respect. It was the same pipe I'd seen him with that time in the Masonic Hall, seeings how I'd never forget how being dizzy and ascared and all could make you sos to remember on a thing. The Agent, he just shakes his head a little, I could tell, because the bowl of his pipe is moving back and forth, and then he says, "Never mind." And then he says, "Stick, tell me about yourself." And me, I start talking up a storm, even though I ain't up on the past much, because I knowed I'd much rather be talking about my past than my future, what was the subject the Agent was first interested in, I knowed, just like I knowed one time and still knowed I'd be the best at three cushion there ever was, but not till the rest of the world knowed it. But what I ain't done yet is I ain't put two and two together. I mean how was I to know I was to have my cake and eat it too? How was I to know that being the boss of myself like I were on my table was going to give me my authority so I could be the boss of myself even when I weren't at my table? And even though I knowed it were the Agent who was in my future near much as the ginks and Floyd, who was standing there mainly because Digger, bless him, was short on pall bearers, how was I to know it were him what would hand me my opportunity? My table was in Freeland, not Lawless nor no place else.

So I talk about me. I talk about the past, beings its easy to talk about the past to people sos they think you're talking about you, not knowing you're not the same gink in the present as they seen in front of them because they ain't used to hearing nobody talk about his future—what I would've had to do to talk about me. So, you see, I din't really have to talk about me atall. I talked, instead, about Mom and Baby Sis. I even show him their stones. Talk, I come to find out, was a lot easier for me than it used to be. Ever since I've had so much practice listening. Ever since the Lord decided to make Wally Phillips something akin to my conscious, what was the one part of the story the Agent weren't about to hear from me. It were a good thing we got cut short in our conversation, too. I was coming to the part of my history where the brain waves and the radio waves together was starting to rock the boat.

The Agent, I could tell he wanted to hear more, beings after the Schoolteacher read the part about ashes to ashes he come over to me and shook my hand, saying he had to go. I think he knowed he din't have to say he'd be seeing me again.

"Stick," he says.

"Yes Sir," I says.

"You're growing up."

I told him I sposed I was.

"You'll have to do something about that handshake of yours," he says.

"Whatchu mean?" I says.

Well, the Agent, he showed me how to grip a hand real firm-like sos another would know you meant it. It come in real handy the first time I used it, what was on the Bear to say I was sorry after what I done, the story what I have to tell you on, ceptings I practiced that handshake one time, there, after the funeral with the Schoolteacher, her robe flying in the breeze and all, and she took me in her hands by the face and pulled my head down to her and kissed me on the forehead. Right there I knowed how tall I'd got. Right there I knowed how much younger she were getting sos when you studied on her face, as I done right then, you knowed she weren't the same Schoolteacher but becoming another Luda Corvus. I watched her from behind, walking across the grass to the parsonage. Her shadow was longer than it should be, I says. It flew beside her across the yard till it got lost in the shadows of the trees. She had her secret what was the Vision of the Flock, all right. But there was more. I'd come to know like I already knowed there was more.

IFING IT'D BEEN up to the ginks, they might've changed Freeland's name to Anarchtopia, but they could see other folks in town wanted no part of it. Me, I weren't too excited about it neither, beings it sounded kind of foreign-like, and what I figured was a name ain't nothing but a name anyways. I mean, there I was, about to join up with the Patriots, what is the high school team name, and I knowed I'd've felt more loyal ifing we was called the Ginks, but even that wouldn't've kept me from doing what I done.

October it was, and I had my pad in my lap, sketching whoever'd come in the shop, and I said to Bob the Barber what would he think about me joining up with the basketball team sos to keep the smart alecks off my back, them upperclassmen with their cars, their fiancées, and their talk about me being a gink and all. I mean I figured I was tall enough, though I ain't measured it none, and maybe the coach wouldn't have me suit up for the away games sos I wouldn't have to give up my practicing on my table ever day.

Well, I knowed it was coming, a little touch of the old envy in the Barber's eye because there weren't no gink what ever got chose for the team, and the Barber, I figured he wanted to real bad when he was a kid, beings he was the kind what would. But, the Barber, he weren't sarcastic about it or nothing. He just said that, with my eye and height, ifing I hadn't joined up, he'd've crippled and drugged me all the way to the loony bin in Lawless by his lonesome, on account of folks would've knowed for sure I was crazy, and that there's where a crazy belongs, in Lawless.

I got to thinking on what he said and real sudden-like I made up my mind to chance it, even ifing the Bear was to put me on the traveling squad, on account of I'd rather shoot baskets in Lawless than weave baskets, even though I knowed we din't play Lawless hardly ever because they was too big and we was too small, even to have a junior varsity.

So me, I joined up. And the Bear, you could tell he was real happy when I done it too, even though we ain't touched a basketball for the first two weeks. What we done was sprints and laps. And the reason he were glad I was there weren't just because I was tall, you could tell, but because them others was always breathing hard.

"Cousin," Bucky Williams would always call me, "don't you never get tired?"

Well, sure I got tired. It was just that in them practices I din't act tired none because ifing you act tired, the Bear, he'd figure you was tired because you wasn't in shape and I figure the way to get you in shape were to run you like you was a loony to Lawless ifing you looked tired.

The next week we done drills, and what surprised me some was I could dribble the ball real good. But it were so much fun to pass behind your back and between your legs that I hardly ever dribbled, cept to draw the *de*fense to me sos I could pass.

I never shot much in the second half. I din't need to since we was always way ahead by a big score. The Bear seen to that. The first scrimmage we had, the Bear, he blows his whistle and he tells me to shoot and to quit passing the ball off. Well, I know I'd better do what he says, but I just can't bring myself to.

"Why not?" he says.

"Because I ain't going to make it," I says.

"How do you know till you try?" he says.

Me, I don't say nothing.

The Bear, he takes me over to the side, and he says, "How do you know you're not going to make it?"

Well, the Bear, I knowed he was about to become the bear he could be, and you know me, I don't like strangers none, so I up and tell him I drawed it in my sleep.

Now the Bear, he weren't so ignorant that he din't know what that meant, because there weren't nobody in Freeland, Bob the Barber says, who weren't interested in the latest edition of my doodles, so he just looks at me kind of queer-like and he says, "Well, what about the second shot?"

"I don't know," I tell him.

"How do you know it's the first shot you'll miss?"

"There ain't no points on the scoreboard," I says.

The Bear, he told me we weren't in no game, we was practicing, we wasn't about to keep score for a while, sos I should shoot the first time sos I could maybe get the first time over with sos I could find out what happens the second time.

So I get out there and we was running picks, and the first time I get the ball I'm at the top of the key and I heared the growl what come from the bench, the Bear what is standing on the bench sos he's taller than me, and the growl says "Shoot!" So I let it fly, figuring it don't matter none anyhow. The ball, it don't hit no iron nor nothing but it's just hanging in the net and ever thing stops.

Well, I knowed they was all looking at me funny-like, sos I says to them I'm sorry. Bucky says he ain't never seen a ball shot from the top of the key what it was shot so soft it got caught in the net, even ifing they was new nets, what these wasn't.

Well, the second time the Bear growls I shoot too, and the ball, it goes through the hoop, rips the cords and falls straight down. Me, I shot that one a little harder, not wanting to show off or nothing. The funny thing is as long as the Bear remembered on to growl, I never missed the rest of practice, not that I wanted to what with my notion to knock the rest of them smart alecks on the team down a peg sos they would know a gink weren't no differenter than them since ifing he wanted he could play basketball. The Bear, I knowed he thought I'd been coached, me knowing how to keep the ball up high and all sos nobody could reach it without they fouled me, just like I begun to think on maybe I *had* been coached. And it hit me. I had been coached. By the Bear. Only it ain't happened yet.

Now I don't mind telling you there was something eating me some. I mean, the way I figured it, I made me that first basket, even ifing it din't fall through the net, what it did, eventual-like. It just took it's own sweet time about it.

The whole thing had me homesick. I mean I'm saying to myself maybe the reason I drawed in my sleep something what really weren't about to happen was because me and the Schoolteacher was separated like we was. And when I thought on how I'd have to give up my income a little sos I'd have time to practice on my table and play basketball too, I got to feeling pretty bad, knowing like I done she wanted me to draw and ifing I was to slack up on my pad a bit that meant I'd see the ginks—what was my second father more than my Pop was my first—even less.

Bob the Barber, he wouldn't have it none when I finally two weeks later get the gumption to tell him maybe it weren't meant I should play ball.

I says, "I mean ifing playing on a team makes a gink so lonesome he wants to quit the team, why for should I play?"

"Stick," he says, "how many points did you score in the home opener?"

I told him I din't know.

"You don't *know*? he says.

"No," I says.

"Just a minute," he said. And the Barber, he gets up out of his chair and does something I ain't ever seen him do. He walks over to his conversation piece, what is the throne what burnt up, and real ginger-like, he sets hisself down in it. Then he says, "I spose you do recollect how many assists you had."

"What of it?" I says.

The Barber, I done thought he caught afire again, because he jumps out of his throne, the papers flying ever witch way.

"What's wrong with *that*?" he says.

"What's wrong with *that*?" Floyd says.

I took over at Floyd, the same Floyd what owns a medicine ball for a head, what has his grin what stretches from here to Lawless.

"Yeah, that's right," the Barber he says to me, "Study on Floyd!"

"Study on Floyd!" come the echo.

"You think he wouldn't've give his left nut when he was a kid to hit twelve buckets in the first half, seven free throws for the game and shoot a hundred percent in both categories?"

"… and shoot a hundred *per*cent in both categories?" was the words coming out of Old You-Know-Who.

Well, I guessed I knowed what he meant. But how was I going to tell him there weren't no satisfaction like the satisfaction to be had on your table. Besides, it were awful hard to be happy about winning when you knowed the others was going to lose. I could see it on the face of the upperclassmen who knowed there weren't no chance of them ever being the star of the team. And it weren't going to give me any more pleasure ifing I was to keep teaching them smart alecks a gink is as good as them. It was something they already knowed now. And then there was the look on the face of them on the Elmville team we played. I hated it when they come up to shake your hand after the game on account of you could tell they din't think it was fair the Law of Averages should've had them and me in the same game, even ifing we weren't strangers no more. I tell the Barber I guessed I were good at it, beings, like he said, I shot the eye out of the basket and all, but how was

I sposed to know that? I mean I wouldn't've joined up none ifing I'd've drawed in my sleep all them long faces, even when I seen all them smiling faces in the crowd when I caught a quick look-see once, what would be, I figured, the grins on the ginks who'd come to see one of their own on a team they never got picked for. Even the Bear was almost smiling after we'd won. And I thought on how that was probable-like a bad sign for me, because how was I sposed to get my practicing done ifing I was to be on a bus once a week instead of in the Masonic Hall where I belonged?

So I asks him. I says to the Bear would he mind ifing I was to sit out them away games, beings it would be nice ifing the others on our team could be the stars sometimes. And do you know what he up and said? Well, he din't say nothing at first, him looking at me, I could tell, even though I weren't looking at him. He just started a laughing and said that was a good one. So when the bus pulls up to my place and honks its horn the night of the first away game, I tell the Bear when he come up to the door that I thought we decided I shouldn't oughta go with them. Well, the Bear, he just started this laughing again. Then he stopped real quick, and he looked at me with this mean look you'd see on the cover of *Field and Stream* up at the shop, what was the look of a grizzly what done just got woke up and were about to have a bow hunter for breakfast. Well, me, I ain't so dumb as to not to know what that meant. So ever body was real mad because my uniform was in my locker and not there, and we had to go to the school to pick it up, because the Bear, he got gentle enough sos he could tell me I had my wires crossed and once you was on a team you was on it for good, unless you wasn't on it no more. And me, I weren't about to quit what with Floyd thinking he would've gave his left one to play and the Barber being my biggest fan and all. I want to tell you, you would've been looking at one sad gink what was torn between hisself had you been riding in the seat I was sat in all by my lonesome in the front of that bus.

The Bear, he was sat behind the driver, and I knowed he was staring at me sometimes, even when it was on the way home again and it were dark. Me, I had me about the most nervous time I'd ever knowed what with the Barber being about the only face I knowed that I'd seen in that gym over at Waterton. And I was sorry since we din't get to warm up all that much what with me not knowing I was on the traveling squad and us being too late.

I mean, how was I sposed to know when nobody tells me? About the only thing what made me happy was I knowed how many points I'd got sos the Barber wouldn't razz me none. They was a real weak team, the Bear found out, so he tells us he don't want nobody shooting but me for the first quarter, and me, I'm sposed to take only one shot ever minute. I never even got fouled. So it was easy to remember on how many points I had after I got to set down at the end of the first quarter on account of what the scoreboard said was sixteen to nothing. It was a real boring game since me, I hardly got to do any of my favorite passes till after the half when the Bear put me back in. The other players on our team, I was glad they was having a good time making baskets, but I guess they din't see why they had to pass to me none since they was doing OK for themselfs. And there I sit the whole last quarter, thinking on how I'd rather have my stick for company, even though least-wise the Barber was there because you could hear him even ifing you wasn't looking up in the bleachers what I weren't about to.

Well, we get back, and the bus, it dumps us off at the high school, and me, I ain't got my bike or nothing sos I start walking for home. I'm about halfway there and I can feel these headlights on the back of my head slowing down. It's Bucky, who ain't a bad sort atall, and he wants to go celebrate the victory with him and some others. Me, I don't want to none, beings I'd rather get some sleep since Saturday is my one day to get some good time in on my table. But Bucky, he's telling me it's pretty important I should come because Jim North and Rich Thompson, the two seniors what had such a big game, would be the ones there, and they might think on I was conceited ifing I wasn't to the party to celebrate. Now, me, I din't care who might say I was stuck up, but I got to thinking on how they'd probable-like feel bad ifing they was the ones who asked me to their party and I din't go. So I'm in the car, and Bucky, he's passing me this bottle and I say no thanks, knowing like I does it ain't no Royal Crown. Ceptings before it's over, I'm taking a swaller what is more like a cherry Coke at the drug store, and beings it don't smell none like Digger's office, bless him, I take me another drink, beings I was real thirsty still after the game. The way it turns out, Bucky and Jim and Rich have got a whole case of it at Rich's house and what is on the box is the words Slow Gin, what I ask them ifing it's named after anything like Euchre, beings I played it a lot. Well, you know I on purpose made a fool of myself, and pretty soon they was mocking me right along with me, me thinking maybe I oughta not be so hard on them when I talk on them to the Barber.

Well, me, I don't see where the celebrating comes in much when there ain't nobody at Rich's place to celebrate, ceptings I don't care much what with the stuff they poured in my glass almost good enough to make a gink want to switch brands. Well, pretty soon the doorbell rings and here comes them fancy two up at the high school what is engaged to Rich and Jim. They don't look at me but once, but I'm sure looking at them and their womanly parts all of the sudden. That's when I knowed I wasn't drinking no cherry Coke, that and for a fact it started to sound like the record player at WGN accidental-like got set on thirty instead of thirty-three and a third.

It ain't but a hour we're there, and them two with their fancy parts is smoking cigarettes one after the other and drinking real fast, and one of them gets sick in the bathroom. Then the phone rings, and Rich, he comes out of the kitchen where it is and says he can't stand the smell of puke so let's go for a ride. Before you know it, the four of us is in Bucky's car with all the Slow Gin, and we done left them fiancées behind, one to play patient and one to play nurse, is the way the Barber might've told it.

We ain't got no cups or nothing, so me, I'm just taking these real small sips from a bottle they're passing around in the car, beings I don't want to wet my pants none. And me, I din't pay much attention to the conversation what with being in the back seat and Jim leaning over the front seat talking with Rich, who ain't driving but giving Bucky directions on where he oughta drive.

Well, me, I just close my eyes and lean my head back ever so often, not about to know where we was, what weren't too unusual I come to find out, beings when we pulled out of Helen's or Peg's—I can't remember witch place we picked them up—all we done was drive around some more, Helen and Peg giggling and drinking till all of the sudden there weren't no giggling, and then there weren't no more drinking neither.

Well, you know me. I got to go to the bathroom for two reasons, what with Helen in the middle of Jim and me and her leg slung up over my knee, and her hand pressing down real hard in my lap while she's making out with Jim.

It ain't but a while in the front seat Peg is pretending she's real hot, you could tell, and Rich says to Bucky to find somewheres. And me, I don't like it one bit when I heared that, beings that Peg, she's moaning like somebody on TV got shot and I know where we are. Bucky, he turns on his signal and slows down and I can see the lane what leads to the storm shelter what houses the flying Vetern's monument and the world's first Perpetual Motion Machine what got squashed by it.

Peg, she pops up for air, and she's looking out the windshield like she were looking through fog and she says not here again, because there's too many bugs. Bucky, he turns off his signal, drives up to the corner, cuts the lights, and then coasts into the cemetery. Me, I got to go to the bathroom so bad that I done something I ain't had the ambition to do before, opening up the car door and sliding out from under Helen's leg and right hand what is still groping for my boner behind her back,

I can see, when the interior light come on. Me, I close the door real quiet-like and run for the corn.

I knowed I could've filled one of them empty bottles of Slow Gin, but I'll be darned ifing I don't get out there in that cornfield and I can't go. I think about them two fiancées, beings they was in the bathroom so long what with me having to go then. Why in the world can't I go now, I says to myself. So me, I just concentrate, what weren't easy with a boner with remembering like mine, I want to tell you. Well, the cornstalks, they was real dry like they was to be picked tomorrow, and final-like I heared this sound of a breeze among them, but then I figure it's me making that noise, beings I'm just dizzy enough not to know when my bladder begun its relief its self.

I ain't sure at all I want to go back to Bucky's car with Peg pretending she's hot and moaning like she is sos to wake the dead, I says to myself. All of the sudden I'm remembering on, really remembering, where we was, and me, I don't like it one bit, but it was like Helen and Peg done to me in Sunday school when I kept coming back for more till final-like I swore off like I swore off pool. I'm about to walk back to that car with a boner in my pants what hoped it would happen that Helen or Peg would help it quit, while me, I hoped heaven would still have me. Then, real sudden-like—Peg, there ain't no more moaning what's coming from her mouth. Me, I figure maybe it's all over and maybe it's safe to go back, beings whatever was going to happen, it was going to be happy and sad. So I make for the car, about to climb in the back seat, when I seen a girl's shoe sticking out of the winda. "Bucky?" I says.

"Yeah?" he says.

So I walk around the trunk of the car and there's Bucky behind the wheel, but I don't see nobody else up in the front seat.

"Where'd you go, Cousin?"

"To the bathroom," I says.

"Yeah, sure," he says.

I thought on how he'd probable-like figure what he'd figure, sos I just up and asked, "Where are them other two?"

Bucky, he din't say nothing, but all of the sudden I heared this click, and there's a big flash to my left. First off, I don't know what I'm seeing, even though I seen hogs doing it a hundred times, beings a hog's hind ain't white like that. But Peg, she were on all fours, and she was doing it just as fast as he could do it. And it din't seem to bother them none when Bucky hit his brights, neither. For a fact, it seemed like the lights was just the ticket for Peg, since all of the sudden she started moaning again, only you could tell this time it was real.

Well, I want to tell you the longer this goes on, the harder it was to think on how ascared I was when Bucky first flashed on them brights, beings I knowed like I did the Schoolteacher lived not more than a hundred yards aways, even ifing the church was set in the way sos she couldn't see. I mean, I'd been thinking how ifing the Schoolteacher knowed what Peg and Helen was doing and that there I was, taking it all in like it were a dirty movie in Lawless, she'd probable-like fly out of her parsonage and bust rulers over all our hind ends. I mean had they been doing it in the dark, maybe there was no chance of us getting caught. But then them lights come on and the thing what stopped me from reaching in through the winda and shutting them off was I knowed Old Crow don't fly at night. Besides, I says to myself, I ain't never seen a dirty movie, and maybe it's time I got me some education on it, just like Peg were getting herself some education.

It weren't till the two of them come apart I begun to see the place they was doing it in. It weren't that I was ascared the Schoolteacher would hear Peg was making me sos I was starting to feel the heartache. It weren't nothing I drawed or nothing. It weren't Slow Gin. I was aching because sudden-like I seen the shadow on the side of the church, what was like a ghost raising amongst the stones, what made me think of the stones, what makes me think on Mom and Baby Sis.

And when I seen what I ain't even heared on account of the fret was coming on, that Bucky was now in the back seat and Jim was up front on the other side, even though I knowed it was my turn, what with another ache in my crotch and Rich walking toward us, shielding his eyes from the headlights for what seemed eternity its self and Peg in the distance, covering herself with her clothes, leaning agin a stone, the ache what was in my heart was worser, sos I just shut off the carlights and walked past Rich like I knowed he din't know I was passing him.

I come up to Peg and there she was all naked under her clothes. The stone, it belongs to Baby Sis.

You proable-like think I wanted to pound on her for what she, Peg, made me watch and where she made me watch it. But I knowed she were innocent as me. I knowed too I wanted to do it to her real bad, but me, I just stood there.

Final-like, I says to her, "Do you want to do it?"

"Do you?" she says.

I din't know what to say now, how I was going to tell her. I stood there for another long time, thinking on ifing her answer had been anything but what it was that by now my sperm would be swimming inside her and that would be one less ache inside of me. "You'd best get dressed and go," I said.

"What do you mean?" she says sos I must've said it funnylike.

"I ain't blaming you none," I says.

"For what?" she says.

"It ain't the Schoolteacher. It's the stone."

Real sudden-like she lurched forward a bit, like she knowed what I was talking about but then she din't know.

"It's my Mom and Baby Sis, Peg."

Peg. I seen what a good heart she really had when she stood up slow-like, still covering herself with her clothes, and then she said she was sorry and she busted into tears, without even looking behind her at the stone, and she run for the car.

I guessed the lot of them knowed I wouldn't be going back to town with them, since they backed out quiet-like and din't disturb my thinking on it none by turning on the headlights or nothing. I spose, now that I think on it, there weren't all that much in my head to disturb, ceptings I had me my new ache in my heart and the old ache in my underwear what weren't about to go away, even ifing I weren't thinking on what I seen but instead remembering on it.

Now how I'm going to tell you on this next part is hard, beings I've to start by saying I weren't drunk and I never falled asleep. Even ifing I had done one or another it would've made no difference because I din't have my pad with me, not that it were something you could draw. I mean ifing somebody was to whisper something to you that you was to pass on, you sure as heck wouldn't draw it none, would you? Especial-like ifing it weren't something you was sposed to tell as much as you was sposed to believe it sos you could live it, something like a new message. And sposing this new message were something you couldn't never believe unless you knowed for sure that the Luda Corvus what were the Schoolteacher weren't the same what was your great grandmother, even though she was too. Sometimes I says to myself what better way would there be to tell me than what she done, beings ifing I wouldn't believe her new message after what she done, then there was nobody who would. Not that what she done wouldn't make me hurt, but not in the way you'd think, beings I knowed that on this Earth—and this I knowed on account of I read it in a science fiction book, even though it ain't science fiction because the book said it's something what happens in a country and not on a another planet—that on this Earth there are lots of strange goings-on, like mothers what feed their children their own urine when the little kid has got a belly ache and mothers what play with their baby's parts when they nurse him.

So there I am of a Friday night in the cemetery laying between two markers what're there to tell the living it's my Mom and Baby Sis under the ground and nobody else, with my heart and my virginity aching inside of me, one hand on each stone, when I hear rustling in the corn again what has me thinking on beavers because they're about the size of racoons what I figure is making the noise. Me, I figure the beavers

what Cromangon Man called critters was like the dead I come
to know and what left for a better world. Well, I'm wrong, and
the way I come to know I were wrong was that it were part of
her new message. Not that the beavers wasn't like critters, but
that heaven were a different place. I mean I oughta've knowed
because there I were, laying on the ground what was used to
cover the only natural Mom and Baby Sis I'd ever know, my
hands on their visible souls, the stones, beings when Mom
and Baby Sis was dead the only souls they had was the visible stones. And it weren't like they was ever dead, really, on
account of they was still alive in the way the Earth's alive. I
mean now that I know her new message, I can see the stones
is alive, just like parts of a cell in a body is alive when you put it
together with other parts. And the breeze what come over me
was the breath of the Earth. The stones was like the bones, the
soil like the muscles. And ifing you was to sit up real high on a
mountain, you'd know that the rivers and cricks was like veins
and the water was blood. You'd know all this because part of
her new message was the Earth was just as alive as a human
being is alive. And ifing I hadn't read me lots of science fiction,
I'd probable-like be thinking right now that the Earth, it never
dies sos critters and the rocks and the people don't never die
neither. But me, beings I am a science fiction nut, what Bob
the Barber has said many times hisself, I know that the sun
what's really a star will grow so big sos to burn us all up but
not before rocket ships carries a sample of ever thing that's
good in the world to someplace else, what I come to figure out
is what Noah and his ark is all about anyways, beings I now
know her new message, and I know that whoever dreamed up

Noah and his ark, never knowed about rocket ships, just like I don't know about what kind of ships there are after rocket ships on account of I ain't yet drawed it in my sleep. And even ifing I don't, somebody will. I know because that's the kind of knowing her new message give me.

But I spose that's not the most important part of the story, beings it's another story, although it ain't really. Because it's the story of how I come to know like Cromangon Man knowed that a man is part of the Earth and that he ain't apart from it. And ifing he is part, and that he is, then all of the people what are dead are still living because all you have to do is look around you and you can see plain as day the world is still breathing. And the world, it ain't but a cell in the body of God, what ain't in heaven but right here, what is the universe what is all the time getting bigger too, I know, on account of I don't read science fiction for nothing.

But all that weren't the most important part of her new message, because I din't even know what the other parts was yet. All I knowed was I had me my aches and pains and my frets. And there I was, laying between them two stones what reminded you of chalk on a blackboard, beings it was so dark, no stars or nothing, not even a sliver of the moon. And I ain't even ascared or nothing, what with this fluttering of her robe above me, thinking as I was just for a second, is it her house robe or her church robe she has on, and I don't move or nothing, beings I got my own wings spread, my fingertips on them stones what are as smooth as a cue ball, reminding me on my table, what I wished I was laying on instead, cept I knowed the hands would be *here*, and she knelt above me and done what she always done with her hands for a real long time, only this time she done more, without saying nothing, her raising up to walk around Mom's stone and real gentle-like to lay down next to me on her elbow. When she took in her hands my face and made me look into hers, I seen her eyes, the pupils so wide sos there were no amount of color in her irises, and I seen and then touched her cheek what was warm and smoother, even, than Baby Sis's stone. I should've been ascared, she looked that young. I should've got up and run. But we was laying there a while, and she'd made me look at her so long sos when she kissed my forehead, it seems so natural-like when she opens her robe and give me her breast what I took it but not before I took it in my hand and felt it smooth and firm, even, as her cheek.

I know you think you know the rest. I spose you do, cept-ings you don't know it all. You couldn't or you'd know her new message and there would be no reason for me to be telling on this whole story. You see, I was as surprised as you. And I was hurting over it too, but not in the way you'd suspicion. I spose that when it happens the first time part of what makes you so happy is you know there is something to look toward that can make you feel so alive. A human being has got so much to fret over, beings they can see the future has got its bad name and times, that they need to know there'll be good things happen-ing too, and what could be better, cepting maybe the satisfac-tion what comes from doing your best on your table. But your table is for your peace of mind. The other is for your body and mind. I couldn't believe it when she told me when we was done that she loved me in another way sos that it wouldn't let us do it again. Well, me, I seen how she seems to like it so much, even when she did go slow and me, I was trying to go slow too. I even heared her crying and felt quivering toward the end after I done it too. And me, there I laid, thinking ifing we couldn't do it ever again, how come we could do it now?

So there we was, done, laying in that grass, and I just can't stand it no more. So I whispers to her, "Is it because you are the same Luda Corvus as the one what had my mother's mother?"

"You already *have* the answer to that," she says.

Well, she were right, but there I am, thinking to myself, she *isn't* and she *is*. And what kind of answer is that?

Just looking at her, I knowed she weren't old enough to be my mother, let alone my great grandmother. So I says to her point blank, "How come you're younger than you was?"

Well, she weren't so young as there's none of the School-teacher left in her, on account of she just looked at me like it was for her to know and me to find out. But then she up and surprised me. She told me she weren't any younger.

What she said I already knowed. She was right about that, too, you can guess, or else I wouldn't've knowed she was the same Luda Corvus what laid out those stones I dug up, the same what bore my mother's mother, the same what just done it with me. But then she weren't the same, nei-ther. Her face weren't the same as her picture. And Floyd with his own eyeballs and photographic remembering what had seen two copies of the same Luda Corvus knowed she weren't the same neither.

Well, the Schoolteacher, she took me over to her parsonage, and it was like we never done it, ceptings I knowed we had and that it weren't no dream or nothing, but we was acting real regular-like like we ain't done it. But there's more. It was in her house she told me the words to call her secret, the Vision of the Flock. She suspicioned I knowed it but not what to call it, and she done something strange-like. She said ifing I ever needed it I could ask her for it. Well, me, beings I inherited the curiosity what she is famous for, I asked her what for, and she tells me I'll know what for when I need it. And then I asked of her ifing she was born with it, and she asks of me was I born with my dreaming, only she din't say it like that. Me, I tell her I don't rightly know. Well, she says the same is true of her, cept it was a Indian what taught her it, the same Indian what were once her husband, I figures, but she din't want to talk about it none, witch was all right, I spose, but I was real mad, but mostly sleepy. I weren't so tired sos I couldn't ask her why we couldn't never do it again, though. Well, she said it again. She said she din't love me in that way. And when I want to know how we could do it the first time ifing she din't love me in that way, I thought I weren't hearing right when I heared her say, her hands square on my face, her eyes what weren't Mom's eyes neither, "I carry your seed, the seed of the mother and the healer."

Then I looked at her hard, real hard, and I knowed I heared her right, and I knowed my next question, like the one before it, had no answer sos I was meant to understand, and me, it made no sense to ask more about the miracle what was happening what with her getting younger ever day. And it made no sense to ask her ifing the Vetern, the very one whose memorial laid in the storm shelter still squashing that Perpetual Motion Machine were my great grandfather, especial-like when I already knowed it was true. Her hands come down, but she was looking at me hard-like too. It was like she hushed me up for good on account of she give me a secret I couldn't even tell, even ifing I was to know what it was. And it made me proud. And it made me not ascared, almost.

IFING THE CONGREGATION had any inkling as to what she hid under her robe of a Sunday morning, even though they was mostly ginks and their families, they probable-like would've voted to call Freeland Anarchtopia from now on sooner than they did. Nobody seemed ever to notice, though, not even when she was in to town for groceries on account of she kept it real quiet-like that she was in a family way and nobody ever seen her out of her robes in June and July when it was me what done her shopping. It weren't hard for me not to hurt so much then or even earlier when I seen her in March right before the tournament and I knowed for a fact it were only me who could know because I ain't told nobody, especial-like no gink, that she were with child, my child, I knowed even though I never really believed it till she sets it in my arms. You see, up till I knowed for sure she was pregnant on account of I could see it, I wanted her and me to sleep together in the worst way, though I knowed it weren't about to happen because she said it weren't and because, though she weren't the same Luda Corvus what was my great grandmother, she was. And she was the Schoolteacher and the live-in preacher.

Come March I knowed *why* she got younger, what with her needing to sos to bear another baby witch was the second she bore, all by herself beings the first was my mother's mother. But what I din't know was how. Unless you said she willed it to happen. Now I spose you think that's pretty far fetched. Well, maybe it is. But so is miracles, I figure. Now, you take your Father who art in heaven, for a fact. That there would be a miracle when you think on it. Yet right there in old Anarchtopia there were a whole congregation full of ginks what was ready to believe on that miracle since the moment they was sprung out of the Earth because that's where the first mother sprung from. But they changed their minds after she proved to them there weren't no Father in heaven beings their heaven weren't anywhere but in their heads, and ifing that's where their heaven was, the Father who art there is in their heads too. And she give them plenty of reason to believe her, too. I mean, after a gink's seen a miracle, he's liable to believe who he seen the miracle happen to. After all, that's how Jesus got his followers, ain't it?

That last sermon she give us, she give it to us from the pulpit, and what she said was her new message she'd been giving to us all along but in pieces sos we could understand it. I mean there I sit in the front pew all by my lonesome, ceptings for the baby in my arms, and how was I to remember it all unless this last sermon was review, mostly. I mean, what she done in all the sermons is first she told us what she was going to tell us. Then she told us, what took about nine months. Final-like, in her last sermon, she told on what she'd told us, Miss Luda Corvus. First she was the Schoolteacher. Then she was the live-in preacher. Teacher. Preacher.

But this funny thing was happening in my head. When she were the Schoolteacher she were more like a preacher than the preacher she become, what was more like a teacher. And what she taught, I tried to teach a little of it to the Bear. We was in class right after I done to him what I done. I says to him it's all kind of like the geometry he'd been teaching us on. Say ifing, I says, you've got a mind and this is the mind. Then I drawed them all a circle on the blackboard. Now say that in the mind there is a picture of heaven and this is the only picture of it you ever seen. And I drawed him another circle inside the first. Now, I says, ifing the Father who art in heaven is in this second circle—and I drawed another little circle inside the other two circles—then what is bigger—the Father or the mind? The Bear, later he told me the reason he listened at first was on account of my circles was so perfect since I'd learned to draw so good, and it weren't till I'd said something else what she'd told us on that he really begun to believe how what I'd done to him was the most important thing in his life. I told him and the class how the Schoolteach-er talked on Cromangon Man and the Indians and how right it was to think a person ain't apart from the Earth but part of it. Now take something bad what happens to somebody else, I says. Now think on them standing there, bleeding. Now ifing you was to think of yourself as apart from the Earth, then you would think on them as apart too. And ifing they are apart from the Earth then they are apart from you. Now a man can jump, I says, but he always comes back down. And you can run from somebody bleeding but you can't run from a picture in your head of somebody bleeding. Once you have you that picture you can choose to be apart, but when you do that, blood has got to be on your mind. And unless you belong in the loony bin in Lawless, you don't like it one bit neither, even ifing that man is your enemy. And you don't like it none because it's happening to you, inside of you sos that you are part of it. Now, because you ain't crazy you want to stop the bleeding, but it ain't you that's bleeding. Let's say you can't reach the person who's bleeding. Do you act real ascared sos that you make him ascared of his own bleeding sos he tries to run from it and when he does his speeded up heart pumps out the blood faster? What you do is you use your will and your courage. You help the person stop bleeding sos the bleeding in you stops too. Now, how do you help him stop bleeding? Well, you've got to picture how. You've to will the picture, and once you done that, it cancels some of the bleeding in you sos you won't bleed more too. And the Schoolteacher, she said another thing, too. She said that beings the Father helps those who help themselfs, it weren't right for us to ask when we prayed, but instead we was to will. "Thy will be done," she said. She said, "World without end. Amen."

Now, while the Bear din't seem to have much problems with that, I want to tell you that it already upset a lot of apple carts in the congregation—mine too. I mean, how does a gink will his daily bread, I says to myself. And I asked her of it afterwards.

"Ask and you will receive," is that what she says to me.

"But you says not to ask," I says.

"Knowledge is power," was what she said, and me, she had me figuring on the Old Curiosity again.

Well, she knowed what she was doing, too. On account of there ain't nothing what perks the ginks' ears more than the curiosity about what's going on with somebody else's business, and the Schoolteacher she made it her habit to keep her business a mystery sos ever body knowed there was something going on in her outside too with her changing like she was so that she was looking more young and beautiful of a Sunday and her voice was getting softer, and, beings it was real strange-like it should happen, she had her even more authority. And like the ginks up at the shop said, it weren't no more that she was the boss of herself alone, but she was perfect for a president ifing we was to start our own country because what she was doing was giving up her authority and getting more. Not that she wanted it. It was just she seemed to know it was time for another hero, beings the Vetern could hardly be pictured no more cept by Floyd, and the trouble was, Floyd, he could remember all right, Lord Jesus, could he remember, but he couldn't draw worth a hoot none but a naked woman.

Me, beings I'd come to know her like I done, I din't feel like drawing much of anything of late, especial-like no gink, because ifing and when I'd do it, it'd remind me of the pictures I'd made of her what was hung on my wall what would just make me more lonesome for her on account of they was real sexy-like.

I don't know. Maybe my practicing on my table and geometry and basketball made me so tired-like there just weren't gumption enough for me to pick up a pencil of the middle of a night and draw with my eyes closed, but when I quit drawing in my sleep, it was maybe on account of I pretty much quit it when I was awake, though I couldn't quit all together, not with my long ago promise to her I'd draw.

Now the reasons I remember when I quit it in my sleep is two. One is I got me this long distance call what was person to person for Mr. Stick Cousins, what I din't like one bit so I hung up right away. But me, my curiosity'd got the best of me, and when the phone rings again, I take the call. Well, dumb me. Who else would it be but the Agent McMillion?

Well, the Agent, he was real nice and all, and he said he'd been reading about me in the papers. And when he said that, me, I got real ascared-like again, what I ain't been for two months, ever since the Friday night in the graveyard.

What I wanted to know was what I done wrong. Well, the Agent, he just laughed. He said it was what I done right. It made me kind of proud when he said they was all talking about me as a big basketball talent what the Barber never tells me till later that day, see, on account of he don't want me to get the big head like Floyd, what got soda in my nose. But there on the phone I got ascared when I figured on there was probable-like people staring at me in the stands and some was reporters.

Me, I want to change the subject, so I says, "Did you catch him yet?"

"No," he says, "but we will. He robbed another bank."

But the Agent, he din't want to talk about that none, beings he was just making a social call. But me, I ain't as dumb as I sound, and later I got to thinking on it that maybe he just up and figured like you might that ifing I had drawed a picture of the robber in my sleep even when I ain't had a good look at him, maybe I was drawing more pictures of that robber in my sleep, even though he was miles away. But no soap. I figures my drawing the robber in my sleep was maybe like I'd heard tell about a radio or a TV station sos that when you got far away from it you couldn't get the signal no more. Besides, I says to myself—and this was the number two reason I remember when I quit it in my sleep—I ain't drawed in my sleep since the night before the first scrimmage at the high school when I shot and the ball din't go through like my drawing said it wouldn't. Ceptings it final-like did. And beings it'd been so long since I drawed in my sleep and beings that when I done it, it weren't true what was to happen, I figures maybe my sleepwalking had been laid to rest. Pop, all he said was that that was a relief. That was the first point in a while him and me seen eye to eye on, I want to tell you.

I GOT TO thinking some on how that slow divorce Pop and me was getting was getting slower. I mean Pop, he told me in a round about way it weren't working out with the woman and her kids up by work. And the reason beings them three was little Dickenses. I told him on what Digger, bless him, says, that trouble it don't come but what it shows up in threes. Pop, he knowed that one, all right.

Well, Pop, he had some vacation time coming so what he done was he saved some of it up sos he could watch me at my basketball playing, what he said he liked a lot, beings I was becoming so famous and that were making him famous too, though what for he din't know. For a fact, it was him what was driving me to the Regionals in Lawless behind the school bus after we won the District tournament. The Bear, he din't seem to mind none, especial-like when I tells him I knowed I wouldn't feel so nervous-like ifing at least some of the surroundings I was in was familiar-like, like the inside of Pop's car with Pop in it when we got to Lawless. And beings Pop, he'd got to knowing how him and me wasn't as close as father and son could be, he up and asked of me ifing there was anybody else I'd like to take along. Well, it were the Schoolteacher who come to mind first, but I knowed, on account of I could tell it on Sunday, that she were with child, so I figured on how it wouldn't be such a good idea. So me, I said Bob the Barber first, knowing he was my biggest fan and all, but I'd right after the Schoolteacher thought on Nooner because I knowed ifing we was to get lost that he knowed his way around in Lawless good enough to get us found again. I'd've asked Digger, too, bless him, but I knowed he wouldn't go, beings how he was first in command since Pyro got creamated and there had to be somebody home to mind the store always, beings Termite was permanent-like out of town too. I'd've asked Floyd, but you already know he weren't no gink, but an adopted one, and I figures ifing we was to show him off in

Lawless, there'd be people mocking him, what weren't right coming from anybody but his own kind, I figured. Besides, I just knowed that the farther away he got kept from the loony bin, the better.

Well, we won on Tuesday night, and all the ginks just knowed that the team we was to play on Friday weren't nearly as good, beings they played smaller teams like us and they wasn't undefeated like us. Bob the Barber, he was even planning on how he was going to close up shop a couple days next week sos he'd make it in time for the tip-off at the Sectionals.

Me, I din't like that talk none, beings going to Lawless to play basketball is one thing, since I had my library card in that town, but going someplace else where I ain't never been before, where I knowed it would be big and full of people staring at you on account of the papers was all talking about you, was another thing. And I don't mind telling you none I was a little worried about the Schoolteacher, too. I mean, what was she going to do, beings she was in a family way like that? I mean, how was we to have a live-in preacher who was in the first place a woman and in the second place a woman what weren't married but about to have a baby? Ifing it weren't for the fact all the ginks knowed she were the boss of herself and had her her authority, I don't think I could've played basketball even on Tuesday. And there it was, of a Thursday, and there was ginks at the shop talking about me like I were a town hero when, ifing they'd've knowed it was part of me swelling inside her, they'd've knowed I was the Devil I thought I was, even ifing I din't really believe it she was with child, beings I sure din't feel or think like no future father what with no income to speak of, homework to finish, and basketball to play beings I couldn't let down the ginks or the rest of Freeland, where we was living an experiment, like the Schoolteacher said when we buried them three what tried to get them some authority by going contrary to nature and building theirselfs a machine the likes of witch ain't been seen anywhere but in the books I'd been reading on.

THE FUNNY THING, though, was I sort of seen how maybe the Schoolteacher's idea of a experiment was about as crazy as a Perpetual Motion Machine. I mean I hoped Freeland weren't about to be squashed too. And the more I thought on it, the more I knowed that machine was them three's idea of heaven here on Earth, what was like what the Schoolteacher wanted the congregation to think on, beings we was to will the picture of heaven in our heads into something others would see as just as good as heaven sos maybe there wouldn't be no need to think on another life but this life. I knowed that because it was part of her new message that I'd hear on Sunday. But what I din't know was how I was going to have me my concentration on my table, what was *my* heaven, ifing I knowed I was going to be a father before I even had me some practice at being a brother. And that made me so sad-like that there weren't no way for me to get right for the game the next night but to bust curfew and be with my stick and my table, beings I knowed there was my salvation, though I have to admit on I was beginning to have me my doubts about how a gink what chose to be a billiard player by trade, one who never bet no money on hisself and never would, on account of it would be like taking candy from a Floyd, could be a billiard player by trade. Even though I knowed I'd already become one in the future. Otherwise, there weren't no way I could be that good, because though I knowed I were good in basketball, my heart weren't in it because my future weren't. So I had me my faith and hope and I were thinking on maybe I'd need me my charity, what I already had some, since I had me my table, where a man could think, beings there weren't no radios around and nothing to make a gink ascared. The same weren't true for basketball, what with them pocket-sized radios and them people staring at you, and you knowing that ifing you was to slip up, they might have you in the loony bin in Lawless before it was over.

The more I practiced there on my table, the better I were feeling, till, me, I all of the sudden notice I done worked up a sweat of a Thursday in March when it weren't hot out or nothing—but dark. I knowed I'd been shooting fast, but I had no notion that fast. I says to myself I'd give just about anything for a Royal Crown, and then I'm thinking on the refrigerator there in the Masonic Hall, but there ain't no way I'm about to open it up, so I go over to the sink and take a drink from the faucet like it's July and I been making hay.

I spose it was the noise of the running water what wouldn't let me to hear him none when I seen his shadow out the corner of my eye, thinking on how it was way past curfew, specting to hear the growl, when I turned around and it weren't the

Bear atall. It were the Agent.

"I can't," I up and says to him like the one half of my brain knows why and the other don't.

The Agent, he's startled-like, you could tell, like a little kid just got his sucker pulled out his mouth from nowhere, him standing there with this blank look on his face and his pipe in his hand. Then he says, "I haven't even—"

"Oh yes, you has," I says. "The answer is no," I says, though I'm only half sure why I says it, though I'm real sure why it is I go over to my table and I set up a break shot. "Now just you watch this," I says.

Now me, I ain't trying to show off or nothing, but I just got to make my point. I had to show the Agent what I could do. So I run me about twenty straight points just as fast as I can, and then I stops, and I turn around.

I says, "Did you see that? Did you ever see anybody alive what can do that. Not even me. It weren't me you seen. That was me in the future. Only a man what's been doing this for years can shoot like that, and I ain't about to change it none. I've got and I'm going to have more things to think on. This is where I go. It's where I *will* go."

The agent, he don't say nothing. But he don't leave neither. I knowed he weren't about to leave, beings I knowed he weren't an F.B.I. man for nothing. "Stick," he finally said.

"No," I says. And I ain't looking at him neither. I'm sizing up my next shot.

"Stick," he says.

Me, I figured I made my message clear sos I wouldn't have to say nothing more.

"Stick," he says, "you'll have to hear me out."

Well, I knowed he was right. So I keep my trap shut. And the Agent, he talks. He tells me he believes me. He tells me he's shot some three cushion hisself. Then he says something that really sparks the Old Curiosity in me. The Agent, he was real smart, all right. He wants to know how a man is going to make a living shooting three cushion in Freeland.

Well, I din't miss the shot I was taking, like you might suspicion, since that there was the moment of truth, but the only reason I din't miss it is because I din't take it yet. Instead I was studying on that shot some when I knowed it was a natural, just like I knowed the Agent knowed it was a natural because he weren't saying nothing. Me, I just stepped back from my table, and I studied on that cue ball now, instead of the shot. Well, the Agent, he weren't saying nothing. He was just standing there. And me, I wanted to shoot, but I couldn't, beings all of the sudden I was thinking on my stick and then on my hands. For some queer reason they was reminding me of the Schoolteacher's hands, and I wanted to lay my head in them, beings I was so ascared, beings I knowed she was going to have a baby, though I din't believe it now, beings I knowed that her having the baby would change ever thing, would make it sos she couldn't just come running when I needed her like I needed her now because without her there was no way I could shoot that shot, a natural, and the Agent knowed it, I knowed, because the Agent, he weren't saying nothing. And I done something wholely contrary to my nature and out of my character, but I done it because there weren't nothing else I could do. I brung my stick so quick-like I din't even know I was doing it up over my head with both hands, and I brung it down and feel it snap over my knee but I never heared it snap like maybe it were a crack of lightning way off on the horizon.

Me, there I stand holding a piece of my cue in each hand like I'm waiting for the thunder to roll in, but it don't come. What come was the Agent's voice, only it ain't got no thunder in it, beings it was real quiet-like.

"Stick," he says.

I don't know that I answered him none.

"Stick, he's robbed again. In Lawless."

I din't want to hear it. "So what are you doing *here*?" I says.

"I need your help," he says, and that's the way he said it, and I knowed he was trying to make hisself my friend when he done it, but I also know in his voice he means it.

I tell him I ain't drawed nothing for a long time, ceptings faces at the shop. And besides, Lawless is too far away for my brain to pick up any signals. The way it turns out, that's exact why the Agent come to Freeland. He wanted me to go to Lawless. And then comes the kicker. He says he ain't got much time.

Well, when I heared him saying that, I know there's a fret coming on in my head on account of I heared him say that once before about a Banker what was a human being, even though he was from outer space. So, me, I ain't saying nothing.

"There's more," he says. "The robber spent time in prison."

I wanted to make like I din't hear him, and me, it was a dumb thing to do, but I started to walk around the room like I was looking for a wastebasket to dump my busted cue.

"Stick?" he says.

I don't say nothing.

"Stick, he's a child molestor too. He's got a little girl."

Well, me, beings I ain't real sure what a child molestor is, I'm thinking the worst, and all of the sudden I ain't pretending I'm looking for no wastebasket. I'm really looking for one. Then the Agent, he calls out my name again, and I get so mad-like inside I just throw the pieces of my stick into a corner and I look at him in the eye, and I'm ready to yell.

"What do you want me to do?" I says. "There's people being dead and disremembered all over the world and I can't stop it none. There's tornadoes what come and squash people too. What am I sposed to do? Sleep in a tornado alley sos I can draw people before they get killed? Besides, I ain't drawed in my sleep since what I drawed din't come true."

I'm really telling him off, all right. I guess I told him so good that he knowed it weren't no use to try to talk me into it, at leastways not now. And the Agent, he din't say nothing. He just went away and left me alone like he knowed what I wanted. But the Agent, he's smart too. I figured he's so smart that he knowed all he had to do was plant the seed in me. And that fret he planted, it backfired, I figures. It were growing so fast and big-like what it turned into was sleeplessness when all of the sudden I remembered on that I'd be in Lawless the next night and this night would be the most ascared I'd ever be, thinking on me, how I knowed I were a future father though I ain't believed it yet. How was I going to face all them faces tomorrow night what with reporters and transistor radios in the crowd when the gym weren't but a little ways from the loony bin? How the Schoolteacher was to help me when I need it, beings she wouldn't have time what with her baby and the live-in preacher's job they might not let her have. And me, how I'd be able to handle it ifing that little girl the robber took got hurt or dead when maybe I could've done something about it.

And there was what I owed to the ginks and the Bear. I couldn't go off with the Agent like I knowed he wanted. I had to get rest for the finals, what was sort of funny, beings I din't sleep a wink all night, not on my table, what I tried to do because I was so tired from bawling like I done when the Agent left, even though I knowed it'd feel sack-religious and contrary to my nature. And when I come home, there was Pop, and it done my heart good to know he was all in a dither about me staying out after curfew, what with him thinking, I spose, my fame was giving me the big head, but him yelling at me what was the first I could remember on for a long time and weren't like no lullaby neither, I want to tell you.

Ifing there were more to the story about that day before the big game what was actual-like two days all rolled into one, you know I'd tell you on it, but it just weren't to happen, beings I was like the zombies on the TV without any will of my own. What ate at me most on the inside sos I couldn't move on the outside was I kept thinking on that little girl, beings I was seeing Becky in her stead, and she weren't alive none. And I seen Nooner trying to tell his little girls how the Lord gives and the Lord takes away or some fool thing the grieving are want to say to the grieving, I knowed, because I heared it from my Pop. And I seen them little sisters of Becky's all crying and thinking they had a right to spit in the Lord's face. Then all of the sudden, towards dawn, I got me my pad and I laid in my bed and thought hard towards sleep, but it wouldn't come, for too many reasons I spose, but beings mostly because I knowed I wouldn't've drawed anything had it come, beings I was too far away and because it ain't something I can just make happen. Maybe there was that other thing of me like a zombie too. I mean who can make anything happen when there is a way but no will? Maybe that's why I couldn't even pray, what I pictured the Schoolteacher might've done. Maybe that's why I left her alone, though I knowed there was another reason, beings what she would've told me was to be brave, what I weren't brave enough to be.

So real sudden-like, it's Friday night in the gym in Lawless, and the team is warming up. I see Pop, Nooner, and Bob the Barber out of the corner of my eye what all got seats up front on account of we come early behind the bus, but I don't remember on us coming none. All I knowed is I ain't slept in two days. The only reason I'm awake, I figure, is I drunk me enough Royal Crown to keep me standing in front of the toilet for a week, beings the Barber cleaned out his machine for the trip before we come.

So we're doing these drills, you see, lay ups and stuff, and I got to go again real bad, so I tell the Bear it can't wait, and the Bear, he sends me down to the locker room. Me, I come out of the bathroom and there he stands, the Agent. He's got somebody with him, too, but I ain't about to look at her.

The Agent, he don't even give me time to think. "Stick Cousins, meet the mother of the little girl I told you about," and he told me her name.

Well, that Lady, you could tell she were a Lady, too, she stepped toward me, and what she done was she slapped my face so hard I din't feel it none till she had both my cheeks in her hands and she was up on her tip toes kissing the left side of my face what was both stinging and numb like a firecracker went off in your hand before you could get it throwed. Me, I just looked in her eyes what was swelled and red. And I looked at her mouth when it whispered, "Please, whatever you can do." And I watched her turn. And I watched her walk away.

The Agent, he din't move none, and I could tell he put his hands in his pockets and was looking down at the floor, even though I din't look at him none.

Well, we was standing there for a real long time without neither of us saying nothing. Finally, I heared myself ask, "What did you say her name was?"

"Johnson," he says, "Mrs. Stanford Johnson. Her husband is dead. She's very wealthy."

"And the little girl?" I says.

"Rebecca. She's almost ten. An only child."

Well, maybe I'm telling you the truth on that the name was Rebecca Johnson and maybe I ain't, because the mom, she never wanted their names in no papers, she was so ascared like that. And even ifing I was to tell you their real names, you wouldn't believe it none because you would say it was a lie. But when I heared their names it was the time I knowed someday I'd have to tell on this part of the story, that I'd have to tell it all true but their names, beings ifing I was to say their names, you'd tell me I was a liar. So what I done was I picked Stanford, I picked Johnson, and I picked Rebecca instead of Becky, sos you might think on this is a miracle and not far fetched, what it was. And the reason it were a miracle what their names was was on account of two things.

One I can't tell you about, and the other was I seen all of the sudden it would be necessary-like for me to tell you about my built-in antenna, even though I don't like talking about it none because ifing you was to know about it, you might say I did belong in the loony bin in Lawless. On account of, you see, I knowed these people real good sos you wouldn't believe me ifing I was to say they was like members of my own family ifing I never told you on my built-in antenna. They don't live in Lawless nor Freeland none, but they had a good reason for being in the bank when it got robbed. They probable-like was the owners of it.

I looked square at the Agent. "Ifing I was to help, would there be a reward?"

The Agent, he just up and said yes.

Well, I want to tell you that that just made me real mad-like and ascared that I even asked it of him. I mean there was the team, the Bear, and half of Freeland upstairs waiting for me to make them real proud-like, and here I was thinking on me and my table and at the same time thinking on that little girl and how she might be murdered to death and all, and I was the one who was sposed to find her. And I all of the sudden I knowed what Freeland would think ifing I was to walk out on them, and that was about what I was to do in my head. They'd think even ifing they knowed I was a future father that I weren't but a whore. I couldn't do it to the Schoolteacher. I'd to get me my concentration before a game back. So I just up and says to the Agent, no, I wouldn't help ifing there was to be a reward, though I knowed I would anyways, on account of the Schoolteacher, she wouldn't want me living with the picture of that little girl or the picture of the mom what was a lady's misery, even ifing Miss Luda Corvus knowed she had to take her own baby and move away, though there still weren't no way I believed she was with child, though I knowed it. And I runned up to the gym and before you knowed it the buzzer sounded and we was playing in the championship, and I seen the little girl what was the picture of Becky in my head and she weren't dead none, and Bucky gets the tip-off, feeds me on the baseline and I'm wide open and I shoot and I miss.

They tell me a whole minute goes by before Bucky could call time out, on account of it weren't us what got the rebound but the other team and they was so surprised to be playing again four and not five that the whole gym come to a hush what with the sound of the basketball stopped and the sound of my shoes walking off the court was all you could hear.

Well, the Bear, he was the first to come down to the locker room, and he don't say nothing at first because the Agent'd followed me down, him just standing there and me getting out of my jersey what seemed so queer-like that it come off so easy, beings I hadn't worked up a sweat, hardly. And the Bear, he come charging over, and I don't say nothing. I just keep undressing, and Agent McMillion, I seen him reach in his side pocket of his suit coat and he just holds up something at the end of his outstretched arm what is leather on the back what I figured was his badge on the front sos the Bear would see it, and the Bear, he stops short and he growls, "What in hell is happening here?"

Well, me, I got such a knot in my throat I can't talk or I'm going to start bawling.

The Agent, I heared him saying to the Bear that I don't *have* to do this, and I want to shout, "Oh, yes I do!" but my voice cracks before I can get it out, and pretty soon I look up and there's this terrible mess of people at the other end of the locker room—Pop and Nooner and the Barber and some others and it weren't till the Barber, who knowed the Agent pretty good, took over sos they all cleared out. And the Agent, he goes upstairs with them and then he comes back.

I asked him ifing the lady was outside or something and he tells me we should go to the Holiday Inn and that he fixed ever thing up with Pop and the ginks, that they'd be staying at the game in my stead.

Well, dumb me, I asked him ifing there was a bed somewheres in Lawless where I could lay down before I falled over. The Agent, he din't make fun of me or nothing. He just said he had him this pad just in case but would I mind ifing it was yellow and it had lines on the paper. Well, I told him not to worry because my pad was in my duffle bag.

I SLEPT so hard it hurt when I waked up to the siren on Digger's hearse, but I was so glad the Agent done like I asked that I got up real quick-like, and even though I was seeing stars and breathing real hard, I could see the Agent open the door for the Schoolteacher and then I seen Floyd's grin. They all come walking up to the room, and Digger, bless him, was carrying two suitcases.

The Schoolteacher, she come right in and put her hands on me, and I says to Digger not to worry because I had the F.B.I. man's promise nobody was going to stick Floyd in the loony bin. But me, I figured I had to have Floyd there ifing we was to have a recording secretary, like the Agent said we oughta, while people talked and I listened because I din't trust myself none to get the facts straight sos I could help the Agent and his men find Rebecca because they already found the loot and the robber, dead like he was, beings his head got squashed on a stop sign when he got throwed from his car when the police seen it and they chased it. And Digger, bless him, I could tell he were glad that was one accident what is out of his jurisdiction.

Real sudden-like I remember on my pad and I run and check it but it's blank. But still it was the middle of the night sos I asked of the Agent ifing we could get started.

Well, there must've been about ten people who come into that room in the next two hours by theirselfs, cept the lady, she din't come none because she was too exhausted, the Agent said, what was all right because Rebecca's nanny was with them when the little girl got snatched by the robber on account of he got ascared when he'd heared a siren what weren't but a firetruck siren anyways. That nanny, she come in the room first and she was like all them others when she got a look at Floyd what was sitting in his chair on the wall. Ifing you'd've been there you might've thought like I thought all them people thought when they first come in the room that Floyd were the psychic they was to talk to, him with his biggest-head-you-ever-did-see and a brain inside of that head. But nobody mocked him none, even ifing he din't say nothing with his grin on. But I got to thinking on it. Why would they mock him when there was the Agent and three of us Freelanders in that room, beings we was shy one of us, since Digger, bless him, he felt sos he should get back to Freeland sos he could mind the store. Now that I think on it, the nanny must've thought she got her the wrong address and was at the loony bin, what with Floyd's big brain taking it all in like a sponge, the Agent apacing and puffing on his pipe while he was asking questions to fill me in, and me laying in the Schoolteacher's lap with her hands on my forehead and the back of my neck and me glancing out the corner of my eye ever so often at first to see ifing she showed with child when she was sat down on the bed. Witch she did, but sos only a future father would know, though I din't believe it none till July. And the Agent, beings he was as smart as he was, he notices something about halfway through all the people I was listening on, because he just kind of looked over at us and I could tell he was staring at the Schoolteacher, and all of the sudden he says to her, "My God, you look beautiful in this light." Me, I din't get jealous or nothing because I look up and studies on that mouth of hers what ain't opened since we been there and what was smiling, and I knowed what the Agent said was the truth and the way he said it was the way you might've said it ifing you would've seen the painting of the Blessed Mother she done herself and what hangs across of the one of The Last Supper in the church basement. Me, I felt so free of my troubles, laying there in her lap, that I says to myself, it wouldn't surprise me none ifing sudden-like I was to believe as good as I knowed that she were with child and the child she was carrying were the seed of the mother and the healer.

Final-like, we was all done listening and it were time for me to do some asking, so me, I go to the wizard, not that I don't trust the Agent none, but he ain't got a head big enough to house a reel of tape like one other person in that room's got.

"Floyd," I says. "Did the robber go west?"

It were good to hear another voice from Freeland again. "Yep," he says.

Well, me, I'm too sleepy, sos I up and ask of Floyd, "Did that one policeman say it was a crossroads or a 'T' where the robber got his head squashed?"

Well, Floyd, he don't say nothing.

So I ask again but this time I ask of him the right way and what I found out, it was a "T" where the robber had his accident but it were a crossroads where the policeman caught sight of him first.

"Floyd," I says, "did the policeman say the robber had him his beard?"

"Nope."

All of the sudden I find myself studying on Floyd's head real hard, beings I couldn't remember none whether the policeman said anything about a beard or whether the nanny or the teller did. "Floyd, did the robber have him his beard?"

"Nope," was the voice of the wizard.

"So the Barber and me was right," I says.

Well, I din't spect Floyd to say nothing then, but Old Floyd, he just up and said, "Yep."

"What are you talking about?" the Agent says.

I tell the Agent I figure the robber weren't living around here, because ifing he was he wouldn't've growed hisself a beard to rob Freeland because Lawless has got *The Letter* what carries Freeland news, and the news would be full of a bearded robber.

"So where does that get us?" the Agent says.

So I tell him I figure ifing the robber was to murder a little girl it would be somewhere where there weren't no buildings on account of buildings lots of times has people around them and the robber, ifing he din't live around here wouldn't know what buildings din't have no people around them of a Thursday morning.

The Agent, he told me I was right about one thing, they knowed the robber weren't living around Lawless. But he told me I was wrong about another thing.

"What?" I says.

He tells me there's no way we know the little girl is dead. "After all," he says, "Nazareth has never killed any of his victims."

Now I want to tell you when I heared on that name Nazareth that's about all I heared for the next minute. Me, I keep looking at the Agent, beings I was ascared of looking up at the smile on the face of the Miss Luda Corvus what I all of the sudden wondered again ifing she weren't a witch. Real slow-like my breathing starts on skipping a beat and my heart is squirming in my chest like a caught fish in your fist.

I can't even talk none, I know, but I don't even try on account of the more my breathing gets crazy with being ascared the harder the Schoolteacher's hands is pressing on my head and neck. Right then and there, I know, was my first asthmatic attack I ever felt. The only thing I could think on was maybe the Schoolteacher din't hear the Agent none sos she could be innocent of that smile I sense out of the corner of my eye. Me, I begun to calm down a bit when I thunk on I was safe in her hands ifing she knowed what I thought maybe she knowed, that the Nazareth the Agent was talking on were not only the bank robber but the same Vetern what disappeared and what maybe was the cause of her powers of healing.

But then I thought on how that would make him a dead Vetern even ifing he weren't a hundred years old, beings he got his head squashed. So what's she doing smiling ifing she is smiling, what I can't say for sure never ifing I'm not to have the gumption to look. So I look. Lord, I'm saying to myself, what a beautiful smile, and all of the sudden my asthmatic attack ain't. It just up and vanishes.

Well, me, I says to the Agent after about fifty years of quiet from me I want to be alone with the Schoolteacher and my recording secretary some.

Well, the Agent, he obliges me, but a lot of good it done me what with me sandwiched between a smile on one side and a grin on the other and no words what would come out her mouth but, "Charles, you must sleep."

When final-like I waked up, the first thing I seen was her eyes what was her eyes and Mom's eyes and the eyes of ever woman you ever laid eyes on, I spose. They was crying-like. First off, I think it must've just hit her the Vetern was gone forever, but then I seen it weren't sad crying atall but the weeping you seen in a woman what was just about as happy as she could be sos you were sure there was wedding bells aringing some place. I look down at what she's looking at, and I see a camera-took picture what seems funny where it is in my pad what she's holding.

The way it turns out I been walking and talking in my sleep and I don't even know it none. The walking I done, it were apacing back and forth asking of Floyd questions what I done in a real hypnotized voice the Agent said, on account of he comes back to the room after I been asleep for a spell on account of there weren't nobody to come and get him back. So I says to the Agent what time is it. And the Agent, he tells me it were dawn before I asked of the Schoolteacher any question what he fell asleep on before he heared on the answer. The Schoolteacher, she weren't talking none now, but I figured on I'd said questions she used the Vision of the Flock to answer on, on account of it were dawn before I asked and on account of the Agent, I just up and asked him ifing he had trouble in his mind because she were so beautiful, and he says all she done was stare at the wall, her smile gone, only she weren't really staring with her eyes going ever witch way and her head still while I'm saying on something about is there any beaches around these parts.

But what I ain't told you on is how I got me a case of the Old Curiosity when I seen that photo in her lap what for the most briefest instant I first thought were a newspaper she were holding in her lap but it was really my pad.

Now that picture, it weren't a picture atall. I drawed it. I made it little on account of I done it real meticulous-like, the Agent said. Me, I'm up on an elbow and I leans over and says to the Schoolteacher, what's that?

Well, the Agent, he remembered on what she called it and so does the recording secretary, but not me, on account of I never heared of no hyperrealism what the Agent and me each in our own curiosity looked up later when I found out I din't disremember dreams no more but remembered on what was coming out of my pencil. And the hyperrealism what I looked up in books in Lawless, they say it don't exist none. Only we figures it don't exist none *yet*. And the Agent, he talked on how I was a pioneer and all.

By now, after the Schoolteacher were done on saying what manner of drawing I done, her crying faucets was turned all the way on and she looks so beautiful I knowed it'd be a sin to turn them off just sos I'd have me my curiosity satisfied, but I says it anyways, "I don't mean what *manner* of drawing did I draw."

Then there was the Agent with his curiosity looking over her other shoulder, and him, he says on how it looks like there was a car dealership parked in front of a hill where the Earth had a bite took out of it. But we'd probable-like to blow it up sos to be sure. Well, dumb me, I says something like, how are you going to be sure ifing you're to drop a bomb on it?

Somehow the Agent, he took a picture of my picture and he made it bigger sos you could see what I drawed weren't no new cars and a hill but old cars and a hill what were a double exposure, and it first turns out what I drawed weren't one picture but two. And what I kept thinking on was when I seen it big it were like the hill were a ghost of itself or the cars was like a ghost of themselfs or they was both ghosts. And knowing as I done that trouble it don't come but what it comes in threes, I figure there was three pictures there, so I says to the Agent, I says, do you spose you could take you some pictures of parts of this big picture?

"What on Earth for?" he says. Then he looks up at me full in the face for about five seconds. I don't know what he seen, but what he does is he just rolls up his picture and leaves again.

Well, me and the Schoolteacher and Floyd, we had us some room service, but there weren't none of us could eat what with the Schoolteacher still crying, Floyd with his grin gone and crying too, and me thinking on that little girl what ain't even had breakfast yet, ifing she could still swaller with her throat.

Pretty soon the Agent, he come back, and the pictures, they was real magnified-like, and it was like they was pictures of sand, and me, I says, "That figures."

The Agent, he says, "Why do you say that?"

Me, I says, "What?"

The Agent, he just gets kind of ornery-like, and it looks like he's about to have him a *can*iption fit when we hears the echo what is in my voice, and we can't hear the Schoolteacher's crying no more sos we turn to Floyd what is like a crying statue in the corner since dawn till now what is a statue what is grinning, and the Agent says to Floyd, "What did Stick say?"

Just like you was talking to the Vetern's monument, Floyd he don't say nothing.

Now I knowed the Agent ain't forgot the code none, but it were like he was about to prove a point, on account of he got tomato red in the face what I figure ain't no mad red but murder red, and he begun yelling on how he weren't playing no games and he din't have no more time and it were me, not him, not Floyd, not the Schoolteacher, not the walls, not the Almighty what said *sand* and what said *it figures.*

Well, I couldn't help it none sos I just start bawling sos maybe we'd have us a trio before it was over. But it weren't no trio on account of Floyd, his bawling were but a carbon copy of mine sos there's a duo so loud now with one half what has got reverberation sos I can't hardly hear Wally Phillips none, and the other half is the Schoolteacher, even though she's up off the side of the bed and she's got her hands on me tight-like.

Soon as she done that, it were like I disremembered I couldn't remember on the sand.

"Agent McMillion," I says, "either I'm seeing things, or is there specks where there oughta be sand on them blowups?"

Well, the Agent, he agreed on they was specks of some sort but they was more like specks and streaks.

Well, me, I don't know what to make of it all, so I just up and asked of the Agent how come he weren't taking us to the junkyard, and the Agent, he says how can he take us to the junkyard when there ain't one in Lawless what's got old time cars what are intact and shining like the Dickens. And the Agent, all of the sudden, he's got an idea, you could tell, on account of his look—though it weren't but a second or two—and he bolts out the door. Pretty soon he's back and panting and herding the three of us in his car. What the Agent done was look up antique dealers in the phone book, ring up the first in the list, and we was on our way out of town.

What we seen when we got there was cars what was took care of real good. There was thirteen on account of I counted. And in the thirteenth one I counted what was bare on the inside and had some real tall weeds growing around it was where a man'd been for a time and then some. We just knowed.

When I heared on that sigh of satisfaction what come out of the Schoolteacher what had her nostrils flared and taking big breaths, I knowed what I had to do. Either we was going to find ourselfs in the loony bin or we was going to be heroes. Me, I couldn't stand the suspense no more, so what I says to the F.B.I. man was we got to go and we got to go fast. And I says to the F.B.I. what I figured the Agent, he was the boss of in these parts, what happens ifing I leads them to the little girl and she's kidnapped and dead, and the F.B.I. knows I knowed where she were. Ain't they going to think it were me what were the Vetern's accomplish?

The Agent, he just looks at me like I'm speaking in tongues. So I says to the Agent never mind and tells the Agent, drive, beings Floyd is in the front seat sos I can whisper my business to the Schoolteacher. Only it turns out I don't need to on account of when I says *drive*, the Schoolteacher, she just puts her hands on my neck and forehead like I knowed my head would glow when she let go, and what I had, I had my first real glimpse of the Vision of the Flock.

Now maybe you're wondering on why it were the School-teacher couldn't just up and tell where that little girl was. Well, the way I figure it is, the reasons, they was two. First, she don't really know on account of it were me what drawed the double exposure of used cars what was like new and a hill what got a bite took out of it. Second, ifing the Agent heared her telling on it, then the F.B.I. would've knowed either she were a psychic and her secret would be spoilt or that she were the Vetern's accomplish. And she couldn't risk that none, not with her and her new message to tell us on yet. And maybe there were something else, a reason maybe I shouldn't tell you on, sos you won't think on she did belong in the loony bin since we was just outside of Lawless anyways. But it was like her tongue got took from her ever since I heared that sigh in her breathing. Only it din't really. On account of she had stuff to tell me later like it were the Vetern what kidnapped Becky and even her, the Miss Luda Corvus, when she were a little girl.

Now I spose you been wondering on that little girl some, but me, I told me enough stories and heared the Barber tell enough to know you don't go telling on the ending before you told on the beginning some. Well, believe it or don't believe it, whatever you want, but I'm going to talk on the beginning some more right now. The little girl what is Becky what maybe it is and maybe it ain't her name none, she were still alive. I knowed because I seen her, just a flash out of the corner of my eye, and I ain't talking none about when we found her neither. And I ain't talking about the Vision of the Flock what I were using to steer the Agent through the country roads until we come to a dirt road I says to the Agent to go down. And the

Agent, he were real mad at hisself on account of he said he forgot to ask of any Lawless locals where there might be a sand pit in these parts because he's so excited on that he could figure out where the used car dealership what weren't really a dealership atall could be.

But it din't make no difference what with him having radar in the back seat of his company car, I figures. Besides, leave it to the Agent, ifing there's a way to do something sos he can test out your powers, he can't help hisself none even when it comes to finding little girls what got kidnapped. Now, I ain't saying he weren't the best F.B.I. man you ever did see, but what I'm saying is ifing the Agent, he's got him his faith and hope in you, then he's one F.B.I. man what is going to go with his hunch.

Anyways, the way it turns out, this were a sand pit what ain't had a bucket of sand took out of it for fifty years, you could tell on account of we come to a dead end on the dirt road, and there weren't no sand but in some muddy tracks what a car recent got stuck in, the Vetern's car, I figures, on account of all of Lawless forgot on that sand pit being there, ceptings they din't forget about the dirt road what was the Lawless lovers' lane. I spose nobody come to wonder none on where that road really went because there was trees and bushes and stuff where it come to a dead end, and ifing you was to know the road were a lovers' lane then that there ought to be reason enough to think on that's where the road would go. I know on account of I seen a rubber.

But the Agent ain't seen one none yet, him too busy ducking when there weren't nothing to duck because the branches, they was hitting the windshield, not us. So when we come to the dead end what was all growed over, the Agent, he just up and said something I ain't about to repeat.

Me, I just quick get out of the car and start walking the road what weren't a road no more, and the Schoolteacher, she come up behind. And I heared them all right, the calls what was the streaks on the pictures of the picture what weren't really a picture but what I drawed in my sleep. And then I heared another call what would be the cry of Old Crow. And me, I pick up the pace some, and I knowed the Schoolteacher, she were right behind me on account of she weren't afraid of nothing, even though she were sniffling some and crying I knowed, because me, I keep looking over my shoulder, not wanting to leave her behind in the brush without a handker-chief or nothing, and I ain't seeing her. I mean I'm seeing her but not her in her face. In her face I'm seeing the girl what her name might be Becky. There ain't no way the Schoolteacher's face could've looked that young were it not Becky, and what I seen was, as we get closer to them streaks what is calling and flying ever witch way over the trees, I seen the Schoolteacher's face changing with my own eyes and changing faster until we get to the clearing some and I look at her and it ain't her face atall no more but of that little girl I ain't even seen. And it were the most beautifulest sight you ever did see, and me, I weren't ascared one bit, but instead I had me my second asth-matic attack so bad sos even with her hands on me like they was, what was the Schoolteacher's hands, you could tell, and not Becky's, me I up and pass out some. And when I come to, I seen first the specks what I seen in the drawing I drawed of cars in front of a hill what got a bite took out of it, and what they was I don't know yet until I seen me up in the sky birds what weren't crows none but was crissing and crossing ever witch way and darting on account of they was little birds what was coming out then returning to the specks what was their holes they made nests in the face of the cliff what was all sand. They was calling too. And it seems like they was ever kind of little bird on Earth on account of each had his own piece to sing what was different than the others.' And when I blinked because I know I ain't seeing double of what is one face on each side of me, beings one ain't got a big head and the other ain't got a pipe in its mouth, I knowed I was privy to another miracle on account of there weren't no mirrors in that sand pit and there was the Miss Luda Corvus on the one side of me with the face of Becky on the other side of me with the face of Miss Luda Corvus. The faces, they was identical twins. Ceptings the one twin, she were a lot older, and the other twin, she were a lot younger. You could tell because one was the face what melded perfect with the body with womanly parts, and the other face melded perfect with the body of a little girl. Both was smiling. Both was crying at the same time with the same eyes what kept up changing color. And the woman with the hands what was on my neck and forehead, she just let go and puts her hands on the face of her twin, and they both changed to who they was before.

And that little girl, she weren't murdered with her throat cut or nothing, so me, I start in bawling too. Pretty soon Floyd come along, and he's bawling, and when the Agent finally come, I seen tears in his eyes too.

There weren't no way she'd breathe such a notion as Anarchtopia yet what with reporters what showed up off and on in town and come to get the story about the psychic what lived in Freeland and what were the whole town's adopted son, but mostly the Schoolteacher's what was real camera shy sos she wouldn't allow no evading her privacy. Me, I weren't too hot on having my privacy evaded none neither, but leave it to Bob the Barber, he up and figures I can make me my retirement speech from basketball on account of my asthmatic attacks was coming real often. And me, this is the perfect time for me to hang my shingle ifing I'm to be a billiard player by trade, he says. But them reporters what showed up to the news conference, they wasn't interested none in my game. They want to know what a gink were. So I tell them on it. And before, they want to know all how I drawed in my sleep. Well, me, I din't have them any answers, so the Agent, he takes over. And he tells them on what you probable-like been working up a question on yourself on account of I knowed *I* was. The trouble is what he knowed about my powers don't amount to a hill of beans, he says hisself. All he knowed was what he seen: The robber, he were dead with a squashed head.

Charles—that's me—he located the sand pit. And the little girl, she was unharmed. Well, me, I knowed what he were talking about on that last part on account of I weren't a farm boy for nothing. But I couldn't believe it one second, not while I knowed what the Schoolteacher herself told me on. That the robber and the Vetern was one in the same. And the little girl, she'd be carrying the seed of the father of the healer what would be birthed and be my relation someday.

"But she ain't old enough," I say to the Schoolteacher.

"Just like I'm not young enough," she says.

Well, me, I've to admit she's got her her authority still, even ifing she ain't hardly talking none after that, saving her breath for her final sermon, I spose.

Them reporters, though, they weren't saving their breath for nobody. But the Agent, he knowed how to handle them. Pretty soon they was all talked out on account of they got met up with Bob the Barber what told them all they was a bunch of quacks, he knowed, on account of he din't read the *Post Dispatch* for nothing. And on account of couldn't they see they had them the story of the century ifing they was to just open their eyes and see me shoot billards. And the Barber, he gets into a big fight with them on how he ain't trying to dictate the news but they is.

I spose when you think on it it weren't the Barber what talked them out of town as much it was they already had them the facts. The facts was the robber had a squashed head and nobody really knowed where he come from, ceptings the Schoolteacher what they din't know. And me. But I ain't about to rent me no rubber room in Lawless by telling them on nothing, let alone the truth. Then there was Becky, and her mom din't let nothing get out but Becky weren't hurt none what the Agent knowed was probable-like a lie from the mom's look at it on account of Becky, she ain't been so happy in her life what with the look of satisfaction always on her face. Still, the mom, she were glad to have her daughter back, and what she done was she set up a trust fund.

Well, it takes me a good long while to figure on what that means. And me, beings I still ain't too hot on strangers, I don't like it none for another long while when the agent tells on the terms. The terms, they was two. Me, I'm to have me my table and my income sos I can be a billiard player by trade, ifing I give exhibitions when I get growed up and take a name what ain't Stick but more dignified-like. Well, I says to the Agent, ain't no gink what is going to call hisself Charles Q. Cousins when that ain't a gink name, sos she can forget it. Well, the Agent, he does him some negotiations, and the lady, she figured she were in the wrong so she don't hold me to it.

Two, ifing I'm to have me my income, me, I've to help the Agent till I'm twenty-one ifing there's any little girls what got lost or kidnapped or anyone else or ifing the Agent needs me. And the Agent, he were the boss of the fund.

Well, I goes to the Schoolteacher real mad-like, and I says to her, the Agent, he don't play fair. But the Schoolteacher, she just real gradual-like smiles her biggest smile, and I knowed I weren't going to get no sympathy from her now nohow, beings she were still the Schoolteacher she always were even ifing she were our live-in preacher with child, I knowed, even though I still din't believe it none even when I seen with my own two eyes she were in a family way, so I goes to the ginks, and pretty soon they was all calling me Crime Stopper, even the Barber and Nooner, ceptings Digger, bless him, and Floyd, beings he's an adopted gink, and he ain't got no say anyways.

But them reporters, there weren't no gink in Freeland what was about to tell them on the trust fund on account of I want it kept to a whisper. Me, I ain't even decided whether I can help no Agent what is so sly like a fox he up and tells all the ginks on the terms sos to make them think I oughta retire my stick and check in a permanent resident of the Hotel Lawless ifing I'm to say no. Or ifing I'm chicken.

So I says to the ginks I knowed I got Free Will on account of I still live in Freeland, just like they done. And me, I figure the Law of Averages says somebody's got to be put to the test once in the while. Sos they shouldn't oughta be prodding me none ifing they knowed what's good for them. On account of what ifing I *was* to accept the terms. Maybe I'd stick around sos to put money in all their pockets sos we could start us a bank in Freeland.

Well, me, I get this idea. What I says to the Agent when he next called were, what ifing I was to say to the lady I got me some terms too? And what I says is, I says, ifing the lady was to buy the bank in Freeland and let me tell her on who the board of directors oughta be on account of they ain't got better reason to want it to fly than they love Freeland, beings they is the boss of themselfs and never want to be the boss of nobody else, then me, I'd accept her terms ceptings the one about me calling myself some such as Charles Q. Cousins. And I says I ain't no dummy sos I knowed it'd have to be somebody else what is the president of the bank on account of who I got in mind ain't going to have time to run it none what with their business to keep, even banker's hours being what they is, but what's important is they be the bosses sos they could hire and fire the presidents. And I says to the Agent, them what I got in mind is ginks: one a barber, one a undertaker, one a bulldozer operator, and one a recording secretary on account of trouble it don't come but what it shows in threes.

Well, that lady, I spose she had her some Free Will too even ifing she don't live in Freeland, and she had to think on it some, but not any longer after she heared on the School-teacher's final sermon what the lady got an invite to, the Agent said, though you couldn't prove it by me because I din't see nobody there with no disguises. Not even no Agents. And no reporters neither, though they was there, but me, I'm sitting in the front pew with my new baby girl in my arms, sos now when I think on it I can say I was more *here* than I was *there*, and all of Freeland is spilling out the other pews in the aisles and out the door, and you don't think much on who'd be behind you when your new baby girl what you never seen and got set in your arms just now is cooing and you're about to be witnessing you a miracle on account of the Miss Luda Corvus what were your mother's mother's mother, though she weren't too, and what were the Schoolteacher, she din't lie none never, especial-like on Sunday last.

And that other lady, that mother of that little girl what had the look of satisfaction always on her face, even when it weren't inherited, you knowed, on account of that lady always had the look of being ascared on her face, what that lady done was say yes, all right, she'd buy the bank, what is another story, although it ain't really, on account of ifing we was to have us a little of the old Anarchtopia, then we'd have to have us a bank.

The funny thing is them bloodhounds for the news, what the Barber hisself calls them to their face nowadays, never has caught on who it is what owns our bank, beings the Agent says the lady's got her name so buried in paper there ain't even a F.B.I. what could dig it out. And you can bet there ain't no member of the board of directors what is going to whisper that secret neither, unless it be a recording secretary what has a delayed reaction echo. Even then them reporters is not about to figure it out on account of they got them a bigger story to always wonder on since some of them seen the miracle with their own eyes and some of them even got the proof what is in the pictures what got took of it that the Barber says ain't no editor would believe, he knowed, since he ain't never seen them pictures in the *Post Dispatch*, though he did see one what must have got took and doctored by some loony from Lawless or someplace like it on account of it were sposed to be something from outer space, what he don't believe in nohow.

"Bob," I says, "*I* believe in U.F.Os."

"What?" he says. "You mean to tell me you ain't learned nothing from her sermon, you who's the principal instrument."

"Wait, I says. "You din't never hear me say I believed in rocketships none. All I'm saying is there's some things what you just can't figure out on account of, like she says, there ain't science enough what can esplain it all. Take them U.F.Os., for a fact. I figures just because they're unidentified that don't mean they're giant saucers what took wing. But I'll tell you another thing, there sure as heck are some people what is from outer space, and me, I figure the Law of Averages says some of them got to be reporters."

Well, the Barber, he din't take issue with that none and neither did Nooner. And I knowed full well ifing they was to know me and Wally Phillips was like Siamese twins sharing the same brain—cept I don't know ifing he can hear me on account of I never heared him use my name on the air—that here is one Barber and one Nooner what would agree there is finonenema-like—and I ain't talking no miracles—what is like the Schoolteacher says in the sermon when she said to Horatio, the gink what runs the filling station, there's more things in heaven and Earth than is dreamed on in his philosophy. I spose, too, what she means is there's things what ain't real yet but is about to be real, just like you might say it weren't Edison what invented the light bulb but it were Edison what found the light bulb. And me, I was figuring on the Miss Luda Corvus, the light bulb she found was the old Anarchtopia.

OLD CROW, I seen him that morning, I seen him the morning of her last sermon, the morning I come to believe as good as I knowed she were with child. I seen him sitting on the charred wood what was shiny black as him the day before when the Schoolteacher had me out to the parsonage, her smile turned on still, that look of satisfaction she wore always like it were the most beautifulest mask that weren't a mask you ever did see, and what she done was she told me to get on my bike and find some firewood. Well, me, beings I don't know where there's any deadwood, I pedal over to Nooner's and ask of him ifing I can have some of the beaver lodge what is hanging in the trees and ain't rotten. Well, Nooner, though he ain't inherited all that much of the Old Curiosity, still, he wants to know how come.

"For the Schoolteacher," I says.

"Yeah?" he says.

"Yeah," I says.

"Well how come?" he says.

I says I don't rightly know, but maybe it's for the miracle.

Nooner, he just shrugs and he says, "Take all you want."

Well, when I get back to the parsonage on my bike, I'll be danged ifing I din't have me the surprise of my life when I seen the Schoolteacher in her most familiest way I ever seen what is all covered in buckskin and beads. And what she done was she builds a cooking fire right near Mom's and Baby Sis's stones, right on the lawn. And what I done while she was cooking something I ain't never smelt but what I knowed it would taste good, what with some kind of herbs in it, was I drawed her like she asked. And while I drawed her some more—it were like I couldn't stop on account of I couldn't get enough down what with her face, beings it were a little new to me—she cleaned up. And she says to me flat out I was to always remember on to clean up the mess before the meal.

Well, I says how come she's telling me on that and not on the Vetern, on account of I want to know more, like what he done with the money he stole, did he give it to the poor people? Is there Indians what needed it? And what about Becky with the look of satisfaction always on her face too? Does she really carry the seed too? And ifing another healer is to be born, who's going to be sick and what part of them needs doctoring?

She weren't about to tell me none, I knowed, on account of she never answered questions you asked direct any more, like she don't even belong in Freeland no more, beings she's on the reservation on her mind, I spose. And there was always a flock of questions I had, like don't it bother her none the Vetern got a squashed head and the place where he got it too, it were real close sos it'd be natural-like ifing he was buried here sos she could take care of him? No, all she done was she smiled.

Well, like I says, Old Crow, I seen his black satin, and I knowed she were looking at me, but I go towards him a little and he up and raises his wings, and just when you think he ain't got flap enough in them, he lifts off the pile of charred wood what was some of it green before it got burned and turned real black. And what I seen was the ashes flying theirselfs and the charred twigs and bits of wood sos it's like some terrible critter what sneaked up on him and some of his feathers got left on account of a fight—feathers what was really charred wood, shiny as coal in the sun. And that's where I lose Old Crow—in the sun.

On account of that, I ain't seeing so good when I go inside, but me, I know my way to the front pew what is the spot on the left side of the aisle I sit of late since she were in a family way. Me, I like it better up there beings there ain't nobody but me ever on account of ginks'll stand on the stoop outside rather than be in the front pew, I spose, and beings I ain't got distraction of my ears and since it weren't like I weren't her best pupil or nothing. And besides, there's got to be somebody to tell you on all this.

Well, me, I still got this blind spot in my eyes, trying to read on her program what is mimeoed herself, even, and I only seen there was a baptismal and the name of the sermon what was "Earth as It Is in Heaven." After I stares at the back of my eyelids for near-like a minute, all of the sudden I heared a hush what was even our organ lady what stopped too. And when I'm thinking on why it were that she, the Miss Luda Corvus, wouldn't put down in the program the miracle what she says the week before was to happen and when, I seen something to my right remembering me on the barber's pole, and I look up towards the alter what is standing before it the same Luda Corvus who's our live-in preacher what has the smile and the eyes, even ifing she does have blood all over her white dress and smells like a birthing, on account of I weren't a farm boy for nothing, and with a naked baby in her arms sos you could see it's a girl with the most thickest, wettest black hair sos you knowed it just got birthed.

And what she done was she walks down the aisle with a baby in her arms, sos to show her off I spose, and she comes back up front and stands in front of me and says straight in my face with eyes what is ever woman's and a smile what is her own, "And what shall this child be named?"

Me, I heared there's a hush still and I says something what I don't know I'm saying till I hears the echo what is coming way back behind me and what is in my voice when it says, "The child shall be named for its mother."

What Miss Luda Corvus done then was kiss the junior

Miss Luda Corvus Cousins on top of her hair so gentle-like there weren't no need for Ludy to wake none nor stir when she got set in my arms, my own little girl what is my baby sis too on account of Pop, he's raising her like she were his own, witch she ain't. But that, that's another story, though it ain't really, beings it's the story of how Pop and me, we put us a hold on the slow divorce we was getting on account of the School-teacher, she give us her books that was real valuable-like and made a trust fund with Digger, bless him, sos Pop ain't had to work none but changing diapers and boiling bottles for near-like two years now, the best two years of his life, I heared him say hisself to the Barber just like he were no different than the other ginks what is now all the boss of themselfs. On account of they seen it too, the miracle what weren't the birthing atall but what was about to get started, you just knowed, by the way she put on her robe-I-ain't-even-seen-yet and what was draped and laying beside me over the pew where I'm sitting with the baby what I believed was there in my arms as good as I knowed she were. And bless Baby Luda, she were such a good baby and still is, asleep when she's sposed to be asleep, even though me, I start on bawling, knowing as I done it it were the Schoolteacher's hands I wanted but she weren't about to give them to me none sos I would learn to be the mother and the healer what heals hisself as good as somebody else.

Well, like I says, the Schoolteacher, what she had to say on she already said before. Only beings she were the School-teacher, she said more. Lucky for us we had us a photographic-remembering recording secretary anyways, I spose, on account of you'd maybe never hear on what she said anew ifing we din't have one, beings folks and ginks say it's my place to tell on all this sos when I ain't got all the details I take me some notes and asks questions of The-One-Who-Knows-and-Ain't-About-to-Forget beings he's so ascared while he's sitting there, the Barber says, him with his big head and all like maybe he feels stuff a lot more than the rest of us put together on account of *it*, his brain like a sponge what ifing you was to squeeze it it'd be full of facts and tears, and he's got him what Bob the Barber says hisself is a aversion to ladies, at least ones what got their clothes on or is about to put them on or take them off. Not that the Schoolteacher was about to do neither once she got her robes on. No, hers were one set of clothes what was about to get hung in the closet for good, beings you was to think there's air what's got a door in it sos like on a cartoon you could open the air and hide inside and the door would disappear when you closed it. Ifing then you was to swaller the key.

On account of that's what our live-in preacher done, ceptings the Agent, he calls it spontaneous human combustion what ain't a miracle, he figures, beings it's happened to people in the newspapers before, unless you was to maybe draw it perfect in your sleep before it happened or tell on the hour it were to happen without telling on *what* was to happen sos not to kill suspense none.

Well, me, I ain't drawed nothing. Ifing I had, I probable-like wouldn't be sounding so surprised now when I tell you on how it was her face looked, smiling and all afire. But not before she says her piece what was no doubt a darn sight shorter than what I got to say sos I can tell you on it. And the reason I figures that is on account of her having perdicted the miracle—what Floyd and me already got a preview of when we seen Bob the Barber burning up—she'd've knowed she'd be keeping her sermon short sos not to belabor the suspense none. And when I asks the recording secretary to repeat it word for word, the voice what is exact-like a recording of the Schoolteacher's voice gets a little bit longer ever time I time it, though it ain't caught up with my version what is longer, beings sometimes I got to pause to collect my thoughts what with me born with a curse of having to tell and no photographic remembering to remember on it, though I know it goes like this, her new message what ain't really new but old, her beings the one what already told on it to the citizens of the congregation in the first place.

It seems the Father witch art in heaven ain't really there atall. Now, was we to believe all of what she learned us on before her new message was a lie? No, on account of unlike Jesus, she never said she believed on it. Besides, we've to know the old truth sos we can understand the new truth, just like we got to live in Freeland before we can live in Anarchtopia, what she told us on, beings it's heaven and Freeland weren't but a town.

Well, who was she praying to all this time? Well, she was praying to the human being what was the supreme being inside her. The same supreme being and brain we all got in our heads. And that brain, what it's got is it's got the land, the clouds what is the feelings, and the sea what is the tears. But they ain't got to be sad tears. They're sometimes glad. They're the gift within what is life, though it ain't really, on account of life, it ain't a gift. It just is, and it ain't sad nor bad, beings it's both good and bad, like the tears what is fathered by the feelings what had got some of the land in it, beings each of us has got some of the land in us, beings ginks is the salt of the Earth. It just is, and it ain't bad nor good but it's wonderful.

Because there ain't no man nor gink what ain't a Earth unto hisself. Sos there ain't none what couldn't be the boss of hisself ifing he was to try and ifing we was to have us some Anarchtopia, some heaven what ain't visible of yet. But we was to get us some, we was living an experiment, and the way we was going to get it is to have us no leader what was powerful. We was to say *no* to power and *yes* to knowledge.

But what about them feelings when we just knowed there was a Creator, she says with the smile still on her face and the eyes what has the knowledge. Take them mornings when the sun is coming trough the winda and you just know on account of you don't read science fiction for nothing that there is stars you don't see what is never ending on the other side of the sun. And even the Earth is so big and beautiful you can smell ever flower sos you just knowed somebody made it all.

Well, like in *Job*, she says, we got to know there ain't nothing we can know whole. The Father is our picture of the Father. The Father is only part and never *a*part. On account of there is limitations to all our talk, to our brains, we need to make new words and pictures sos the new truth ain't seen as the final-like truth. We got to see what Old Crow sees. And there is other critters what ain't birthed yet sos we can't know what they'll see for a good long spell.

So what do we know about the Father? There ain't no

mystery about what ain't. And the Father *ain't* on account of there ain't no heaven but what is like a tropical island in the mind. And the Father, he's bigger than that, beings he's all, ever thing, just like it says in the Good Book. And that's why you can't see him none, on account of he's so big, he *ain't*. You can only catch a glimpse ifing you was to not look for him in the *all* but in the one thing, like maybe your table.

Well, me, I don't think she's talking on ginks when she says ifing you want to know the universe, you're to look at the Earth. Ginks are peculiar that way, I spose, but sposing one did want to look at the universe. A gink's of a mind same as a man's what ain't such sos it can see ever thing. I spose it's like a buckeye tree what you ain't never seen until you studied on a buckeye some. Or a war movie like one I seen at the shop through the Barber's Motorola. You can't see the war till you seen a battle what you can't see unless you was to see one soldier with the camera in his face.

In other words, there's meanings even Old Crow don't know. The pair of docs is that one buckeye you come to know you can know only ifing you find it in the same planet where there is buckeyes. Sos you've to run into something like a buckeye tree before. In other words, you got to know a little about ever thing sos you can get to know some one thing what gets you knowing on ever thing.

And knowledge got by the Old Curiosity is real important-like, beings you then remember on the Earth where you are, not like you was somebody from outer space looking down on the planet, I spose, on account of here you feel genuine joy, a kind of happy like what comes from your science fiction books, what is science and art both, you figure, and what ain't really about outer space atall. Or your table what is science and art and science fiction too ifing you was to shoot billiards like me, Bob the Barber'd say hisself.

Me? I feel real proud-like when the Schoolteacher says it were me what was her picture of the powerful what had no power by the knowing—not even the believing, though I ain't sure I believed *that*. And all of the sudden she up and says it were my monomania for my table what was still to happen on account of it were already here like it had to be ifing it was to be there so strong in the future too. It were my obsession with my stick that Sigman Floyd would say made her sos she'd like me, beings I was all growed up in my wanting to be a billiard player by trade, even ifing I'd the body of a boy and the manner of a gink. But she suspicioned it for years I'd chose the gift within on account of my handwriting what was real small and exact-like, beings it were a sign I concentrated real good. Then she tells them all I'm the disciple for her new message, me. Ifing she was Jesus, I'd be the Peter what never'd betray, beings I'd be the Thomas what chose to doubt. I'm the one who knows on account of it's me what will tell and tell all. And what I'm to say is the answer is the question. That's reason enough to ask the question, she says. She says, Truth is absolute, but there ain't no absolute truth. Courage you need on account of a human being can get squashed. A gink can die happy only when a gink knows he can die happy. He gets done being ascared when he knows some things there is what you can't control none, and you swaller that like you swaller the medicine what tastes bad but is good for you. But most important is you ask the question even ifing you is ascared, even ifing there ain't no answer but the question. That's what Job done, she says. The Old Curiosity.

And where is the Father? she says at me like I'm already sposed to know, like the answer is the question. Well, I up and tells them where the Father is in the refrain we always say what ifing you wanted to hear it exact-like, you'd call up your recording secretary with photographic remembering. Anyways, it goes like this, the question what would be in her voice and the answer in mine, though I ain't believed yet it were me talking that way none, like I done took lessons, like it were Wally Phillips what gived them.

Where is the Father?

The Father is not.

Where is the Father?

The Father is part as the daughter is part.

Where is the Father?

The Father is music without sound, wind without air.

Where is the Father?

The Father is a man. In a silent storm.

Where is the Father?

The Father wears a robe and hood, both made of wind. The Father is not here—only there.

Where is the Father?

The Father is the crow at night like a phantom seen in fog all around, cloud you are surrounded by and surround.

Where is the Father?

The Father is the moment whose time has not come nor ever will. The Father is invisible sculpture. A net full of water. Form itself—the more intricate, the less exact, without content. Or content without form. The Father is steam. The Father is a block of cold—chiseled and stacked. What soil without seed cannot become. Or seed without soil. Memory you can't remember. The Father is the ghost of fear.

But where is the Father?

The Father is where He is not.

So where is the Father?

The Father is the hollow reflection of a mirror in a mirror.

Where is the Father?

The Father is reflection.

Where is the Father?

The Father is in the mind. The Father cannot be got. Father is. The Father is not.

Where is the Father?

That witch is not lost cannot be found. The Father is found in the question, Where is the Father?

Where is the Father?

Yes, Where is the Father?

Where is the Father? Oh, Where is the Father?

Yes, Where is the Father. If the Father is found, the Father is not. If the Father is not found, the Father is. And is not.

Then, Where is the Father?

The Father is. And the Father is not. You are the Father and you aren't. Like the atom that is and is not, you *are* and you are *not*. Thy will be done. Anarchtopia without end. Amen.

Then what she done was she burnt up. But it weren't horrible or nothing unless maybe you wasn't a gink or a F.B.I.

man who seen it coming. You just sort of sat there with your hymnal in your lap or—ifing you was me—your new baby in your lap and watched.

And what you seen when it was over was a almost pile of ash behind the pulpit, beings there was something besides the remains of what was left of the Miss Luda Corvus what was my mother's mother's mother, although she weren't really, on account of she were and she weren't, and the same Miss Luda what was our live-in preacher and the Schoolteacher, beings that that *something* what were left, it were a shoe of hers what din't leave with her. And it were that shoe what stayed behind bothered you the most on account of dumb you was awondering how she'd make do with only one shoe to walk with.

You see, it weren't like no crucifixion where Jesus was suffering pain. No. This is one Miss Luda what had a smile on her face and what burnt up about as fast as your Christmas tree might ifing you was to forget to burn it till July. And Digger, bless him, when he goes to sweep up the ashes, what they done was they just keep on sifting down to littler ashes sos after about five minutes they'd all broke up to them atoms or beyond, he figures, on account of when he was done he had a boxful of nothing but a brand spanking new high-heel shoe what were unscorched just like the carpet under her feet weren't even scorched none. And the trouble is, even though we buried her shoe under a real plain marker with *Corvus* writ on it, Digger, bless him, he ain't been able to remember none what the color of that shoe was, up late of certain nights with the question still on his mind, though we been telling him it must've been black on account of it looked all gray with her ashes all on it. Until final-like, the ginks at the shop and Digger, bless him, all dig it up one moonlit night sos to tell on the color, but the shoe, it were missing now too, even though the box it's in were set in poured concrete, the vault Digger made hisself what had his initials in it and were in tack when we dig it up. And Digger, beings he wouldn't lie none, you just knowed what you seen was another miracle, beings all he could say now was, "Anarchtopia without end. Amen," as ifing at that second he knowed what it all meant, beings he knowed she wouldn't be coming back, beings we din't need us no leader ifing we was to find out there weren't no chance something what *ain't* ain't ever again going to return to be something what was, even though she weren't and she were, and we was to turn into Anarchtopia without no mayor or nothing on account of we was mostly the boss of ourselfs. Even the ones what ain't had no gink upbringing on account of they seen the miracle too.

So what part do you want me to tell you on now? Well, I spose I should say I ain't drawed of late, ceptings when the Agent, he needs me to draw some. Me and Floyd, we even got us a free train ride too one time, even ifing we din't get to see Wally Phillips none on account of Floyd, he got sick and we come home, but that's another story, although it ain't and it is but mostly is sos you'll have to remind me sometime and I'll remember on it sos I can get the facts straight.

Nooner? He's done added to the litter twice. And Nooner's Becky, she's starting to get her her womanly parts what looks real good on her ifing she don't get too sassy.

It's been pretty quiet here in the old Anarchtopia, what is the way Digger, bless him, likes it, witch you can't blame him none what with him having enough to contend with, beings there's the Barber to listen to on his new throne and Royal Crown always in the machine to help you stay cool when the Barber takes out his sarcasm or whips you at Euchre. Them two is contrary of late, especial-like when there's a grass fire and they got all the volunteers to impress, what the number of them is dwindling on account of there ain't no *big* fires no more. For a fact, the last big one they seen was the one I and ever body else in the congregation seen beings she were a mass of flame before anybody could lift themselfs up off the pews, her in her robes with her arms outstreched to her sides and her fists clenched and that smile still on her face and her chin up, like she couldn't get any younger and still be a woman, let alone no mother.

Weren't nobody what tried to put her out, neither. I mean who's about to fight a fire what ain't natural but a miracle what got told on in the first place of a Sunday before? Even them reporters quit taking pictures, they was so stupified not on the miracle but how beautiful she become, so beautiful she final-like burst into flames—not like a star or nothing with fire shooting out all ways at once in outer space where there ain't no gravity around ceptings its own gravity in the middle, but flames going up like it would happen on the Earth, ceptings the ceiling, it weren't scorched none neither. And it ain't leaked a drop since. What reminds me on another part I've to tell you on.

Them reporters, what they thunk was they had them some real news. Well, the one, he couldn't bring hisself to write on it none, he up and says at the shop where he stops on his way to Arizona. And the Barber, on account of he ain't never since seen the Schoolteacher's name in print, he figures what happened was the same what happened to the other reporter what has come to Anarchtopia for good to start hisself a newspaper, what is ever time he goes to write his story on what happened, the paper, it starts asmoldering in the middle just like you was holding a magnifiying glass to it in the sun, what is another baby miracle, the Barber figures, till that paper, it's all burnt as black as your marsh-mellow what falled in the fire, ceptings the ash of that paper, ifing you was to so much as breathe, it'd take wing in tatters, like any flock of crows might ifing accidental-like you was to come up on one of their conventions, I figures. I knowed it on account of I tried it myself. And all of the sudden I know how come we got us a recording secretary what is to live forever, beings he don't ever volunteer hisself for no loony bin, what ain't likely again nohow.

And Bob the Barber, he just about has hisself a *can*iption fit laughing ever time he remembers on his joke of them reporters hosing down their typewriters what caught afire all by theirselfs.

Well, me, I take about all of his sarcasm I can take for about six-months-after-a-miracle, and what I done was I up and told him I din't see what was so funny.

Well what on Earth was I talking about, the Barber wants to know.

So I tell him, and I tell him good, beings it weren't of necessity none I says a word, beings I got props. What I done was I says, "Bob, ifing you think that's so funny, just you take a little dictation next to that crossword puzzle."

So I tells him "A" and he writes "A" on his *Post Dispatch*.

So I tells him "N."

And so on.

Right after he done writ down the third "A," the Barber, he's up from his new throne and he's slapping that newspaper hard on his conversation piece like it was crawling with spiders cept these are spiders what turns to smoke when you squash them.

Well, the Barber, he just looks down at his complete crossword puzzle page what ain't no more, and he looks up at me like he don't quite get it yet.

So I sets down my pad and goes over and around the other side of his conversation piece, and I breathes real hard and long on the mirror, mad enough sos I about get me an asthmatic attack. "Take a look-see," I says, and I scrawls the letters in the mist what was hanging on the mirror real good until I scrawls the last letter, when the mist, it up and vanishes just like that.

Well. Sometimes the smartest Barber you ever did see ain't got savvy enough.

So then what I done was I say to the Barber has he got hisself something solid he don't want no more and a nail. And what the Barber done was he come out of the back room like he ain't took eyes off me yet with a old cue ball in his hand and the nail what holds up the calender of near-naked ladies. And what I done to make a barber savvy again was scratched the old *Anarchtopia* on the surface and quick-like rolled it out in the street where it blowed up, albeit quiet, sos you'd've suspicioned something ifing you ain't seen it gone to smithereens with your own two eyes, you'd've said it were talcum what got spilled on the pavement.

And Bob the Barber what he figures is not only am I the Thomas what doubts and the Peter what din't betray none, but I'm the John the Babtist what has still got a head on his shoulders and Bob ain't one bit ascared it's me what's the one to tell and show the world there ain't no reason to fear ifing you got you a Anarchtopia where you are the boss of yourself in your own backyard.

And real sudden-like I ain't mad no more on account of I ain't but a little ascared. Who'd've knowed it were the Barber what would be the one what give me the goosebumps when I thought on how it were me what was just like the Vetern what weren't about to leave Freeland after he come on account of he knowed a good thing when he seen it? Ceptings he had to leave, and me, I could stay. Ceptings the only way I could really stay was to leave. And only by leaving could I stay. I got goosebumps telling you on this when I think on what I know now I din't know. As long as you got you a picture of the future, even ifing you ain't got the *de*tails, there ain't no reason to be ascared none, even ifing it's the picture of you dead with questions still in your head, beings you can have only what is possible, beings you're part and not *a*part, beings there's spirit but no soul, beings the gift is within—never without.

So HOW COME am I the Thomas what still doubts? On account of what I knowed I ain't really knowed till I believe it too. Oh, I believe in miracles all right. Miracles ain't nothing but what happens what is contrary to nature. Take your ever day Floyd, for a fact. You just know on how he's going to live forever on account of he ain't dead yet, beings by rights he oughta be, beings he's so old and all with a big head what would've broke another creature's neck. But when the Schoolteacher done told me on my mom, "Your mother can see you too," when I'm looking in the eyes of the Miss Luda Corvus what is and ain't my mother's mother's mother, I ain't believed it none on account of it ain't no miracle what I seen, but the eyes of ever woman.

Well, you know me. I don't believe in ghosts none, ghosts what ain't even contrary to nature ifing you can't see them none. Take Floyd, for a fact. Now right there is something contrary to nature. On account of he's what you might call a ghost what you can see. Now take Mom and Baby Sis. Ifing the Schoolteacher was specting me to believe on a dead person could see, then she's got her her doubting Thomas. Floyd, on the other hand, ain't dead. Besides, how would you like the looks of Old Pyro, Termite, and the Banker maybe staring at you from peep holes on the other side? Them is more strange than strangers, given where they're gone to, I figures. And anyhow, I ain't felt the Schoolteacher's eyes for nigh on two years now, ever since she burnt up. Anyways, I know the Schoolteacher wouldn't lie none, so I spose I know Mom can see me too. But there ain't a loony bin alive but what the threat of sending me there could make me *believe* it. Ceptings maybe ifing you was to say she can and she can't.

Come to think on it, though, that's maybe what I'd've said ifing you was to tell me the critters ain't left none—they has and they ain't. Just ask Pop and Little Ludy what was fishing at the crick on her first birthday, sitting there on a big oak what got felled by lightning and not critters. Little Ludy was in Pop's lap when they just caught themselves the biggest bass you ever did see with a spider lure of rubber, and Pop, he's about to cast to see ifing the bass has got a daddy when all of the sudden Pop sees out of the corner of his eye a reed in the water what is making a wake and what is moving down stream on account of it's faster than the current. Pop, he suspicions something all right, and what he does is he just holds that pole quiet sos not to flick his wrist and cast or nothing on account of he don't want to disturb the waters none sos he can figure on what's this reed traveling here all by its lonesome in the middle of the crick like the mast of a little straw boat what got sank, floating straight up instead of on its side.

Well, Pop, he sees the waters start to roil where there ain't no rock and instinct tells him drop the pole and tumble back, Little Luda tucked all snug in his lap and all sos she din't get hurt none. And instinct done right by him, I want to tell you, on account of what he seen before he knowed what it was, that reed, it were a *breathing* periscope.

First off, what he thought he and Little Luda seen when they peeked over the log were something like the Lock Nest Monster, arising out of the water, the creature's back to them what had all sorts of weeds and mud plastered on it. Then, he just knowed it were a ghost when the figure real slow-like turned around and Pop was staring smack dab in the face of Cromangon Man.

Right then and there was when the miracle what melted Pop's heart started, when Little Luda, she begun to giggle and laugh like she just found her daddy, me, what got lost. And there I am, over a mile away bent over my table and I heared her just like she were in the Masonic Hall herself sos I just got to drop my stick and ride on out to her and Pop. By the time I'm there, Cro, him and his *breathing* periscope is gone down stream, but Little Luda, from acrost the pasture I heared her laugh and then I heared words in the sound of her laugh. And when I get closer I seen Pop propped up agin the log with the back of his head laying on it, and she had her hands on Pop, one on the back of his neck and the other on his forehead, and Pop, he's bawling like a baby hisself, what just had a heart attack, witch he probable-like did on account of Little Luda, she was *atalking* and it weren't no baby talk, but she was saying it in sentences-like. And I come running and she sees me and starts wobbling to me, her arms throwed up to be picked up, and I says *Pop*, and Little Luda, she says, "Stick," just as plain as day. And me, I stops in my tracks and

look straight in her mouth. "Stick," she says. And dumb me,
I says, "What?"

"Where is the Father?" she says.

And double dumb me, by habit I says, "The Father is not."

"Oh yes, he is," she says, and she points to Pop.

And I says, "What?"

And she says, looking at me, "You are the Father and you
are not." Then she looks over, points to Pop, and says, "He is
the Father and he is not. His father is the Father and he is not.
The Father is and the Father is not. Stick," she says, just like
she knowed it ever since she got birthed, "Earth is the Father.
Water is the womb."

Well, you just knowed it would've happened sometime, the
Little Luda letting loose like that, even ifing Cromangon Man
ain't showed up. But showed up is what he done all right, and
he ain't a ghost or nothing, and whether the Schoolteacher had
designs on him showing up at that moment I spose we'll never
know. But what we do know is what the Barber said of Digger
what had him complicity in the matter on account of he signed
that death certificate what the Schoolteacher talked him into
beings Cromangon Man, he'd been in the loony bin in Lawless
ever since Digger, bless him, says, beings we knowed it, beings
ifing you can't take the loony to the loony bin, the loony bin takes
its ownself to the loony, them crazies in white suits blowing into
town now ever so-often, looking for their volunteer what up
and unvolunteered hisself and is back where he belongs, I spose,
ceptings who knows where he stays in winter time, unless Old
Cro's folks got complicity in the matter too, what Digger, bless
him, he ain't saying. It's like I says before, that family of crit-

ters, it's like they is and they ain't. They ain't on account of you can't see them. They is on account of maybe Cromangon Man can. Least ways, that's what Becky says, beings she's Nooner's tallest and the one what sees Cromangon Man by the crick the most. I know on account of Becky, I'm teaching her on billiards some when Nooner brings her up to the Hall for her lesson and leaves, what don't bother him none, even ifing she's getting her womanly parts early, what she is, and even when he knows I weren't a farm boy for nothing. Nooner, he knows I love her like a little sister, and he figured on what the Barber hisself tells me, that ginks got to have the counsel of a woman. Never mind Becky ain't one yet.

Well, I spose Bob's right on that, on account of Becky, it's real natural-like talking with her on how I oughta handle the Agent, beings let's not forget she were one of the Schoolteacher's pupils too, even ifing she weren't no real gink but a girl. Besides she's so sweet and all about me and the future what she figures I got to someday get an education for, beings she figures on how the Agent is giving good advice when he says we should just leave Cromangon Man alone and that goes for the loonies what is employed by the loony bin. Besides, she says, how does a mind get healed in a place like that? And she figures that's what the Agent has been saying to hisself. And why he's kept it quiet is we all know Old Cro, he's come back to live with his kind.

But what Nooner nor nobody but Becky and Pop knows is it ain't just Becky what is for a whole year now been giving me the advice what I need. It's Little Luda, what we figures we shouldn't tell no one on account of us being ascared she might become a curiosity for the reporters. I figures it won't matter none ifing you knows it were her what convinced me there's two kinds of believings, one gradual-like and one like lightning. On account of she'll be older, ifing not a lot older when you hear on this. That's why it won't matter none what she says about my real gift ain't billards atall on account of what's more important is a picture of the future what turns out true beings I got will, beings I'm to be the boss of myself, even when I'm to draw for the Agent.

And ifing you should be the first to hear these tapes what I'm making just for practice and not on account of I'm still real ascared-like and what the Agent tells me is to be hid in the bank vault in his safety deposit box, beings he were the new bank's first customer—maybe what you already knowed on account of the Agent's last will and testament. Whatever you do know, don't forget *this*, beings the Agent don't even know it because he promised he wouldn't listen none ifing I was to put it all down in the only words I knowed best, don't forget to don't go scrawling *Anarchtopia* nowhere just sos you can try it out. You won't get hurt or nothing on account of ifing you don't believe in it none.

Me, I'll still be here should you come visit, awondering, most likely, on the healer to come and the one after him, maybe, cept when I'm gone on exhibitions and all, for the Agent, even after I turn twenty-one. But that's another story, although it ain't really.

Well, Anarchtopia without end. Amen.

The end.

Karl Elder is Lakeland College's Jacob and Lucile Fessler Professor of Creative Writing and Poet in Residence. Among his honors are the Christopher Latham Sholes Award from the Council for Wisconsin Writers; a Pushcart Prize; the Chad Walsh, Lorine Niedecker, and Lucien Stryk Awards; two appearances in *The Best American Poetry*; Lakeland's Outstanding Teacher Award; and grants from the Illinois Arts Council for poetry and fiction. For many years and from its inception, Mr. Elder has been associated with the literary magazine *Seems*—originally as a contributor, followed by poetry editor, and, since 1978, editor and publisher.

82478168R00159

Made in the USA
Columbia, SC
17 December 2017